FRACTURED EARTH

Viceroy's Pride Book Three

CALE PLAMANN

MOUNTAINDALE
PRESS

Copyright © 2022 by Cale Plamann

All rights reserved.

No part of this book may be reproduced in any form or by any electronic or mechanical means, including information storage and retrieval systems, without written permission from the publisher, except for the use of brief quotations in a book review.

This is a work of fiction. Names, characters, places, and incidents either are the products of the author's imagination or are used fictitiously. Any resemblance to actual persons, living or dead, businesses, companies, events, or locales is entirely coincidental.

ACKNOWLEDGMENTS

When I started writing in late 2019, I never thought I would get a single book actually published. Sitting here at four is a humbling experience, and there are a number of people I'd like to thank.

First and foremost, my wife and family who have been supportive of the long hours I've poured into my computer. Then my friends, they know who they are. Many of them aren't huge fans of the genres I write in but they humor me nonetheless when I talk about developments both in my books and in the process of getting them published.

I also want to thank the various online communities such as LitRPG Forum, Silver Pen, the Quinlan Circle, and Bad Cat Hangout. I've spent probably more time than I should being non-productive on their discord servers spending quality time with other readers and writers. Without them, I'm not entirely sure I could have maintained my sanity throughout this entire project.

I'd also like to thank everyone at Mountaindale Press. Both for believing in me and for being incredibly supportive/helpful along the way.

Last but not least I'd like to thank you, the reader. Without you books like this couldn't be possible. In particular I'd like to thank some of the readers that were most helpful/influential in the process of writing/editing this book: Eli for supporting me from the start, James and Ari for believing in my vision the entire time, and Sesharan for always having a kind word.

CHAPTER ONE

Prologue

Lieutenant Colonel Hans Bowman crumpled the report in his hand in disgust and threw it to the ground. He snorted.

He should probably stop calling himself a Lieutenant Colonel while he was at it. The army that granted him that rank had already disintegrated into a collection of isolated warlords, ruling over disconnected chunks of what had once been the United States. Sure, some of them still worked for the local civil authorities, but it took everything in him to not sneer at their foolish weakness.

Politicians were what led humanity to the brink of destruction. They argued and bickered amongst each other, trying to score petty political points while they let problems linger and grow. The country was left to run on autopilot for decades at a time, a couple of yearly speeches during the elections hardly a substitute for leadership.

Distrust and dissatisfaction reached the point where you could shake the entire system with a puff of fresh air. The Coalition for Human Transcendence was much more than a stiff breeze; they were a hurricane.

In the moment of humanity's greatest triumph, after it finally fought off an extraterrestrial invasion, they swooped in and tried to seize power. The coalition approached him as soon as his task force came back from Brazil.

Their pitch was attractive. Highlight the architects of humanity's victory and install them as political leaders to clear away the detritus and litter of a past age and forge a glorious new future for the entire planet. As one of the more prominent figures that would have been granted political power in this new order, Hans stood to benefit immeasurably.

The only problem was the people giving the pitch. Oil, telecommunication, and information technology executives had to be convinced, along with a couple fossils who literally did nothing but horde and trade vast quantities of stock. The same figures who exerted influence on the previous government would expect to control him from behind the scenes, too.

Hans knew exactly what the future they were seeking to create would look like. It would be the same as before except with new masters and without even the veneer of paying attention to the common man.

Not that he cared about what the common man thought. He did once, but learning magic changed that. Compared to collecting mana, day-to-day concerns about political parties and divisions paled to a shadow of its former importance.

Honestly? Hans couldn't care less about whining complaints of food shortages and bandits springing up. In Brazil, he killed honest-to-god monsters. As part of a team, they'd brought down at least two elves. Those moments, covered in hot blood with his breath coming in fast frantic strokes as mana washed over him, put everything into perspective.

Compared to those moments, food tasted like ash and sex lost all meaning. Some of his men tried to warn him that it was addictive, that the sensation clouded his reasoning. Even if that was true, he could feel the power thrumming through him, letting him perform superhuman feats.

He knew better than to listen to the doubters or overcomplicate things. There was no question in his mind. The coalition was lying through their collective teeth when they promised a utopia free from "the corruption of the past."

There wasn't anything noble or well-meaning about their goals. The coalition wanted to rule the world, and they wanted to make him a cog in their machine. Instead, they would rather twist him to their will through lies, threats, and blackmail.

At least Hans could admit the truth of the matter to himself.

He wanted power, naked and white hot. There wasn't any need to wrap it in pretty words. There wasn't any need. Might was an end to itself.

Bowman walked outside the penthouse suite he had appropriated for himself into the thick, humid Florida night. The bodies of three defectors littered the balcony, discarded and useless. He had already taken their mana last night,leaving nothing but their useless husks of meat.

In the middle of the bodies stood a wooden frame bearing the only survivor amongst the defectors draped across it. His hands and feet were lashed to the wooden planks by blood-soaked razor wire, every movement no matter how slight eliciting another groan of pain from the man. Hans' heartbeat accclerated as he approached the prisoner. Even from here, he could almost taste the mana flowing through the man's veins.

He bit his lip, trying to quell his urge to simply kill the man and take his mana. He hadn't been able to restrain himself when his guards brought the man's companions to him, but Bowman needed answers from someone.

With the previous round of prisoners, he hadn't even asked them questions, instead tearing them apart and reveling in the rush of mana that the act of destruction brought him. Ultimately, it was a mistake, but Hans was under a lot of stress. It was understandable if he periodically needed an outlet, given how many things were going wrong.

"Private William Ritter." Bowman tried unsuccessfully to

steady his breathing as he approached the bound man. "You've been caught trying to desert in the face of the enemy. I'm sure you know the price for your actions?"

"Desertion?" The soldier chuckled, wincing as the movement reopened the wounds on his wrists. "That's what you're going with? When our government needed our help, you decided to set yourself up as the tinpot dictator of Florida. Any JAG officer worth their salt would blanch at the things you've ordered us to do in the name of 'maintaining martial law and order.' You forced us to crucify children, Bowman!"

"They were looters, Ritter!" Bowman screamed, slamming his fist into the frame. The dull pain from the blow barely registered as he raged on. "The animals of this state simply can't understand the order I'm trying to provide for them. Outside our boundaries, chaos reigns. The Louisiana bayou is swarming with frog aliens, and warlords rip apart the very heart of this country for a couple precious shards of lucre. I don't care how old the malcontents are; if they rebel, they must take accountability for their actions."

"We just wanted to go home to our families, Bowman," Ritter spat out. "The war was over, and the government was collapsing. I have a wife and a son. I can't trust the local police to keep them safe; they needed me home. I didn't sign up to help you live out your delusions of grandeur."

"Your family needed you?" Bowman grabbed the slumping man by his throat, pulling him close. Ritter gasped as the razor wire dug into his wrists. "Your oaths of service needed you, Ritter. Your duty needed you. Now, tell me: who convinced you to defect? Who in my camp is working with the enemy?"

"What?" Ritter asked, incredulous. "No one told us to run away from base. We all just saw the news. The new aliens are landing everywhere, and all of the warlords are too busy fighting each other to keep our families safe. Hell, my family isn't even in your territory. The next wave of dissenters you order me to string up might include my son."

"I will not listen to your lies, Ritter," Hans drew the knife from his belt, stabbing it through his captive's forearm. "Tell me who convinced you to defect, and I will make this quick. If you don't cooperate, I'll take my time and enjoy myself, like I did with your friends. The choice is yours."

"Respectfully," William Ritter squared himself up, looking Hans in the eyes. "Get fucked, Colonel. Even if I had help, I wouldn't rat them out to you. You're a stain on our uniform, and my biggest regret right now is that I won't live to see someone cut that smirk off of your face."

The knife in Ritter's forearm vibrated, as if rapped with a tuning fork. Mana flared from the bound man. Bowman's eyes flicked to it just in time to see it jerk out of the prisoner's arm in a fountain of blood. He threw himself to the side, and that was all that saved his life. The blade seemed to cut an arc through the air in slow motion, slicing deeply into Hans' cheek. He staggered back a step or two, eyes wide as he slapped his hand to the still bleeding gash.

"Damn," Ritter sighed. "It was worth a shot. How far gone are you, Colonel, that you'd give a knife to a metal mage? You just couldn't stop yourself when you thought about torturing me. You're making mistakes, Bowman. A lot of them."

Hans shrieked in rage, pulling out his handgun and emptying it into Ritter's immobile form. Shot after shot slammed into the prisoner, rocking him against the wooden frame. Then, the hammer clicked on an empty chamber. Bowman looked at the gun blankly for a second, his ears ringing, as he finally realized that the gun's slide was locked open. He set it down on a glass table and stepped toward Ritter.

The wave of mana hit him like a fluffy pink cloud, wrapping him in its embrace. Jolts of lightning flowed down his spine, causing Bowman's entire body to spasm with pleasure. His breath came in short, sharp gasps. Hans sank to one knee, the cool cement of the rooftop grounding him as the rest of his world whirled and spun. He closed his eyes, sinking into the gauzy cotton candy arms of the mana.

All too soon, the sensations came to a stop. Bowman shivered despite the humid heat of the night. Ritter's body hung limply from the wooden frame, silent and unable to answer any questions. Hans sighed, picking up his handgun from the table. He ejected its magazine and replaced it with a fresh one before racking a round. Traitors and enemies surrounded him, and it was better to be safe than sorry.

He stalked back into his penthouse, pausing for a brief moment to admire the artwork that its previous owners had selected. It was a shame that they wouldn't turn over their residence to him peacefully.

He had never been a violent man, but there was something about a mundane human defying him that just angered him. Their deaths, just like those of so many others that had followed them, were unfortunate. If only they'd stopped aggravating him, driving him to extremes--

The elevator to his penthouse opened with a chime. Bowman stepped inside and pressed the button for the ground floor. When the coup failed and the government collapsed, he had quickly taken over Miami. Some of the local forces resisted, but an efficient and brutal application of magic quickly brought them into line. Now the entire state of Florida was in the hands of his Reformed Army of America.

The door opened, and Hans stepped out to fearful salutes from the handful of soldiers working in the building's ground floor. Many, like Ritter, doubted the need for the RAA. Bowman knew they were wrong. Democracy and leniency were chinks in the armor humanity needed to don if they were going to weather this storm.

Already, the amphibious Orakh were landing all over a world torn by civil strife as power-hungry forces fought over the trappings of power. With no one to order them, half of the world's army units refused to move, while the other half attacked haphazardly, without any planning or organization. In America, only the RAA was able to successfully hold back the alien landing in the bayou.

For now. Bowman ran a hand through his thinning hair. It seemed like every day there were more of the greyish-green brutes. Troops were beginning to run low on munitions, and without a centralized government to purchase more, eventually the RAA was going to end up using their empty rifles as clubs. Already, they were raiding stockpiles and private homes to bolster their armories.

Of course, the citizens complained when the RAA seized their guns. They even tried to start a pro-second-amendment protest in downtown Miami. He had put a stop to that rather quickly. A handful of magically enhanced special forces operatives hanging the protest's leaders from light poles took the vinegar out of the rest of the protestors.

He didn't have any time for them. The RAA operated recruitment centers all across Florida, calling on patriots to volunteer against the alien menace. Anyone who sat around at home, letting firearms and ammunition go to waste in the face of such a threat, was useless. Hell, half of them weren't even working. With the alien invasion and the fracturing of the government, most companies shut their doors. Even those that tried to stay open were plagued by uncertain logistics. No one really knew where or when goods would arrive, and there was growing confusion as to what currency could be used to pay for it.

America needed to be made whole again, and this time without the imperfections that marred the first attempt. The nation would pass through a crucible, burning out its imperfections and corruption until it could truly stand on its own once more. Until then, the common citizenry couldn't be trusted with something as weighty as governance. The last thirty years of politicians proved that.

Still, for Bowman's dream to come to fruition, he would need to beat back the Orakh. He had one of the strongest armies on Earth, but he didn't have the magic or expertise to fully defeat them and seize power. As distasteful as it was, he would need to seek help.

He stepped into the ground floor conference room, a forced smile on his face.

"Merella Amberell," he intoned, nodding at the elf lounging in an overstuffed chair. "I've heard so much about you. It's a pleasure to finally make your acquaintance."

CHAPTER TWO

Bayou Country

Daniel Thrush's sword whistled through the air, redirecting an Orakh warrior's poleaxe with a quick tap and a clang of metal as he danced to the side. Time trickled forward at a crawl as he bent backward, letting another axe blade swish through the space he'd occupied a second before. Dan had his spellshields active, but as he quickly found out, the raw strength and weight behind an Orakh's halberd would make short work of his defenses.

Of course, that was if they managed to hit him. An Orakh next to him pirouetted glacially, a smoking hole in its shoulder. Dan smiled as he darted forward, sword removing an enemy's leg at the knee as the report from one of the heavy fifty-caliber rifles built into the armored battle suits they'd looted from Thoth headquarters assaulted his ears. The gunshot was good news. It meant Abe was nearby, and he'd fought his way clear enough of his attackers to provide fire support.

His feet sank into the springy soil of the marsh as he threw himself into a roll to the side, avoiding his injured foe as the crippled Orakh tried to tackle him. Unlike Abe and William, Dan didn't wear the heavy, powered armor developed by the

Thoth Foundation. Instead, he relied upon his mobility. Most of the time, it was a good strategy, but against the heavier Orakh, he needed to avoid being dragged into a grapple. His magically enhanced strength might let him hold his own in a one-on-one wrestling match, but his current fight wasn't one-on-one.

Dan came out of the roll and launched a Fireball into the cluster of five Orakh that had been trying to bring him down. The resulting explosion staggered and wounded all of them, leaving them easy prey for Dan. He hit them like a tsunami of precisely targeted sword strokes and Forcebolts.

Over the past two weeks since the Orakh landed on Earth, Dan had become adept at the dance. Each swing of his sword took a limb, and each Forcebolt slammed into a joint, occasionally breaking a bone but mostly knocking the amphibious Orakh off-balance so they couldn't capitalize on his attack. Then he was on the other side of the gaggle, the swamp littered with writhing limbs and crippled Orakh behind him.

They would survive. One of the first lessons humanity learned was that Orakh could survive a lot. Their bleeding stopped quickly, and as a species, they just didn't go into shock the way that mammals did. Worse, severed limbs could regrow onto their stumps given a couple of hours. The combination meant bullets weren't as effective as they should be. Sure, a head or organ shot would kill an Orakh, just like it would a person, but without blood loss or shock, more than one soldier had died to an Orakh they disregarded due to "fatal" gunshots.

These days, anyone hunting the Orakh made a point of confirming kills before they moved on. Still, William needed help with the Orakh Shaman he was keeping suppressed with a combination of 20mm cannon fire and liberal use of the flamethrower mounted into his power suit's other arm. Technically, Dan had awakened William's ability to use magic, granting him a water and an earth affinity, but the old man didn't really trust the magic.

Apparently, that distrust of magic didn't apply to the series of runes Dan carved into William's armor at his daughter's behest. Jennifer knew logic wasn't going to sway her father. Instead, she convinced Dan to inscribe enough strengthening and defensive runes into both Abe and William's armor to bring both of the suits onto another level entirely.

The shaman let out a silent scream, a wave of force mana rolling toward William across the uneven hillocks of the swamp and threatening to spill him off of the narrow island that they were all fighting over and into the bayou itself. That would be a problem. As troublesome as the Orakh were on land, they were completely at home in the shallow water of the bayou, moving with an ease and agility that even Dan couldn't match. Luckily, they were usually simple-minded enough to follow humans up onto swampy islands, once provoked. Otherwise, clearing them out of the bayou would simply be impossible.

William stomped down with his right leg, digging it into the moist soil and crossing his arms. Dan could sense the flood of earth and force mana as he activated his runes to counter the shaman's spell. The wall of force slammed into William, but the runes activated, generating a shield in front of him and quadrupling his weight. The Orakh's spell still generated enough force to knock the old-timer onto his ass, but William's countermeasures broke the back of the attack.

Dan raised his hand and shot a lightning bolt into the shaman. Whatever charm it was using to approximate a spellshield flashed, but it clearly wasn't optimized for dealing with elemental energy. A second Lightning Stroke brought the shield down. Despite his massive reserves of mana, Dan was beginning to run dry. Gritting his teeth, he fired a third Lightning Stroke, burning through most of the shaman's chest and dropping its twitching and smoking body to the ground.

Sighing, he toggled his time dilation rune off. Immediately, the world sped up, and the dull bass roar turned into music. Abe had insisted that his suit have speakers. He claimed that fighting to "tunes" inspired morale. Dan didn't particularly care; it wasn't that hard to reconfigure the suit's PA systems to play music. It was just that, in the current state, they couldn't ensure proper access to streaming apps. That meant Abe was stuck using an old CD player and collection of CDs he'd fished out of an abandoned car a week ago.

"Big wheel keep on turning," Abe shouted, off-key and with enthusiasm. He pointed the cannon arm on the power armor at an Orakh that was trying to flank Jennifer as she fought another two.

"Rolling!" Abe fired the 20mm cannon twice, throwing the Orakh to the ground. "Rolling on the river!"

Jennifer used the distraction to quickly bring down the remaining Orakh, leaving them all panting on the otherwise cleared-out island. Well, Dan assumed that Abe and William were panting. It was hard to tell through the towering suits of armor.

"Can you cut the music, Abe?" Dan called out to the man. "We've got a job to do, and I'd prefer to not alert everyone and everything within a mile that we're here."

"Come on Dan," Abe responded. "We can take pretty much everything we've seen since the landing, so long as we can stay out of the water itself. Plus, we have to listen to Creedence down here. It's basically a rule."

"Abe," Dan pinched the bridge of his nose. He wasn't sure if his headache was from mana exhaustion or the soldier's exuberance. "We can win against everything we've seen so far, but I don't think we can handle the numbers the Orakh are capable of throwing at us. Plus, now that there are enough mana-activated individuals in the area, it's only a matter of time before the local wildlife begins changing. I'd prefer not to be surprised when some sort of magic-using mega alligator pops up for the first time."

"Fine buzzkill," Abe replied with a chuckle as he wandered over to a pile of writhing Orakhs. Methodically, he lifted the heavy boots of the powered armor, bringing them down on the Orakhs' skulls, crushing them with a fairly satisfying crunch.

"That's Mr. Buzzkill, Sir to you, Abe." Dan rolled his eyes at Abe's gleeful behavior. "If we're going to make this entire mercenary company thing work, we need to have some sort of chain of command."

"I still don't see why I'm not the one running this show," William interjected, crossing the arms of his powered suit across his chest. "I mean, I'm the one that actually used to be a general at one point."

"Because none of this works without Dan, Daddy." Jennifer shook her head as she walked away from her father and began finishing off the wounded but regenerating Orakh. "Plus, he could take all three of us in a fight if it came down to it. You can be in charge of planning and operations, but the person who can command the elements and ignore bullets gets to be the commander. That just seems common sense to me."

"Same," Abe agreed, continuing his happy stomping.

"Thank you for your votes of confidence, everyone." Dan smiled slightly. William was a bit of an ass, but he didn't mean much by it. At this point, Dan suspected that the old man was simply giving him a hard time out of spite. He almost seemed relieved to not have to deal with the boring politics and logistics of command anymore.

Mana began to flow into him as the rest of the team butchered the Orakh he'd injured. Dan gritted his teeth against the influx of pleasure as he grew stronger. He slipped back into a meditative state and quickly began partitioning his personality to prevent it from impacting his thinking. The worst part about the mana was how seductive it was. It was easy to know that too much of it was bad for him, but the minute he touched it, Dan couldn't help but think about how much easier it would be to just let a little more in.

Still, he knew where that path ended. Addiction, and in all likelihood, becoming some sort of serial killer, like the gang running Miami right now. Even as the Orakh tried to take over the world, yet another problem reared its head, demanding that he solve it.

Dan stared off into space and triggered his status. It had

been some time since he'd had the opportunity to access the system and take stock of his gains over the last month or so.

<USER> Status
Rank 7

Body 6(8)
Agility 7 (9)
Mind 8
Perception 7
Spirit 67

Skills
Swords 11, Brawling 5, Archery 2, Runecrafting 8

Affinity
Space 13, Lightning 11, Fire 11, Gravity 10, Force 13

Enhancements
Armor Rune V, Strength Rune +2, Agility Rune +2, Thermal Resistance Rune, Temporal Dilation Rune 10:1

Runes+

Spells
Shocking Fist 10, Spark Field 2, Lightning Stroke 11, Spatial Shield 8, Flame Jet 4, Gravitational Easing 10, Fireball 13, Force Bubble 12, Spellshield 10, Forcebolt 9, Flame Aura 3

He blanked out the status. He was close to another rank up, and already the extra kick from the steadily increasing level of his spells and affinities was having an impact. Once upon a time, Lightning Stroke would simply stun an opponent. Now it killed them. He wasn't where he needed to be yet, but Dan was well on his way.

Shaking his head, Dan focused on the moment. Jennifer was

cutting off the ears of the Orakh they would need to fulfill their contract with the Mayor of New Orleans. The country was in chaos and at this point; no one really knew who was in charge. In some states, the governor ran the show, but in others such as Louisiana, control was much more local. The Mayor of New Orleans had declared emergency powers and set herself up as a borderline autocratic ruler.

Still, most of her efforts were devoted toward keeping her people safe and the Orakh away from the city. When Dan and his team arrived, she was ecstatic at the idea of a trained group of veterans of the Brazilian campaigns against the elves stepping in. Even if paper money was of dubious value, she was able to offer up enough food, gold, and electronic equipment, including solar generators, that Dan's team wouldn't be able to replicate on their void ship, the *Viceroy's Pride*, to make helping out worth their while.

As Dan glanced up at the sky, the sun's rays promised plenty of light left in the day. That meant more Orakh to kill and more mana to earn.

CHAPTER THREE

Recruitment

"Look, Mr. Thrush." Bessie DuBlanc spoke to him in a tone of voice that promised disappointment. "The City of New Orleans appreciates everything you've done for us. Hell, we know that your team has been the only reason we've been able to catch a breath from those damn swamp monsters-"

"The Orakh, Mayor DuBlanc?" Dan asked, waiting for the other shoe to drop.

"Whatever they call themselves," Bessie waved a hand dismissively. "They've encroached on our farming and scavenging operations more than once, killing our citizens and tying up our security forces. The people are sick of it, and they're demanding answers.

"Your intervention has bought us enough time to arm and train the local police with heavier weapons." Bessie leaned back in her chair, ignoring the creak of warning from the distressed piece of furniture. "More importantly, we've had the time to mobilize and secure supplies for the national guard. Finally, we're about ready to make a major push to get them out of the bayou. If you're in, that's great, but if you're not, I'm not sure how much work we're going to have around here, once we clean 'em out."

"What about that warlord out of Florida?" Dan furrowed his brow. "He doesn't seem like the type to play nicely with his neighbors."

"He sent us an emissary." She picked up a sheaf of papers from her desk. "Long and short of it is that he wants to unite the South with some sort of mutual defense pact. I'm not sure I buy it, but he's willing to coordinate an attack on the toads, and for now, that's enough. I'm not inclined to let his soldiers anywhere near the city, but that doesn't mean we can't cooperate to get rid of the aliens."

"Honestly?" She shrugged. "He seems like a piece of work. But even if he's as big of a sociopath as the rumors say, only an idiot would let those fucking monsters fester. There's more of them every day, and even if we can hold them back for now, it's only a matter of time before they manage to overrun everyone."

Dan glanced back at Jennifer, indecision flickering across his face as he weighed his choices. They needed someplace to use as a base for their voidship, and so far, New Orleans had seemed like the best option. Pretty much everywhere else in the English-speaking world was under the sway of some oligarch or another, most of them too focused on arms races with each other as they struggled to collect as much of the Thoth Foundation's old technology as possible.

The various local governments near the Orakh invasion sites were largely left to their own devices. In the former United States, that meant that New York City and Louisiana were on their own. The Manhattan invasion was at least partially contained. Dan had been more than a little surprised at the number of NYPD and national guard members that purportedly showed up to fight off the Orakh, but apparently he was the only one. According to Jennifer and William, the NYPD had about 38,000 officers and would be around the world's 40th best-funded army if they were included on the lists. Between the police and the New York national guard, they were able to keep the Orakh confined to Manhattan.

Jennifer nodded quickly. Really, their options were New Orleans, New York, or overseas. With as much time and effort as they'd invested in the area, it seemed like an absolute waste of resources to just move on.

"We're in, Mayor DuBlanc." Dan's forehead furrowed slightly. "But we're going to need to work out some details."

"Well, the troops will be glad to have you." Bessie smiled, the corners of her mouth crinkling slightly. "Now, what sort of details were you thinking about? We can certainly provision you for the attack and continue with the usual payments of ammunition, food, and medicine. Beyond that, make your offer, Thrush."

"That's most of it," he said with a chuckle. "The only other concession we're looking for is the ability to set up our home base here and recruit from your population. Right now, there aren't a whole lot of us who are fighting fit, and our plan is to turn this into a full-on mercenary company. We'll need volunteers and a place to lay our heads for that."

"Half of them are out of jobs, anyway." The mayor smiled, extending her hand to Dan. "Some of the plants are still employing people, but no one knows if the other states are buying or even what they'd buy with. Layoffs have been hitting the area really hard. If you're willing to step in and employ some of my out-of-work citizens while providing security for the area, I'm not going to say no."

"I'm glad we're on the same page then," Dan took her hand, his tanned skin contrasting with her dark mahogany. "Just let us in on the planning, and we'll find a spot where we can do the most damage."

"Be ready in ten days," Bessie agreed, waving a hand toward the door. "I'll have someone from the defense force get into contact with you in the next couple days so we can see how to best utilize you. Until then, feel free to set up a recruitment stand on Bourbon Street for all I care. You have my permission to hire anyone who wants to work for you."

"That went well," Jennifer chirped cheerfully as Dan and her left the mayor's office. "She's insisting on a stupid and potentially deadly course of action, but other than that, we're all on the same page."

"She has to have seen the reports from the deserters coming out of Florida," Dan frowned. "No one is saying anything good about Bowman. It sounds like he's gone completely off the rails."

"I never got why Dad liked him," Jennifer's mouth twisted into a grimace. "He was always either pompous or dismissive. Like, the only times he would talk to me were when he was being condescending. He was always an asshole at parties. I guess without anyone keeping him in check, he can finally be himself. A glorious piece of shit."

"I'm not going to argue." Dan chuckled slightly. "I fully expect him to betray us the second he gets a chance. Still, what do you think about her proposal, setting up a stand on Bourbon Street?"

"Well," a mischievous grin flickered across Jennifer's face, "Abe did lose the last squad game of hold 'em, and he has been a bit insufferable lately. It would only make sense that he pay off his debt in a suitably painful way."

The next day, Dan sat at a folding table, head in his hands. About ten feet away, Abe was dancing to bad R&B while wearing a sandwich board advertising "Thrush's Raiders," absolutely having the time of his life. Next to him, Jennifer was absolutely laughing her ass off.

"COME ON, MY GOOD MAN!" Abe shouted, puffing for breath as he pointed at an unsuspecting stranger. "The world's falling apart around your ears. Are you going to do something about it, or are you going to just sit here jumping at shadows?"

"What?" The man stared back at Abe blankly.

"Do you think that the ladies are gonna like you just sitting around and getting fat?" Abe shimmied, making Dan even more uncomfortable. "They're going to want a provider! Someone that can sling lightning with one hand and punch an Orakh in the face with the other!"

"I'm married-" the stranger began, confusion wrinkling his brow.

"Then you, ma'am," Abe turned from the lost-looking bystander to a woman who had stopped to take in the spectacle. "Do you want to be some sort of shrinking violet, or do you want to get out there, seize life by the throat, and set it on fire with your mind?"

"What do you mean, 'set it on fire with my mind'?" she asked, her head cocked with a bemused expression on her face as she approached Abe.

"A lady after my own heart!" Abe stepped forward, grabbing her hand in both of his before getting down on one knee. "We are here to recruit the most august and noble of individuals to become mercenaries. The benefits include access to advanced and dangerous technology, as well as the ability to access and learn magic. Before long, you'll be able to wield the very building blocks of the cosmos themselves as you smite your enemies."

"Magic?" She glanced down at Abe's hands on her own incredulously. "You're gonna need a better pick up line than that. Unless you can actually start something on fire with your mind, I've got to get home."

Abe pivoted on his knee and pointed at Dan expectantly. Grudgingly, he raised his hand, firing a Flame Jet into the air. Most people knew that magic existed now. There were too many videos from the conflict in Brazil for anyone to believe otherwise. It just wasn't a common sight anywhere outside of Florida, where most of the campaign's veterans had ended up.

Almost instantly, the clamor of people going to and fro stopped. Within thirty seconds, their table was surrounded by bored individuals, out of work and looking for some sort of show or entertainment.

"There is your magic, my dear!" Abe sprang to his feet.

"The world is falling apart, and the Orakh are at your doorstep, but we aren't helpless! Thrush's Raiders are on hand, ready to hire those who are willing to fight. We will arm you, train you, and inch-by-inch, we will reclaim our nation from the aliens, with your help."

"Aren't you guys the team that's been clearing the way for our patrols?" A male voice shouted from the sudden crowd surrounding their table.

"I'm glad you asked, good sir!" Abe pointed in the general direction of the speaker. "Mayor DuBlanc has contracted with us on numerous occasions to keep the Orakh's numbers down, but soon we will be pushing into the heart of their nest. For that, we need volunteers. Plus, once New Orleans is safe, we'll need to free Manhattan. After that, New Zealand, Madagascar, and Ceylon all need help. In this new and troubled age, there will always be a need for a strong and steady arm, and Thrush's Raiders are angling to be the first and best answer to that need!"

Dan leaned over to Jennifer, who was doing her utmost to avoid snickering. "Do you have any idea where this came from? I thought you said you were trying to punish Abe, not us."

"I probably should have guessed that he didn't have a sense of shame," she replied, her eyes fixed on Abe's antics as she hastily covered her mouth. "I honestly don't know how he's doing this. I'm assuming he drank a couple hurricanes before he got started."

"Of course, I'm the one that he keeps pointing at to perform tricks like some sort of trained monkey." Dan rolled his eyes. "I swear to God, Abe missed his calling as a used car salesman to work in the special forces. No suburban window shopper would've been safe from him."

"Now, line up, men and women!" Abe jumped to his feet, waving excitedly in Dan and Jennifer's direction. "Together we're going to clean your swamps of the invaders and take back what is rightfully humanity's! With a little skill and daring, you could be a vital part of that process and earn some coin and learn a trade while doing so."

Quickly, the crowd converged on their table. Over the course of an hour, they took at least eighty names and numbers of interested parties. With William's help, they were able to cut those numbers in half.

It still took Dan a couple hours to awaken all of the candidates, but once they tossed out the individuals without a magical affinity, they were able to focus on the physically fit and those with dual affinities. Another day passed before Sam had the twenty selected for the company fitted with a copy of the system.

Dan was worried about her. Sam wasn't the same vibrant and brash person he remembered. After he pulled her out of Ibis' compound, she just wasn't the same. Withdrawn and quiet, she did the work they assigned her, but she never smiled, secluding herself from the rest of the team.

Once they got a minute to calm down and talk, Dan was going to make her see a therapist. Sam had been through a lot, but dwelling on it wasn't going to fix anything. She needed professional help if she actually wanted to improve her situation.

CHAPTER FOUR

The Raid (I)

Unfortunately, a week wasn't anywhere near enough time to train the twenty or so new additions to the team. They did have enough suits of power armor for all of them, once Sam made some repairs to the equipment salvaged from Thoth headquarters and Dan updated their runescripting, but having the equipment didn't make the new hires combat-ready.

Abe and William had all too much fun drilling them on how to use their suits. Dan wasn't entirely sure if the "drill sergeant screaming in your face" thing was real or just a movie schtick, but both of them seemed to get a kick out of using it on the fresh blood. Once things settled down a bit, Dan would instruct them on how to use magic. But, in the meantime, all they had to do was pour mana into the simple runes of the armor in order to fortify it.

The Orakh weren't as agile as the elves. They were fast, but in the sense that a human athlete was fast. Other than their Shamans, most of them responded to bullets of a large enough caliber fairly favorably. True, you needed to confirm the kill, but a couple shots from a high-caliber weapon or a flamethrower was more than enough to bring them down.

The real problem was that the Orakh didn't attack in small groups. Near the edge of the bayou, you'd only run into five or ten at a time, but the closer you got to their landing site, the larger the swarms you'd encounter. On a solo scouting mission, Dan had seen clusters of 200-plus Orakh, and he didn't even make it that close to their main base. Worse, those groups were led by much larger and stronger variants of the Orakh that he hadn't encountered yet.

In short, they were going in blind. Planes doing flyovers confirmed that there were "a helluva a lotta toads," but beyond that, they had no idea as to the enemy's numbers, composition and location. Due to potential logistical concerns regarding ammunition, all of the recruits were taught how to use melee weapons. Most of them had some knowledge of street fighting or brawling, and one or two practiced an actual martial art. They were given enchanted weapons to complement their skillsets, usually a knife or stiletto.

Regardless of their skill, all new soldiers were given enchanted axes with reinforced hafts and blades. Without the reinforcement, the powered armor's enhanced strength would cause the weapons to shatter and their blades to deform after only a handful of blows. Hopefully, the axes would be a weapon of last resort, but if their team did have to rely on them, Dan wanted them to last.

The actual journey to the bayou was a strange affair. Half of the troops were just folks from the city, recently laid off or looking for some adventure. They'd been given AR-15s, about two weeks of training, and had been dubbed militia. Dan didn't have any faith that they'd hold when the New Orleans Army, as it had taken to referring to itself, came into contact with the enemy. The militia spent the drive joking and sharing snacks. A couple of them even tried to shoot nearby wildlife from the back of the pickup trucks and school buses they were being transported in.

The actual professional soldiers and police forces, on the other hand, were fairly grim. They'd been out to the bayou, albeit much closer to the city than Dan and his team. The national guard forces were especially upset that they would have to abandon their armored vehicles at the edge of the swamp. They knew at least some of what they were in for, and they weren't excited.

When they arrived, they were greeted by an engineering unit that had been on site for almost the entire week, putting together a motley collection of rafts, pontoon bridges, and boats. The plan was for the New Orleans Army to advance as a rough line, periodically checking in with each other via walkie talkie to ensure that no unit got dramatically ahead of another. Dan's group would be taking a spot in the center of the order, where combat was expected to be the thickest. Behind them, reserves from the militia would be moving forward at a more measured pace via the pontoon bridges.

Dan wasn't sure how much he liked the idea of using the militia as reserves. He'd worked with the guard and police units in the past and respected them. They might be in over their heads, but they knew how to keep their cool and work as a unit. He figured that the militia units were about as likely to run or panic and shoot his team in the back as actually fight the Orakh.

Admittedly, an AR-15 shot to the back wouldn't do much more than scuff the paint on their suits and annoy Dan's group, but at the same time, those sorts of distractions could cost them in the heat of combat.

The only good news was that the 122nd Air National Guard Squadron would be able to support them. William, Abe, and Jennifer all seemed to agree that the F-15Cs wouldn't be the most helpful. Apparently, the jets were optimized for air to air combat and had minimal air to ground capabilities. Unfortunately, the bombers at Barksdale Airforce Base were sitting the battle out after receiving conflicting orders from the Governor and a smattering of federal representatives. They had observers working with the 122nd to see how things went, but Dan wouldn't be able to rely on a B-52 to pull him and his team out of trouble if things went awry.

With a sigh, he opened the door to the semi they'd requisitioned for the ride out. He scrambled down, tuning out the tumult of voices and accents. The militia bragged and chatted about local sports teams while the professional soldiers were much quieter, only occasionally asking questions of their superiors about the supply chain. Dan grimaced slightly, sharing their concerns. The militia was supposed to be handling the supply chain, admittedly a better idea than actually throwing them into combat, and Dan wasn't entirely sure how well that would work out for everyone.

Regardless, his team had their own pair of boats, laden heavy with ammunition and fuel for the resource-intensive powered armor. Two of their more nautically inclined recruits would be piloting the boats while another two manned the .50 caliber machine guns welded to them. Remy Bushear, the team's new resident alligator hunter/poacher and all-around bayou expert simply looked at them and grunted, "too heavy." The hope was that the powered armor could be used to pick up or drag the boats over shallow areas of the swamp.

A couple of the locals approached, whistling and admiring the powered armor as they loaded it off the back of the truck. Sam was already quietly opening each of the back clamshells on the carapaces on the twenty-two suits so that their pilots could climb in. Dan frowned slightly as the new recruits shot the breeze with the other units, obviously bragging about their new rides. He didn't mind a little fun here and there, but the entire engagement seemed to have taken on a carnival air for too many of the soldiers.

"Ready to watch them pop their cherries?"

Dan jumped as Jennifer's hand came down hard on his shoulder.

"If we had more time, we'd beat it out of them, but we needed numbers, so their training had to be accelerated. At the end of this, they'll be soldiers or corpses. Not a whole lot in between out in that meat grinder." She flicked her head toward the waiting swamp.

"I just don't like to see them goofing off like this." He pursed his lips, taking in the bawdy jokes being swapped between his troops and the militia. "They haven't even fought yet, and already they're bragging about how many Orakh they're going to bag. It just doesn't seem right."

"Let 'em." Abe joined into the conversation from fifteen feet away where he checked over his armor. He was wearing the tight polymer catsuit used by the suits' pilots. It made him look ridiculous, like he was wearing a full body speedo. "Before something like this, you're either nervous or an idiot. Either way, they're gonna need to brag and tell jokes. We'll have a better idea of which category they fit into on the other side."

Before Dan could reply, the walkie talkie he carried crackled.

"Thrush, you read me, over?" A man's voice asked, slightly marred by the static of the finicky device.

"This is Thrush," he replied. "Who am I speaking to, over?"

"Major Champlain with General Richard's staff," the man answered. "Captain Anderson and I will be in charge of coordination and communication throughout the offensive. Keep your walkie talkie fixed to this channel, and somebody will pick you up on the switchboard if you make a request or a report, over."

"Sounds good to me," Dan responded. "What's the time table? My team will be ready to go in about twenty to thirty minutes, but I don't want them in their suits until we're ready to move out. Otherwise, they're just going to be sitting around wasting fuel, over."

"We don't want to keep anyone waiting too long." Champlain chuckled, his voice scratchy through the walkie talkie. "The militia are liable to get bored and crack open a couple beers or start a barbeque if we don't put them to work. Right now, the plan is one hour and ten minutes. We still need to get the artillery and command and control set up before we send you into that mess, over."

"Understood, over," Dan made eye contact with Jennifer and Abe.

"I'll talk to the boys and get them ready," Abe supplied, nodding to Dan as he walked past him toward the rest of the unit.

"ALL RIGHT YOU DICKLESS WASTES OF CARBON!" Abe immediately began shouting at the recruits, interrupting their bravado-laden yarns. "WE HAVE ONE HOUR UNTIL WE HIT THE WATER, AND THAT MEANS I NEED EACH AND EVERY ONE OF YOU TO DOUBLE CHECK EVERY SYSTEM ON YOUR SUITS AND ENSURE A FULL LOADOUT. A SINGLE SUBSYSTEM INSTALLED INCORRECTLY OR ONE RUNE OUT OF PLACE COULD BE THE DIFFERENCE BETWEEN YOU BEING RICH OR ORAKH FOOD."

Dan winced slightly, turning back to Jennifer. "I really think he enjoys that too much," he said dryly.

"He really has let a load off since we met him in the Jungle," she shrugged. "I think replacing all of the military's red tape with you, someone who actually listens, really helped his mood."

"It only made your Dad more cranky." The corner of Dan's mouth quirked up into a half-smile.

"Dad was always cranky." Jennifer rolled her eyes, turning away from him to walk toward the boat launch located at the edge of the swamp. "I'm pretty sure he was the red tape that Abe needed to get away from. Now, check out the boats with me. We don't want to get halfway out into the bayou only to find out that one of the locals siphoned our gas to run a grill or something."

Dan chuckled, following her to the waiting vessels.

CHAPTER FIVE

The Raid (II)

The steady chatter of machine gun fire drowned out the usual sounds of the swamp. Both of the .50 calibers mounted on their landing craft's prows swept back and forth across the island, trying to clear enough space of the Orakh for the rest of the team to disembark. Occasionally, the staccato thump of a suit's arm-mounted fifty caliber repeater marked one of the soldiers gunning down a submerged opponent before they could board a boat.

More than anything, the swimming Orakh were what worried Dan. Filling the boats with heavy battle armor made them ride much lower in the water than he'd like. Even though the Orakh wouldn't have anything to push off of, enough of them could potentially capsize one of the vessels, spilling all of them into the water.

It wouldn't be catastrophic. The suits were airtight and waterproof after all, but it wouldn't be great. The Orakh were optimized to fight in the water, their webbed limbs giving them a strange sort of fluid grace that they lacked on land. Worse, the murky water robbed most firearms of their effectiveness after a couple feet. Clearing the bayou was daunting enough without having to fight their seemingly endless enemies where they held the advantage.

Dan's mouth settled into a grim line as he took in the fairly constant stream of Orakh swarming over the island. If this kept up, running out of ammunition was a certainty. Their team didn't even know how much farther they had to go; aerial reports only came back with vague reports, such as, "you're a bit over halfway."

"System," he said softly, not wanting to distract the others. "Send a message to Group 'Battlegroup.' Text 'stop firing at the island on a five count.' Include a five-second timer."

With a musical *ding*, the message was sent. Many of the soldiers either flinched or stopped what they were doing for a second as they processed it. Dan shook his head. Once this was over, he would need to find someplace isolated and drill them. Their lack of discipline and training was more than a little worrying.

At precisely five seconds, Dan mentally crossed his fingers that his team could follow a simple order and activated Gravitational Easing. Then, with a pulse of mana to his strength runes, he jumped. Behind him, the boat rocked from him kicking off, but Dan didn't have an opportunity to truly worry.

In the air above the Orakh, he flung a Fireball into their midst, activating his spellshield as he landed. The heat from the explosion washed over him. Just outside the Fireball's impact crater, Orakh kept charging. Dan flowed forward, slipping between their clumsy attacks and removing limbs with the nonchalance of an arborist pruning a tree.

Behind him, both ships used the gap he'd created to land on the island, disgorging their soldiers in a matter of seconds. Quickly, Jennifer slipped next to him and began her own dance through the enemy forces. Without speaking, they fell into an easy rhythm, quickly clearing their area of the island while Dan periodically dropped spells on any cluster of Orakh that looked likely to overwhelm anyone else from the team.

Abe had the recruits fighting in pairs, one using melee

weapons to conserve ammunition while the other strategically gunned down Orakh to keep their partner from being overwhelmed. One-by-one, the tandem groups worked their way up toward where Dan and Jennifer fought. William and Abe ran freely, using short swords to pick off any Orakh that broke through the first part of each pair.

After about ten minutes, William called for a switch, allowing the front row of power-armored soldiers to step back and let their partner take over. The former front line took a quick break, breathing heavily. Dan smirked slightly to himself. All the cardio Sam put him through back at the Thoth Foundation was worth something. At this point, he could fight for another half hour or so before he even started to slow down.

They fought for almost another fifteen minutes before the first shaman showed himself. As soon as Dan saw him, he let out a grateful lungful of air. The fight was going well. The team's gunners were mostly resting to save ammunition while their melee members staved off the Orakh onslaught, but Dan had noticed an unforeseen issue. The bodies of the Orakh had piled up to the point that the melee soldiers were beginning to have problems with their footing. A low berm of bodies literally led up to the battle line, stacked almost waist deep. Sooner or later, Dan would have had to act anyway.

The shaman introduced himself with a shower of acid over the front line, dousing raider and Orakh alike. The acid did little more than remove the paint from the powered armor and slide off Dan's spellshield after Jennifer jumped behind him, but the Orakh fighting them almost uniformly fell to the ground, clawing at their skin and eyes. Apparently, the acid vaporized on contact, creating a cloud of acidic mist around the targets struck with it.

Darting over the unfortunate Orakh, Dan flashed ahead. The shaman spotted him, its narrow yellow eyes swelling as it frantically tried to cast another spell. Earth mana gathered around the Orakh when Dan's Forcebolt slammed into its spellshield, spilling the creature onto its back.

Dan followed the magic, slamming his sword down with enough force to drain the spellshield before following up with a Lightning Stroke. The Orakh spasmed, body twitching and frothing slightly at the mouth. He plunged his sword and sawed to the side. A second later, the light left its eyes, and Dan sighed slightly.

He looked back at the rest of his team. Jennifer was just finishing off her own shaman while Abe and William almost toyed with another. Apparently, the three creatures had tried to spring an ambush on their team while they were occupied with the rest of the horde. The average recruits were just finishing off the last of their enemies before mopping up the injured and regenerating Orakh.

Abe walked up to Dan. Just as he approached, the facemask on his armor split down the center, bisecting itself to expose his concerned face. Abe briefly glanced over the still-steaming Orakh bodies before clearing his throat.

"There are a lot of Orakh out here, Dan," Abe said blandly.

"Yeah," Dan replied, pulling out a bottle of water and trying to replace the sweat he'd just lost in the sweltering fight. "Every time we knock over one nest, it seems like there's another warren of the things just itching to give us a hard time."

"I'm pretty sure that fight was roughly two hundred and fifty of those things." Abe paused for a second, eyes going blank as he stared off in the distance. "If this keeps up, we're going to be out of fuel in three fights and out of ammo in four."

"And that's only at the present rate." Abe fixed his grim glare back on Dan. "Maybe you and Jennifer can step up a little more, but it only looks like it's getting worse. Each fight brings more of the grunts. Hell, this is the first fight we've seen with more than one shaman. It's like they're banding together, and that really can't be a good sign."

"No," Dan replied, wiping the sweat from his forehead with a frown written across his face. "We barely know anything about Orakh society, other than that it's 'bad,' but none of this looks like a good sign. I'm worried about how the rest of the army is doing, if we're hitting resistance this stiff. I'd take enough rifles against Orakh grunts, but none of them fought in Brazil. I'm not sure if they'll be ready to deal with magic and spellshields."

"Just a friendly word to his commander from a long-suffering soldier." Abe flashed a dark grin at Dan. "Check in with command. If we push too far ahead, we're going to end up surrounded, and the Orakh will be able to slip through our line. We'll be fucked, and the militia behind us will be surprised and then fucked. I'd rather not be stuck out in a swamp overextended while waves of monsters try to kill us, and our supplies run low."

Dan shrugged, fishing out his walkie talkie. They really weren't struggling that much yet, but it didn't hurt to give the troops a short period to catch their breath while he touched in with home base. Plus, they would need some of the militia to run a resupply out to them sooner rather than later. Even if he didn't have to call now, he was only putting off the inevitable.

"This is Thrush, calling for New Orleans Command, over." He waited for a couple seconds while fishing out his laminated map of the swamp and checking his position's coordinates. "This is Thrush to command, is anyone there? Over."

"Thrush?" An unfamiliar voice asked back, the speaker's gender and voice a bit difficult to make out through the walkie talkie's static. "What unit are you with, and where are you located? I can't seem to find you on our org chart, over."

"We're the mercenaries. We've stopped to rest, and we'd like to request a resupply before we push on," Dan replied, trying to massage the frustration out of his temples before reciting his coordinates to the confused soldier.

"Mercenaries?" Dan could barely make out the voice's confusion as the machine's static ate everything else. "Wait, where did you say you were? That's almost three quarters of a mile ahead of the line! Confirm your location, over."

"What do you mean?" Dan tried his hardest to keep his voice calm, hoping that the static would supplement his poor acting skills. "We're on schedule per the timetable. Surely, someone would have let us know if the operation was bogged down. Given that everyone is fighting out of sight of the other units, there's no way we would have known we'd gotten ahead of everyone else. Did you try to contact us? Over."

Abe shot Dan an "I told you so" smirk that dug under his skin as they waited almost fifteen seconds for the communication officer on the other end to respond.

"Well, uh," the voice on the walkie talkie stuttered for a second. "Your unit isn't on any of the Army org charts. None of us knew to reach out to you. Plus, you must've been slowed down by the swarm of toads, too. There are hundreds of them on each island. How in the hell have you remained on schedule?"

Dan waited for about ten seconds, glancing back to Abe, whose grin had faded into a frown. Consciously, he unclenched his jaw and struggled to regulate his breathing.

"Uh, over, sorry about that," the voice filled in sheepishly. Before the other person could cut the connection, another voice burst out in the background.

"Captain Anderson," Dan could barely make them out through the static. "I think we've got them on the ropes. At least half of the forces in every engagement between Cypress Ridge and Lamonte's Channel are disengaging. We're pretty sure they're about to go into a fighting retreat, if we--"

The voice cut off as Anderson stopped transmitting. Dan frowned; something about that exchange didn't sit right with him. Whatever their faults, the Orakh weren't cowards. They didn't retreat. The only thing he could think of was that they were heading toward more appetizing prey.

"Uh, Boss," Dan couldn't see even a hint of a smile on Abe's face as the soldier handed him a map. "I think you need to see this."

Dan's frown deepened as he saw where Cypress Ridge and Lamonte's Channel were located. The two locations were just over a half-mile apart. In the exact center of those two points, fair ahead of their support, sat Dan's team.

"Anderson, you little shit!" he shouted into the walkie talkie. "They aren't retreating, they're attacking us en masse because you were too busy taking a smoke break to check up on my unit! Get me some fucking support, and get it to me now!"

"Uh..." Even through the static, the Captain's unadulterated panic rang out loud and clear. "I'll uh... The General has to make that decision. I'll have to, uhm... I"ll have to talk to him. No one will be manning my post while I get him. Goodbye, over."

Dan stared at the walkie talkie in disbelief as it went dead. Abe elbowed him. On the three islands surrounding theirs, the Orakh were silently gathering. He began trying to count them but quickly gave up. A hulking Orakh, just shy of 10 feet tall, pulled his attention away. It pushed the others out of the way and took position at the crest of the low ridge that made up its island. The massive creature planted an axe the size of a man in the soft earth and stared down at them, arrogance and challenge in his beady yellow eyes.

CHAPTER SIX

Ambush

The giant Orakh shouted something incomprehensible at Dan while clearly pointing at him. He grimaced slightly, wishing he still had one of the translation helmets that they used on Twilight. Even after he returned to Earth, there hadn't been any need to fish a spare helmet out of storage. After all, his System understood Elvish well enough, and it wasn't like the average Orakh talked.

Apparently the shamans could, they just rarely bothered. When they did speak, it was usually a couple grunted phrases, urging the common warriors to attack. They never addressed anyone outside their warbands.

Except this one did. And now it was making a clearly obscene gesture at him. This one was almost twice the size of the Orakh surrounding it and bulging with muscles. He was pretty sure a swing from its axe would be enough to bisect an unarmored human in a single stroke. Whatever it actually was, the thing wasn't a garden-variety Orakh.

Dan opened his mouth to shout instructions to his team when one of the suit's speakers crackled. "Looks like it's frog legs for dinner! Light 'em up, boys!" a woman's voice echoed across the swamp.

He whipped back toward his squad. They were already opening fire *en masse* on the clustered Orakh. Abe and William were trying to make themselves heard and assert some order on the squad's chaos, but nobody was listening.

The Orakh charged through the hail of heavy .50 caliber rounds, throwing themselves into the water and swimming toward the squad. A brief flash of light signalled the first soldier igniting a flamethrower. Seconds later, the water of the swamp was boiling as most of the squad fanned the surrounding area with their flamethrowers.

"Stop fucking firing, you simpletons!" William screamed, his voice amplified by his armor. "Your flamethrowers have limited fuel. We'll need them to clear out clusters of Orakh once they land! Right now, you're wasting most of your fuel heating up the water!"

A couple of the troops stopped on their own. Dan could almost see them blinking in a daze underneath their helmets. They were all struggling through the first mana rush of their lives, the sensations gradually growing stronger as the team advanced through the swamp. Evidently, they didn't have the self-discipline to handle it. He sighed. That's what he got for recruiting directly from Bourbon Street. Still, he needed bodies for the armor, and he needed them fast. As bad as things were, they'd only be worse without the rest of the team as backup.

Abe grabbed a soldier that was firing their arm-rifle wildly, barely even bothering to aim into the oncoming Orakh. They stumbled, turning toward him and bringing the wrist-mounted gun up toward him. Dan tensed, preparing to intervene, but Abe simply cuffed them upside the head with a loud metallic clang.

"Get your shit under control, Sally!" Abe screamed at the dazed soldier. "Quit barking at me; there are more than enough Orakh for you to kill to get your fucking fix. You need to take a second to aim before you fire. Just like in practice."

Then Dan did have to move. The sporadic and slightly inaccurate fire hadn't been enough to slow down the waves of oncoming aliens. He dropped a Fireball into the mud on the shore of their small island, the gout of flame throwing three of the monsters that were pulling themselves out of the water backward into the air. His sword flicked forward, removing a hand before its backstroke took the head, too.

He could vaguely see Jennifer and William on other sections of the island, doing their best to kill the Orakh as they tried to land. If they could get the rest of the team to pull their heads out of their collective asses, they just might have a chance. Every monster took a couple seconds to pull themselves out of the water and onto the island's shore. In that time, they were almost completely defenseless. Even the incredibly raw new recruits could club an Orakh senseless in that moment.

Abe tried his hardest to knock some sense into the rest of the team. They didn't need all twenty of the recruits firing at the surrounding islands. There would always be more Orakh, and the primary concern right now was preventing them from gaining a foothold. If this turned into a stand-up fight, they would run out of ammunition long before the enemy ran out of expendable monsters.

Dan kept moving, killing or disabling Orakh after Orakh with his sword, while occasionally tossing a Fireball or a Force-bolt into a cluster of the creatures. One-by-one, dazed soldiers staggered down to the edge of the water, their melee weapons at the ready. Eventually, all of them managed to make it to the shore of the island, where they robotically began killing the oncoming Orakh. Luckily, the armor gave them enough strength that, so long as their fuel supplies held, even an inexpert blow packed enough force to hammer an enemy to the ground.

The fighting continued for another five to six minutes before Dan retreated to the center of the island. There, William and Abe were spotting the swimming Orakh and using the suits' built-in radios to alert the recruits that enemies were incoming.

On the next island over, the gigantic Orakh was ringed by three shamans, but other than that, it hadn't moved. Its axe remained planted in the ground as it surveyed the ongoing fight as if it was beneath it.

"How are we doing?" Dan asked Abe, taking a swig from his water bottle. More than anything, Dan wanted to wash the grime and sweat out of his hair. But, the way things were going, hydration took precedence. Ever since his stint hiding out in a tree with Jennifer, soaked in his own filth, Dan had been a bit more fastidious about his cleanliness. He wasn't going to catch dysentery anytime soon, thanks to the System, but that didn't mean that he wanted to embrace being gross.

"Hard to tell, Dan," William grunted. "The men are holding for now, but I don't see any end to the Orakh in sight, and that big one over there looks like bad news. I don't think that anything without spellshields is going to hold up against that axe. The armor makes all of us sitting ducks. Hate to say it, but I think you're gonna have to take him."

"What William said," Abe replied, his gaze trailing back over to the other island. "I think they're trying to tire us out, and I hate to say it, but it might work. The recruits shouldn't get too tired; their armor is doing all of the heavy lifting, after all. That said, constant fighting will wear on the mind. It's only a matter of time before they aren't sharp anymore and an accident happens. We've bought ourselves some time, but you're going to need to figure something out, or we're all going to be in trouble shortly."

"That's only if a couple of them don't go mana-mad first." William quickly surveyed island. "It's hard to tell when you can't see people's faces and eyes, but they've killed a lot of Orakh for newbies. Most of them are probably higher than kites right now."

Dan opened his mouth to reply, but the earth beneath his feet trembled. An influx of earth mana swirled around the island with the enemy commander. Around him, the three shamans danced wildly, waving wands laden with gems and skulls as they channeled mana. In Dan's vision, he could practically see a vortex of translucent sand and dirt surrounding the giant Orakh, quickly coalescing on the creature's axe. For the first time, it lifted the axe in the air.

"Watch yourself!" Dan screamed at the recruits guarding the corner of the island nearest the enemy commander. He'd never know whether they heard and ignored him, or if he simply didn't scream loud enough.

They didn't react as the Orakh brought its blade down, causing an avalanche of earth mana to slam into the side of the island. Only two of the soldiers were caught in the attack, but both of them were slammed into the bayou as a large chunk of the island simply disappeared. Immediately, the Orakh around them pulled them to the floor of the swamp, repeatedly stabbing at the joints of the powered suits with knives as they tried to find a point of weakness.

All three shamans didn't slow their frenetic dance. Already, Dan could feel another swell of earth mana building around the huge Orakh's axe. Frantically, he cast around for options.

"Get him, Dan!" Abe shouted, clapping William on the back. "William and I will cover you. I don't know how much good it will do with the shamans over there, but with any luck, they're too distracted by the spell they're casting to give you too much trouble."

Dan nodded quickly to him and gave himself a running start. At the last minute, he activated Gravitational Easing and cranked his strength rune up to its high-performance mode. He jumped into the air as Abe and William opened up behind him. Unsurprisingly, their shots ricocheted off of a massive spellshield surrounding the enemy commander and the shamans. Mentally, Dan made a note to start making some enchanted shells for the suit's .50 caliber repeaters. They'd be a hassle to manufacture, but a couple of them would probably have been enough to knock a hole in the shield.

He created a force bubble in the air to extend his flight. Just as he prepared to jump off, the lead Orakh locked its beady gaze on Dan and gave him a grotesque smile, all fangs and tusk. Then he swung the axe at Dan, rather than the island.

Swearing to himself, Dan jumped to the side, flinging a Fireball at the enemy commander as the wave of brown and gold energy overwhelmed and destroyed his force bubble. The explosion on the enemy island was soon joined by a handful of shots from armor-mounted rifles. The spellshield was beginning to show signs of wear and tear, but it would still take a bit before it would crack.

He created another force bubble, wincing as the hastily created spell crashed into his chest. Wrapping his arms around it, he pulled himself back up. Luckily, in the aftermath of the Fireball, the Orakh had lost track of him. Even now, its gaze raked the swamp, presumably looking for where he had fallen.

Dan jumped again, landing just outside the edge of the spellshield. He thrust out with his sword, pouring mana into it until its purple light shone brighter than the sun through the heavy cypress forest. The Orakh turned to him, but then the spellshield shattered. He rushed forward, temporal rune active as he absently batted aside hastily cast spells from the shamans. They were all but spent. Each of them was pale and panting from constantly casting the powerful earth spell for their commander to use.

The commander swung his axe horizontally, a rockslide of mana rumbling toward Dan. Almost without thinking, Dan threw himself at the ground, burying his face in the squishy, wet soil. The spell thundered into the top of his spellshield, almost completely draining it in a single, targeted strike. Behind him, the shamans had no such defenses. The earth mana rammed into them with the force of a careening boulder, turning all of them into paste.

Dan pushed off of the dirt, using Gravitational Easing to reach his feet in one smooth motion. The Orakh looked at him dumbly. It glanced at its gigantic axe, still held casually in one hand. It shook the axe, looking for all the world like someone jiggling a cable to jog some electronics into working.

Failing at its task, it snarled at Dan and swung its axe at neck-level. Even with the time dilation rune, the axe was moving very fast. Dan knew better than to meet it head on, instead ducking under it and slapping it upward with his sword while firing a Lightning Stroke into the Orakh's leg.

The axe whistled through the air above him as the jolt of electricity slammed into the commander's leg. Almost immediately, Dan noticed that, although it did burn his opponent, the creature was far from disabled by the blast. He stepped forward, only to stop abruptly and lean back as a clawed hand blurred through the air where his torso used to be. As bad as the axe was, he was pretty sure that he'd end up inside that thing's mouth in a second if he let it grab hold of him.

It jolted back, a fist-sized hole appearing in its shoulder as its suddenly unshielded body caught a fifty caliber round. Growling, it brought its axe up for a double-fisted overhand swing.

Dan jumped backward, slamming a Forcebolt into the same leg as his previous Lightning Stroke, knocking it off-balance. Another bullet slapped into its chest with the grace of a hammer shattering a watermelon.

For the first time in the fight, it stumbled. Dan blew up a Fireball under it, scorching it and knocking it off-balance once more. This time, he closed the gap, and his sword flashed, leaving a deep cut in its chest. The Orakh swung one of its hands, the axe long since forgotten, but Dan easily slipped past the clumsy blow.

Then a bullet struck it in the side of the head. Dan wasn't sure what the thing's skull was made from, but the blow only concussed the monster. His sword whipped through the air, decapitating it.

Gritting his teeth as he fought for breath, Dan braced himself for the wave of mana.

CHAPTER SEVEN

Setbacks

Dan trudged toward the sound of yelling. Around him, the seventeen remaining recruits were stacking Orakh bodies under Abe's supervision. The work was dull, sweaty, and occasionally messy when a body would twitch a little too much and have to be re-killed. He wasn't one to pull rank, but the good thing about being the boss was that nobody asked you to contribute to the crap work, so long as you didn't volunteer. A smile tugged at the corner of his mouth as he watched the soldiers stack the bodies. Right now, that was something he was okay with.

"What do you mean you only have one-third of the requested supplies!" William thundered, verbally abusing some poor clerk from the militia. "We just fought off a quarter of the toads in this swamp; we're sure as hell going to need more than this! Hell, with the amount of fuel you brought, we'll only be able to fight two to three more times, tops."

"Y'all can take what we've got, or we can just leave it here," a man holding a battered-looking deer hunting rifle replied while shrugging. "This is what headquarters sent us out with. If it's too little, take it up with them."

"Do you see how many bodies they're stacking over there?"

William's face was growing an unhealthy shade of purple-red. "Last I checked, we just killed something like 700 to 1000 of those things, all because you boys cocked things up and let us get surrounded! I need to talk to whoever is in charge of the provisions. We need to get this fixed up, or this unit isn't going anywhere."

"Go ahead and do that," the soldier cradled his rifle under an arm as he lit a cigarette. "Just lemme know whether you want what's on the boats. The boys'll want a break, if you're gonna turn it all down in a hissy fit." He hooked a thumb toward where another four soldiers were struggling to unload a crate onto the island while another two stood guard behind them.

"We'll want all of it," Dan stepped between William and the insolent militia soldier. "That said, what's under the tarp? Sure looks like there are some supplies piled up in the back of your boat that didn't make it into the accounting."

The soldier glanced at the back of his boat uncomfortably. The cheap metal hung noticeably lower in the water near the engine where a tarp covered a fairly decent-sized pile of some-thing. He scratched the back of his neck sheepishly.

"Dermot!" He shouted at one of the soldiers standing guard while Dan watched on impassively. "Looks like we accidentally didn't prep all of the shipment for offloading."

Dermot, a shorter man with scraggly black hair, looked back in confusion before noticing Dan and William. Immediately, his eyes shot to the tarp in the back of the boat, drawing a smile from Dan. Nervously, Dermot walked over to the tarp and pulled it back, revealing a handful of gas canisters and a pair of ammunition boxes. Dan nodded at him and turned back to the militia member with the hunting rifle.

"What is your name, young man?" William was fuming again, the metal of the suit framing his face as he screamed at the soldier. "This was clearly intentional. I will let your superior officer know that you were attempting to deprive soldiers in the line of duty of the tools that we'll need to win this godawful fight!"

"James Smith," the man replied smoothly, taking a pull from his cigarette. "Tell the boss lady whatever you want. She ain't the one out here risking her neck to play pony express to a buncha thugs with some toys."

"Well, Mr. Smith," William's chest was barely a foot from the man as he screamed down at him. "These 'thugs' are busy doing the actual work of fighting while you're off playing soldier. We both know that you're going to brag about all the Orakh you've killed when you get back to town in order to get some trim, but we also both know that you're nothing but a glorified errand boy!"

"You, my friend, need a shrink," the militia soldier replied, putting his cigarette out on William's armor. He turned back to the rest of the militia team, cupping his free hand over his mouth while still clutching his rifle. "Alright, boyos. Break time's over. Time to get back to camp before the boss lady sends us to bed without our suppers."

William's face was completely blank as he tried to process what had just happened. He reached for the militia soldier as the man began to walk away, only for Jennifer to step in from the side and push down the wrist of his armor.

"It wouldn't accomplish anything." Her voice lacked its usual warm and joking tone. "Even if he did try to short us on supplies, all we can do is contact the base camp and see what the holdup is."

They didn't speak for a moment as the militia's engine drowned out anything they might say. Then William turned to Dan, his eyes sparking.

"Give me the radio, Thrush," the older man could barely choke the words out through gritted teeth. "I need to call up your major and give her a piece of my mind. Between letting us get overextended, then not keeping us in supply, I want to know what kind of three-ring circus they're running over there."

"Sure," Dan handed the walkie talkie over to William. "Just don't embarrass yourself by ranting about James Smith."

"I damn well will complain about that insolent son of a bitch," William spat out, delicately picking up the radio in the giant gauntlet of his armor. "Not only was he incredibly rude, he tried to short us on supplies when the load was already far too light."

"His name isn't James Smith," Jennifer intervened, her face still notably more wooden than usual. "The name came out too smoothly while he was in the middle of provoking you. None of the militia soldiers were actually using their names, other than that Dermot guy. But we don't even know if that's a first name, last name, or nickname. They were trying to avoid getting caught if we wised up to us shorting them on their supplies. I'd bet anything against James Smith being a real name."

"Fine," William sighed in dejection. "I'm still going to try and report him, even if it's hard to pinpoint exactly who 'he' is."

"Be my guest." Dan spat on the ground. As even-keeled as he was, the constant foul-ups from the New Orleans Army were rapidly burning through his patience. He knew from Abe and William's stories that even the best-organized armies had their share of mistakes and confusion, but so far everything about the clearing of the bayou left a bad taste in his mouth. If William wanted to chew someone out on his behalf to let off some steam, Dan was hardly going to rein him in.

He slumped as he inspected the three twisted wrecks that used to be powered armor. Especially not now that they suffered casualties, something they could have avoided entirely if the operation had proceeded as planned.

Dan wasn't as close with the three dead soldiers as William and Abe were, but the entire situation reminded him of Brazil, and not in a good way. Soon. Soon, he'd be able to deploy to a combat zone with a fully trained team at his back and appropriate support from their employers. He was sick of good men and women that he was responsible for dying due to rookie mistakes.

"I don't fucking care if Major Champlain is busy!" William shouting into the walkie talkie jolted Dan out of his woolgathering. "You need to get her right now, or we're jumping in our goddamn boats and driving back to HQ right now. Then *I'll* get her. We signed a contract with the Mayor that said we would be fully supported. I'm not sitting here to get in 'glass half full or half empty' debates with you, but our fuel tanks only have half as much as they're supposed to in them!"

"But, Mr. Finch," the man on the other end of the line began, only for William to cut him off again.

"But what?" he shouted into the radio. "But it was an 'honest accident' that you let our unit get overextended and 'weren't able to secure reinforcements in time?' We lost two men and a woman because of that. Hell, I still haven't seen the reinforcements we were promised almost an hour and a half ago!"

"Sir," the voice from the radio squeaked nervously. "The other captains were unsure if the toads had completely retreated. They've been proceeding cautiously to avoid an ambush. I'm sure you under-"

"Oh I understand that their leadership failed both them and us!" William growled. "That means you, son. Where are the recon flights? Where are the helicopters bringing supplies and spotting for enemy movement? You own the skies, and we're fighting absolutely blind."

"One of the pilots had someone shoot shards of ice at him," the man on the walkie talkie replied hesitantly. "The rest of them were reluctant to go out after that, and we didn't want to push the issue."

"I think you pushed the issue by letting us take on the brunt of the fighting!" William's eyes were flashing again. "Then, when it was time to resupply us, you only sent about half of what we requested. Hell, your couriers even tried to steal some of our fuel and ammunition. Left a tarp draped over it and pretended they didn't know any better."

"Sir," the officer quavered through the walkie talkie. "Those are serious accusations. We will certainly look into them, but given the gravity of your claims, an inquest will need to be formed."

Dan sighed and snapped his fingers at William, motioning for the walkie talkie. If he let Finch have his way, he'd just keep yelling at some poor stooge for the next hour or two, and nothing would get accomplished. As satisfying as that would be, it wouldn't get them anywhere.

He took the radio from a fuming Finch and spoke into it, his voice much calmer than he felt. "This is Daniel Thrush here. I am hereby declaring the Army of New Orleans in breach of their contract under clause IV(a)(3), negligent management and supply by a rightful officer. That means you can either put your General on the radio to dispute my charge, or we will stay put. Your army can handle the rest of this on their own, and we can go back to New Orleans for our payment, including losses and damages that come to about $180 million directly traceable to your office. I'm not a lawyer, but I seem to recall that those losses triple if I can show that they were caused by mismanagement, and I'm pretty sure I can."

"What do you mean?"

Dan swore he could hear the man hyperventilating.

"You've been ordered to push forward! We're less than 3 miles from the landing site, and your team are the only ones with the kind of armor we'll need to breach the Orakh defenses without a bloodbath!"

"Then kindly shut the fuck up and put someone with more authority on the line!" Dan shouted into the radio, trying to ignore the looks of sympathy from Jennifer and William. "I've already lost three people for no reason because your command isn't ready to run an operation of this size and complexity. I'm sitting right where I am until I have some assurance that you have someone other than the lunatics running the asylum."

CHAPTER EIGHT

Negotiations Under Fire

They waited. Honestly, Dan wasn't very upset. Jennifer, Abe, and he ended up playing cards while William kept an eye on the recruits to keep them from doing anything stupid under the influence of mana. Of course, Jennifer wiped the floor with both him and Abe, but Dan knew what to expect by this point. Abe, on the other hand, became more and more comically unhinged at his losing streak before storming off to "take a leak."

No more supplies came, and HQ didn't radio back. In the entire time, they didn't see another Orakh. Either the previous engagement had cleared out the entire area, or the Orakh were backing off to plan something big. Whatever it was, he figured it wasn't his problem anymore. After almost an hour, the drone of outboard motors informed Dan that the rest of the army had advanced past them.

Briefly, they paused the game to walk to the edge of their island and watch the boats going past. The New Orleans Army looked ragged. Most of the soldiers were covered head to toe in mud and more than one of them had large gashes cut in their uniforms. Only one or two even bothered to look up at their team and ensure that there were no nearby Orakh before they returned their gaze to the swamp itself. Dan tried to wave at them, but there wasn't really a response. Eventually, they returned to playing cards and waiting for headquarters to call back.

He looked back down at his hand. Jennifer was smirking at him as she reorganized her cards. Whatever she had in store for him, it almost certainly wasn't going to involve him eeking out one of his rare wins. Really, things were looking just like the stint in the tree all over again, except this time, he was covered in mud rather than literal shit.

The rattle of distant rifle fire provided Dan all the excuse he needed to throw down the cards and walk to the edge of their island. Abe stood next to the two boat pilots, still in their armor, staring out into the dim afternoon light of the swamp. He looked back over his shoulder as he heard Dan's footfalls.

"Sounds like something's going on, Thrush," Abe jerked his chin toward the sound. "Mostly sounds like .223, AR-15s, and M-16s. Every once in a while, you'll hear one of the boat-mounted guns let loose. The real problem is that it's coming from everywhere. This isn't some isolated engagement or island-hopping. They're hitting serious resistance all down the line."

The drone of engines drew their attention as some of the older militia ships started passing their island. Some were loaded down with supplies, but many just had grim-faced Cajun soldiers, knuckles white as they held their mismatched weapons. They weren't going to the front to resupply materials. They were there to provide fresh meat.

"How are our fuel levels?" Dan asked Abe as the whine of the engines was drowned out by the distant gunfire. "Are the suits ready to go? I wouldn't be surprised if someone important suddenly remembered that they have a potent military asset waiting to deploy."

"We're good to go, even if ammunition and fuel are lower than I'd like." Abe shrugged. "Given the sound of things, I wouldn't be surprised if that's the same story for everyone right now. Things must be pretty dire if they're sending in the militia. Hell, half of them were using shotguns. I really don't think the New Orleans Army is ready to resupply them if they run out of whatever ammunition they're carrying."

Jennifer strode up to the two of them, glancing past them toward the sound of gunfire.

"Any excuse to get out of losing another hand, Dan." She shook her head while chuckling at him. "They aren't even close. If it's really a problem, HQ will call us and beg us to come back. If it isn't, we did more than our fair share already. They wouldn't have gotten this far without us clearing the way."

"I, for one, hope they don't need us." Dan nodded to William as the older man approached on foot, his armor split open along its spine for easy access near the center of the island. "That last fight was bad enough. As far as I'm concerned, we're owed a break of some sort. Of course, I'm not opposed to hearing offers. We could always use more food and equipment."

"Boy." William shook his head at Dan. "If they call us up, you let me do the negotiating. After watching you fight, I have to admit you know what you're doing there, but I'm gonna be honest. You barely know what it takes to keep a unit running, and you couldn't negotiate your way out of a wet paper bag."

"You could at least be a little bit tactful about it." Dan chuckled sheepishly.

"I'm too old to be tactful." William snorted. "You can scrap with the best of them, and you're not a megalomaniacal nutcase. That makes you officer material, in my book. That said, you've just spent the last however many months doing nothing but killing shit. You're good at it. You just need someone else to handle the logistics and business side of things."

"Hate to break it to you, Dan." Jennifer shrugged. "Daddy has a point. We've been driving fair bargains so far, and look at what's happened. New Orleans has taken advantage of us and left us in a lurch. Maybe it's time to stop being fair and actually push for our market rate."

"I know this isn't a democracy," Abe interjected. "But I'm gonna have to agree with the Finches. We're gonna need to pay our troops soon, and that's gonna need to be in something other than food and antibiotics. Same with expanding. I'd like to avoid street performing in the future, if I could help it. We're gonna need more rigorous screening and training facilities, if the plan is to keep this mercenary thing up."

Almost on cue, the walkie talkie chirped. Dan glanced down at it and back up at the rest of the team in indecision. Silently, William extended his hand. After a couple seconds of unanswered chirping from the walkie talkie, Dan sighed and wordlessly handed the device to William.

"William Finch speaking." William winked at Dan. "Who am I speaking to, over?"

"This is General Richard," an angry masculine tenor with a slight twang replied. "What the hell is this I'm hearing about your unit refusing to advance? You were given direct orders, and by God, I'll have you all caned for dereliction of duty if you don't get your sorry asses to the battle line in the next ten minutes."

William simply held onto the walkie talkie. Dan frowned, opening his mouth to say something, only for the ex-general to raise an index finger to his lips, shushing him.

"Are you done, General Richard?" William asked bemusedly. "I didn't hear you say over, so I just assumed you had more to say."

"Now listen here," Richard sputtered. "We're in the final stretch, and I can't have a unit sitting around lollygagging. We are under martial law, and I will have your entire unit dragged outside the city and shot at dawn if you don't get your asses moving."

After a pause, during which Jennifer did her best to avoid audibly laughing, Richard ground out the word "over." With the way he dragged the word out, Dan could have sworn that William had just smothered his dog in front of the man.

"Interesting," William replied cheerfully. "You do know that our unit isn't part of your Army, right? As in, your only authority over us is related to the contract that we signed with the Mayor? Over."

"What?" Richard half shouted and half questioned. There was a pause during which screaming could vaguely be heard through the walkie talkie as the General "interacted" with someone else on his staff.

"So," Richard was notably calmer when he resumed speaking through the walkie talkie. "You're the guys with the robot suits that I've heard about. I'm presuming that you're holding out for a better contract from us, now that you know that we're up against a wall. State your terms, but if you try to milk us too hard, I swear to Jesus, Mary, and Joseph that I will have your entire fucking unit executed for profiteering once this is all done, over."

"Funny story." William was smiling a little wider than Dan was comfortable with. "Your ops team 'forgot' to tell us that we were almost a half mile ahead of the rest of the line and let us get ambushed. When we radioed for help, no one came. When we radioed for a resupply, we got half of what we asked for, and the militia team bringing the supplies tried to short us, presumably to sell them on the black market."

"What-" Richard began only for William to cut him off.

"I did not say 'over,' General, I am not done!" William's voice grew heated as he revved himself up to properly chew out the officer. "We cleared an entire chunk of the front on our own, and without the support we were promised. Because your men didn't get off of their asses, we lost 15% of our infantry. They would still be here today if anyone bothered to help. Then, when we asked to speak to you about the issue, we heard nothing. Now, here we sit, still undersupplied due to incompetence or malevolence on the part of your staff.

"We do not live in your city," the old man's voice ground out with all the warmth of gravel being crushed into dust. "We don't owe you anything. Right now, our contract has been voided by my commanding officer for gross negligence on your part. Over."

William spat the last word out with relish. Abe brought his fingers to his lips and made a chef's kiss motion. Even Dan had a hard time keeping a straight face. He did have to admit, William tearing into the obviously in-the-dark general was exactly the level of catharsis he needed right now.

"Why is this the first I've heard of this?" Richard asked, confusion clearly audible through the static of the walkie talkie call. "I didn't even hear that your unit was nearby, until I questioned my staff about unoccupied units, and Major Champlain mentioned that you were in the area, over."

"We've only been talking with Captain Anderson," William replied darkly. "I think the little shit screwed the pooch. He more or less admitted that he forgot about us and didn't give us a call to slow our advance earlier. Then, every attempt to talk to either you or Major Champlain met interference from him. Eventually, we just told him we were sitting pat until someone other than him got on the line, over."

"Shit," Richard replied emotionlessly. "I've never trusted the little weasel. Endangering an entire operation just so he could cover his ass sounds exactly like him. Now, I get that you're mad, but what is it going to take to get your men moving? Over."

"We aren't unreasonable, General," William's grin was borderline inhuman in the way it grew across his face. "We've lost a lot of custom one-of-a-kind equipment, and under the circumstances, you're already responsible for triple damages. In short, $540 million. After that, well, you just triple our pay for the mission, and we'll call it good. Over."

"How much?" Richard practically choked. "Jesus fucking Christ, man, what are you going to ask for next, my daughter's hand in marriage? My fucking car?"

"You already owe us the $540 million," William winked at

Dan. "Our agreed-upon pay for the operation included normal wear and tear for the unit, and it came out to about $20 million. As for your daughter, well, isn't that usually the prize the heroes win for saving the kingdom? Over."

For almost a minute, there was no reply over the walkie talkie. Dan began to fret. They were talking about a lot of money. Maybe New Orleans didn't even have what it needed to pay them. Maybe William had overplayed their hand and asked for too much.

"Fuck you," Richard's dejected voice crackled back at them from the walkie talkie. "We'll pay you the $600 million and not a penny more. I'm gonna have Anderson shot for this, and when you get back to New Orleans, you're buying me a drink. Least you can do for fucking me like this, over."

"A pleasure doing business with you, General, over." William threw the walkie talkie to Dan, who caught it, an amused expression on his face.

"And that," Abe said, clapping Dan on the back, "is how it's done."

CHAPTER NINE

Earning a Paycheck (I)

The boats were silent other than their outboard motors as they drove toward the sounds of shooting. Dan took in the murky afternoon light and the brackish swamp water as they wove through the cypress trees. He wasn't exactly excited to go back into combat without a full resupply for the suits, but General Richard had been adamant. The Army of New Orleans was getting hit hard up and down their battle line, and they needed immediate relief.

Dan grudgingly agreed. His team was carrying about half of the fuel and ammunition he would have liked, but from the sound of things, supplies were starting to run low as well. Even the militia was being pressed into service as reinforcements for the actually trained guard troops. Beyond the rough sketch of the situation given to him by Major Champlain after the General hung up, they were going in blind.

The major didn't even have proper orders for him. The constant fighting draped the entire front in the fog of war. Dan got the impression that the Army didn't even know which unit was where. They just wanted all hands on deck to weather the onslaught of Orakh, and Dan's team was the largest untapped force in the area.

He rapped Abe on the metal pauldron of his shoulder. The Army of New Orleans might not mind throwing his team at the Orakh like a bucket of water on a forest fire, but Dan did. If they were going to go in, he wanted to have a plan of some sort. The last couple hours proved the futility of the half-assed approach.

Humanity had plenty of advantages over the Orakh, namely that the toads couldn't handle ranged combat nearly as well as the elves. Really, their only response was to try and charge fire teams, overwhelming them with sheer numbers. Up close, things weren't as human-friendly. The average Orakh was built like a gorilla and could hack apart an unenhanced human fairly easily. Theoretically, a human could fight them off with a knife or an axe, but for the large part, once an Orakh was in melee range with a person, that person was lunch.

Until this point, outside of Dan's team, battles had been a series of one-sided engagements. Humans dominated at range, gunning down large swaths of Orakh without any retaliation. Up close, the tables turned and battles would end in seconds as the Orakh simply slapped aside rifles and overpowered their human prey. Generally, that meant that you should aim your boat toward where you heard firing. If guns were shooting, it meant people were still alive and that the Orakh were probably at range. Probably.

Dan frowned, rapping his fist against Abe's shoulder pauldron once again. This time, his fist bounced off with a dull 'thonk,' stinging his knuckles, but getting Abe's attention. Abe shuffled slightly, careful to not tip the boat with his armor's huge bulk and split his face plate.

"What's up boss?" He cracked a brief smile. "I just got a little distracted taking in the scenery. I didn't hear you if you were trying to talk to me."

"I was just thinking, Abe." Dan scratched at his chin where

stubble was starting to grow in. He hadn't had a chance to shave properly in the last couple of days, due to the constant training and runecrafting, and he had the scraggly and misshapen beginnings of a beard to show for his efforts. "It sounds like the plan from HQ is for us to set down on an island and shoot until our guns run dry, then hack things apart with melee weapons until we run out of fuel. If we're lucky, the Orakh will run out of bodies before we run out of supplies."

"You know," Abe replied pensively, glancing out into the swamp. "I haven't seen a whole lot of supply runs go by, lately. I think we're running low on bullets, and that makes what you're describing a shit plan."

"I don't think anyone knows what's going on." Dan grimaced. "That call with HQ undermined any trust I might have ever had in them. They're just praying and throwing a Hail Mary right now, and I have a sinking feeling in my gut that we're their last desperate attempt at actually solving this mess."

"Well," Abe glanced back at him, chewing at his upper lip. "Fuck."

"I'm getting the feeling that things won't get better unless we make them better." Dan returned Abe's unhappy look. "If we settle down on an island, waiting for the Orakh to bury us with their numbers, we'll be sitting ducks. I think our only real bet here is to stay mobile. I'll be able to drop Fireballs on the Orakh at a pretty good clip without wasting anything but mana, and at this point, that recharges fairly quickly."

"That would take some pressure off of the other units." Abe glanced out toward the sounds of gunfire in the encroaching gloom. "I'm not sure how I feel about that, though. Our boats aren't exactly patrol ships. They can move, and they have guns on them, but behind that, I wouldn't want to put them through quick maneuvers. We have too much metal piled on top of them that could easily tip into the bayou. As some of that metal, I'd prefer to avoid that possibility."

Dan nodded. Abe had a point. The military had more specialized boats that could strafe the Orakh horde, and presumably they were doing that right now. Either that, or it wasn't a good plan, and the ships were already hacked apart and resting at the bottom of the bayou.

"Do you think the Orakh are stretched thin right now?" he asked Abe, still mulling over his options.

"If they aren't," Abe said with a shrug, metal rubbing against metal on his armor, "we're so fucked, it hardly matters, anyway. Theoretically, the crazies from Florida are attacking at the same time. We don't have any idea what the Orakh numbers look like, but from the amount of gunfire I'm still hearing, I'd estimate we've put a pretty good dent in whatever that total number looks like." Abe eyed him suspiciously. "Why? What are you thinking?"

"Well..." Dan shrugged sheepishly. "When things got rough in Brazil, Jennifer and I just kinda pushed through enemy lines."

"What?" Abe's eyes widened. "Do you know how many of those things are out there? Of course you don't! No one does. I've already decided how I'm going to die, and it involves a heart attack during a threesome at the age of ninety three. Getting eaten by space frogs after I stupidly stuck my head down their metaphorical throats is not part of the plan."

"Come on, Abe," Dan wheedled, a hint of a smile on his face. "If we set up shop on an island, we're just waiting to be overwhelmed. We might as well push through the front and get to the Orakh landing craft. Most of the Orakh are probably still swarming the battle line. If we push through them, they probably won't be able to catch up with us. We'll be able to hit the landing craft and do some serious damage before withdrawing. It might even be enough to get us through this mess."

"You sound like every dumb lieutenant on his first posting combined into one person right now, Thrush," Abe replied, his eyes closed. "Seriously man, it's uncanny. You can probably monetize that ability to make a fortune. Somewhere else. Where you aren't leading me on a suicide mission."

"Give me another choice then, Abe," Dan probed. "It's not

my favorite plan, but the other options are to turn tail, likely letting New Orleans get wiped out after the army falls, or we stand and fight and probably get wiped out with the Army. Not the best options in my book, so I figured we should try and Kobayashi Maru this."

"As much as I want to call you a nerd for that..." Abe opened his eyes and shook his head. "I don't think I have any better options for you. It could work, so long as we don't run into a big cluster of them. We haven't been able to find any long-distance communication enchantments or spells so far. Doesn't mean they don't have it, but I doubt they'll be able to radio for help in time. We'll probably be able to beat word back to the landing craft that we're on our way."

"There's that optimism I expect from you." Dan chuckled, slapping his open palm against the suit.

"I'm still not happy about this," Abe grumbled, flashing a hint of a smile. "It doesn't help that you're right about every-thing. I just expect that'll make you all the more insufferable later."

Dan smiled as Abe began using his suit radio to coordinate the change in plans. As much as William wanted to be his second in command, Abe was the one that actually knew what he was doing. He'd organized and coordinated small units for years, and Dan suspected that Abe knew more about tactics than he'd ever manage to learn. As for Jennifer, she was like Dan: good at killing things, not planning things.

The ships slightly changed course as Abe pushed his way to the front of the ship, motioning for the gunner on the .50 caliber to step aside. Even through his suit, Dan could see Abe flexing and relaxing his hands. It was sort of refreshing, actually, to see someone with as much experience as Abe getting pre-battle jitters. He was always collected, ready to break the mood with some stupid pun or dark joke. Watching him psych himself up for a tough stretch of combat humanized him to Dan in a way he had never realized he needed.

Before long, muzzle flashes cut through the murky light. The Army held out on a ragged string of islands, firing at the Orakh swarming toward them through the water. Periodically, the hulking shadow of an Orakh would make landfall, only to be torn apart with gunfire from a squad-operated weapon.

Individually, the New Orleans' Army's M-16s didn't do much against the Orakh, the small, fast bullets knocking them around but frequently failing to do fatal damage. But, in large numbers, they did the job adequately. More effective were the larger squad-operated automatic weapons that occasionally stuttered, bringing down a handful of their opponents as they sawed through their numbers in a quick burst. Despite the weapons' effectiveness, most of the fire coming from the islands was from the M-16s set to single shot. Without rifles of their own, the Army didn't need to focus on suppressing Orakh return fire and instead opted to conserve ammunition.

Dan couldn't quite make out how many soldiers were on each island, somewhere between a platoon and a company. Their boats sped by, raking the Orakh forces with heavy machine gun fire. Not to be outdone, Dan threw a trio of Fireballs, one after another, into the masses of Orakh preparing to dive into the waters of the swamp. He never saw how much damage their fusilade did to the cluster of Orakh, but he felt the trickle of mana that indicated something, at least, had died from his spells.

Just before the sun set, they made out the shape of the landing craft, a jagged spire of metal and rock sticking up almost thirty feet from the swamp. Given the vessel's shape, size, and weight, Dan was willing to bet the mission's payout that the ship extended almost as far underground as well. It glowed in the darkness, torches, and bonfires littering its outside and illuminating the milling swarm of Orakh that had eluded them on their trip past the battle line.

Dan blew out a quick breath to steady himself as he began preparing another Fireball. Abe glanced back at him, his face concealed by the heavy metal of his power armor's mask, and gave Dan a thumbs up before turning back to the machine gun and chambering a round. They were about to charge the city of New Orleans an exorbitant amount of money. It was time to prove they were worth the expense.

CHAPTER TEN

Earning a Paycheck (II)

Both of the .50 caliber machine guns opened fire at the same time, drowning out the boats' engines. The bullets scythed through the band of Orakh milling aimlessly about the landing zone. Abe didn't even have to aim; the Orakh were so densely packed that most of the bullets passed through one monster and hit another.

The disorganized mob of monsters tried to charge off of the embankment of dirt and mud surrounding the ship toward Dan's team, but it only served to pack them closer, making them easier targets for the gunners.

After a brief period of hammering fire, the entryway to the landing craft was littered with bodies. Dan could almost feel his ears tingle as the System's nanites repaired them while the ship jolted to a halt, running aground on the dirt outside the Orakh vessel. Abe jumped off the ship, causing it to rock back and forth as he stabbed his shortsword into the nearby Orakh corpses. Another soldier jumped off after him, using their armor-enhanced strength to pull the boat a foot or two up onto the embankment.

The rest of the team began filing out of the boat, their

metallic bulk slowing Dan while Jennifer and William shouted from the other boat, trying to speed them up. Periodically, a gunshot would ring out as a soldier used a wrist-mounted rifle to bring down an Orakh that came too close. Dan frowned. Even if they'd cleared out this mass of Orakh, that didn't mean things were secure. Already he could vaguely make out the forms swimming toward their ships.

Unfortunately, they couldn't split their forces enough to defend the beached ships and raid the enemy vessel. Unless Dan left half of his forces behind, there was just too great of a chance that they'd be overwhelmed by the Orakh forces slowly congregating on the site of the firefight. They were going to have to move fast, smash what they could, and perform a fighting withdrawal.

Dan sighed as his feet hit the springy mud of the shore. By now, Abe and Jennifer had finished going through the Orakh bodies to ensure that none of them would move again. Abe wiped his blade off on a towel he kept tied to his waste. The rest of the soldiers milled about nervously, occasionally taking potshots at anything they saw lurking in the water. He jogged past them to stand next to the heavy and crudely crafted iron door into the voidship and turned back to his team.

"Listen up!" He shouted, shunting mana into his sword to make it glow purple and draw the recruits' attention. Once most of them turned their faceplates to Dan, he began speaking. "Right now, we're far behind enemy lines. I wouldn't be surprised if their troops at the front have already turned around to deal with us. The good news is they will be stuck swimming. We have enough of a head start to get into the landing craft and do some damage. That said, we don't have a whole lot of time. Everyone set your System clock to ten minutes. We are leaving at twelve minutes, regardless of who is in the boats. That includes me.

"Now," Dan continued, flicking his wrist so that the sword hummed meaningfully. "We're going to split up once we're in there, so we can cause the most damage possible. I don't want any teams smaller than three, and you all have short-range radios. Use them. If you run into something you're struggling with, give us a call. Someone will help you out. Do any of you have questions?"

One of the suits raised an armored gauntlet in the growing twilight.

"You're going to have to tell me your name." Dan cracked a brief smile. "I can't really tell who is who through the oversized power suits."

"Ahm Remy Bushears, Sahr," the man replied, his thick Cajun accent rasping through the suit's speakers. "What are we tryina break? I know wirin' prettah well, but other than that, I ain't got the slightest."

"Good question, Mr. Bushears," Dan replied, mentally making a note to see if the System could clear up the thick local dialect for him. "The answer is anything that looks important. Machinery, crystals, or foodstuffs are a good guess. I will say that, if you see a large crystal, about six feet tall and thrumming with mana, let us all know before you do anything. That's probably a mana forge. If you blow that up, there's a good chance we'll all be part of the same mushroom cloud together."

He looked around the clearing. Most of the suits were nodding seriously. Well, Dan liked to think that they were nodding seriously. It was hard to tell through the impassive metal. Seeing no further questions, Dan took a deep breath to steady his nerves.

"Let's do this, then." He slammed his sword into the door, sawing it through the hinges holding it to the vessel's wall. "Remember, you have ten minutes to get back to the boats, and we leave in twelve. I don't want to leave anyone behind, but we need to keep moving, or we'll end up as food."

He pumped mana into the strength runes as he kicked the door, knocking it inward into the interior of the ship. Inside, the ship was dark. Not quite as dark as the swamp outside, but there were only periodic lights, simple green crystals that glowed weakly. The rest of the ship was a combination of dark stone and wrought black iron, giving it a half-finished and oppressive aura.

Dan surged forward, starting his own timer for nine minutes. A small Orakh variant, barely waist-high, tried to flee from him, but he brought it down with a Lightning Stroke before cutting it down with his sword. Behind him, the clatter of metal rang out on stone as the rest of the troops followed him in.

He set off running down the hallway in front of him, quickly outpacing the heavier armored suits. Wordlessly, Jennifer fell in beside him. He nodded at her then jerked his head toward a door lining the hallway.

Together they stopped, and Jennifer put her right hand on the door latch. Her left held up three fingers. She put down one. Dan refreshed the mana flow into his spellshield and prepped a Fireball. She put down another finger. He readied himself as she threw the door open and jumped aside.

Immediately, Dan almost gagged at the smell of offal. The room was gigantic, almost twenty feet wide and sixty deep, and the entirety of its flickering interior was filled with more of the waist-high Orakh's moving to and from large stone tables covered in butchered animals. Dan wrinkled his nose. One thing was sure, the Orakh weren't picky. Some tables had gators on them, missing legs and tails. Others were covered with half-dismembered boars.

Most distressingly, Dan made out one of the tiny Orakh running off with what appeared to be a human arm. Frantically, his gaze darted around the cavernous room. It only took him a couple seconds, but he made out a pile of human bodies in the corner, still clad in combat fatigues. He frowned. Apparently, the rumors about the Orakh eating their victims weren't just rumors.

Dan ignited his flame aura, immediately lighting up the room as he stalked forward, launching Fireball after Fireball across the room. The smaller Orakh began screaming and running away from Dan. One-by-one, he set them on fire, and Jennifer quickly dispatched those that made it past him.

She stood in the doorway, watching his back and observing the inferno. Unlike Dan, she didn't have a thermal resistance rune, so actually entering the torched butcher's hall was far from a good idea. Still, her flickering blades of force got a good workout cleaving apart the smaller Orakh.

Finally, Dan calmed down. The fire had erased any trace of the massive amount of animals. He exited the room, frantically trying to rub the foul-smelling soot from his outfit.

"Feeling any better?" Jennifer asked, cocking her head slightly to the side.

"I suppose," Dan replied, smiling weakly. "I've seen a lot of shit, but the idea that these things are eating people really doesn't sit right with me."

"Well," she smiled back. "Maybe killing a bunch more Orakh would cheer you up. There should be plenty more to go around, if you need a pick-me-up."

Dan led the way once more, the occasional gunfire of his soldiers echoing indeterminately through the ship's hallways. Randomly, he pointed to another door. Jennifer opened it in the same fashion, revealing an almost identical scene.

This time, it didn't hit Dan as hard as he walked through, igniting everything in the room. The tiny Orakh didn't even try to fight him. It was strange how different they were from their larger and almost suicidally arrogant brethren. He supposed that they must fulfill a different role in Orakh society, but it hardly mattered. Between Jennifer and him, they cleared the entire room in under a minute.

He checked the System clock as he marched back to Jennifer. Just under five minutes left.

"One more room?" He questioned, cocking his head slightly to crack his neck. "We only have five minutes left. I don't want to risk running late, even if we get turned around trying to get out. Plus, I would prefer to leave first. Hopefully, we can clear the boats of Orakh before the rest of the team gets out. I'd prefer to be ready to go the instant the clocks hit 12. This entire thing was supposed to be a diversion. I don't want to get overwhelmed by Orakh reinforcements before we can get the hell out of here."

"One more," she agreed, glancing down the hallway, sizing up the various doors before they disappeared in the flickering green gloom.

"Shit!" Dan's walkie talkie squawked. "Oh fuck, is he huge! We need backup as soon as possible." Gunfire erupted in the background, followed by a deep, bellowing snarl.

Dan glanced at Jennifer. He'd heard that one without the radio. She took off, Dan following her as they tried to track down the sounds of battle.

"Oh god," the walkie talkie continued, the clang of metal on metal complimenting the steady thud of gunfire. "He has some sort of shield that's just eating up gunfire. He-"

The man gulped over the air before speaking. "He just cut Billeaux in half. Like, the defensive runes flared. It should have stopped him, but he had an axe as big as a fucking sedan."

Dan and Jennifer rounded the corner, and suddenly they were in another oversized room. This one was a hall, the walls covered in Orakh trophies: pennants, weapons, and skulls. At least ten Orakh warriors stood in the hall, but it was hard to really notice them.

In the center of the room stood the biggest Orakh Dan had ever seen. Fourteen feet of muscle and anger towered over his subordinates, at least a head taller than the commander Dan had beheaded earlier. The behemoth of an Orakh held an axe in his right hand, maybe a little smaller than a sedan, but close enough that Dan wouldn't begrudge the panicked soldier. His left held the metal helmet of a power-suited soldier, whose feet kicked helplessly, suspended almost a foot off the ground. At his feet were two torn-apart suits of armor, great rends ripped almost through them by the axe on his shoulder.

The Orakh made eye contact with Dan and smiled, an ugly thing of chipped fangs and tusks, before his body pulsed with mana. Then he closed his left hand, crushing the suit's helmet and the soldier's skull.

"Good," he ground out in heavily accented Elven. "An actual challenger. These suits of metal are interesting, but they're piloted by grubs. Not even worth taking a trophy. But you, human. I can feel the deaths swirling around you. You'll make this shit invasion worthwhile."

CHAPTER ELEVEN

Boss Fight

The remainder of the Orakh spread out, allowing Dan to approach but cutting Jennifer off. They formed a rough ring around the hall, blocking Jennifer out but not taking any action against her. The gigantic Orakh dropped the armored body and hoisted its axe, quickly crossing the ground toward Dan with long, casual steps.

"I can feel the mana pulsing off of you, human," the Orakh said, his voice a deep rumble Dan could feel in his chest. "You feel more like an elf than these animals playing around with their toys, but that shouldn't be the case."

"Tell me," he commanded, hoisting his axe. "The elves believe your kind can't accumulate power past a certain point. Obviously, they are wrong. Tell me who you stole this power from, and I will make your death and the death of your mate quick. Resist, and I will feed your limbs one-by-one to my men while you yet live."

Dan let his mana flow into the sword, igniting it. The purple light illuminated the room eerily, casting the huge Orakh in front of him and the large metal throne behind him into flickering relief. The creature's eyes lit up as it focused on the blade.

"So, you've killed an archmage." The Orakh's mouth curved into a bestial smile. "You are powerful, but not that powerful, human. I've been in battles against archmages. I've seen Orakh fall by the dozens as spells ripped their bones from their bodies in order to buy our warriors enough time to smash their way through the elf's shield."

"Tell me how you did it," he continued, his eyes gleaming with a feral light. "No archmage would abandon their blade. But, at the same time, there isn't quite enough magic in you to overcome one. What is the trick, manling? Tell me now where this power came from."

"I earned it on my fucking own." Dan rolled his eyes as he increased the mana to his strength rune. "By spell and sword, one dead monster and elf at a time."

Some of the anger of the past couple weeks bubbled over. Days of stomaching overly rushed schedules and incompetence on the part of his employers. The constant skeptical comments when he spoke of using magic. The lack of discipline on the part of his new employees that led to their deaths and the destruction of hundreds of thousands of dollars' worth of equipment.

All of that, and here he was once again with an enemy talking down to him. The same cliche lines and doubts. Being underestimated might give him an advantage, after all. An arrogant enemy was an enemy you could easily trick, but Dan was fucking sick of it.

He triggered a Fireball into the ground behind him, counting on it to engulf the Orakh surrounding him. Given an opening, Jennifer could handle ten Orakh on her own, so long as she wasn't surrounded. With any luck, the Fireball would provide her that opening and let her leverage her mobility to keep the traditional Orakh off-balance.

The Orakh Lord bellowed his defiance and anger at Dan, swinging the axe at a speed the half-ton weapon should've been incapable of. He hastily ducked under the weapon as it whistled through the air. Dan gritted his teeth. Even with his enhanced reactions, dodging was far more difficult than it should have been.

The Orakh moved elf-fast as he stomped on the ground, knocking Dan off balance from the impact as he jumped backward. In the air, the towering Orakh pointed his gauntlet-clad right hand at Dan.

Dan stumbled to his feet and looked up in shock as dark mana coiled around the Orakh's hand. Energy curled around the creature's metal glove, a wreath of purple sparks that arced and crackled as power accumulated.

With a muffled curse, Dan dropped mana into his temporal rune, eyes tracking the crude bolt of oscillating darkness that spat forth from the Orakh's gauntlet.

His sword traced a crackling line of purple light through the air. The slowed time made the action maddening. The sword crawled, even with his enhanced muscles only able to drive the weapon forward at inches per subjective second as the bolt of darkness moved at almost three times its speed.

Sweat beaded Dan's forehead as he pushed with all his might, dragging the tip of his sword infinitesimally faster through the molasses air. The blade barely caught the bolt of darkness, its purple aura hissing and crackling as it deflected the bolt to the side where it slammed into and disintegrated a stone chair.

Dan gasped for breath, eyeing up the Orakh as it glanced dubiously at the wrecked chair. His spellshield could have taken the blow, but it would have almost entirely wiped out its mana. Whatever that attack was, it packed a punch.

A punch that the Orakh shouldn't have. To date, their race had divided itself neatly. The shamans were smaller and weaker, but they could use mana. Warriors came in different sizes, but they were straightforward. The only tactic they employed was charging toward you with an axe and hoping for the best.

This Orakh was different. He talked, reasoned, and used magic. Dan had already been preparing to counterattack once the thing overextended itself in the first charge, a common quick victory tactic he'd used against Orakh to date. Instead, it had anticipated his actions and tried to trap him, a worrying sign that his fighting style was growing stale and predictable.

They circled each other warily, eyes locked on the other. Behind him, clashes and clangs announced that Jennifer was fighting the ordinary Orakh, but he couldn't pull his gaze from the enemy before him. Even a moment's hesitation would give it the opening it needed to bring him in range of that axe.

Dan launched a Lightning Stroke with his free hand, catching the Orakh in the upper right portion of its bare chest. He sprinted forward, temporal rune pulling heavily at his mana reserves once again as he tried to take advantage of the spell's distraction.

Unfortunately, it did next to nothing. The heat from the electrical arc burned a portion of the Orakh's flesh, but there wasn't the usual disability for him to take advantage of. No spastic twitching, no muscle spasms, not even a loss of focus. Instead, what remained was three tons of pissed off Orakh with a small burn on its chest.

It swung its axe at knee level, almost flush with the floor, forcing Dan to jump over it. Immediately, he realized his mistake, as the Orakh used the momentum from swinging the axe to spin around and deliver a backhand straight into his spellshield while he hung helpless, suspended in the air at the apex of his jump.

He managed to create a force bubble in the way of the Orakh's fist, which dampened the blow somewhat, but even with the spellshield, he rocketed into the chamber's wall, leaving a cracked crater in the heavy stone and iron. Dan shook the fuzz from his vision, tossing a Fireball into the air where he suspected the Orakh would be charging while he tried to regain his bearings long enough to escape.

The Orakh, singed but not seriously injured, stormed through the Fireball just as Dan managed to sprint away from the wall, narrowly dodging the axe blow that cleaved through it like it was made of soggy cardboard. He jumped over the stone table in the hall, trying to ignore the way the floor tipped and jerked under him as his scrambled brain tried to regain some semblance of balance.

The alien bellowed in anger, once again charging dark mana around its gauntlet. This time, Dan didn't give him a chance, firing a string of Forcebolts into it before finishing with a Fireball.

Despite his incredible size and strength, the Forcebolts managed to stagger and distract the massive amphibious creature enough that it lost control of the dark mana. The Orakh took one step backwards, the closest thing to a victory Dan had managed to earn in the battle to date, when the Fireball detonated.

Dan sprinted forward once more, the translucent light of force mana glittering around his left hand as he charged. So far, the Orakh had mostly shrugged off his elemental attacks, but at least force mana knocked it around a little bit. Pummeling it with force bolts might not do much damage through its thick skin and dense muscle, but at very minimum, he should be able to keep it off-balance.

Once again, the axe blurred diagonally through the space that he was about to occupy, forcing Dan back a step. The Orakh grunted, his normally moist body hissing and smoking as he burst through the wall of flame created by Dan's Fireball.

Time slowed as the temporal rune gave him the seconds needed to line up and launch a trio of Forcebolts into the gigantic axe, knocking it slightly to the side. Dan adjusted his course, twisting his body past the descending axehead as it buried itself in the floor without any resistance from his spellshield.

The Orakh's eyes went wide with surprise as Dan ducked under its guard. His sword flashed, cutting deep into the meat of its left forearm, severing tendons and shattering bone before his strength and momentum ran out, and Dan had to brace himself to withdraw the blade.

Feeling rather than seeing the dark mana swirling behind

him, Dan ripped his sword out of his enemy's arm and threw himself at its ankles in a desperate spinning roll. The bolt missed, carving a hole in the room's floor and creating a torso-sized hole into the chamber below. Then, his spellshield crackled as the Orakh's shin crashed into him, sending Dan skidding on his back across the chamber.

Dan stood up, taking in the four remaining ordinary Orakh as their leader bellowed, gauntleted right hand clasped over the deep wound leaking ichor from its left side. Jennifer was partially surrounded, but she was holding her own, still without help. It would be some time before she'd be able to assist him.

"Duck!" he screamed at her, simultaneously triggering a force bubble over her dropping body and detonating a Fireball almost directly above her. She'd likely end up slightly crispy from the blast, but it was the quickest way he could think to resolve the stalemate.

The Orakh around her staggered back, clawing at the third-degree burns that covered their bodies. Dan turned toward the Orakh leader that was already trying to line up another bolt from its gauntlet at him. Silently, he cursed himself for focusing mostly on flashy area-of-effect and stunning abilities in his spell research. In a battle of pure strength, he needed something more dedicated: the ability to target the meanest SOB on a battlefield and make them hurt.

Filing the thought away, Dan ran at the Orakh once more, a zigzagging serpentine designed to deny the alien a clear shot as he peppered it with Forcebolts. Silently, he prayed that he could finish the monster off before he ran out of mana. Already, the constant spell and rune use was putting strain on his reserves.

A quick stutterstep and another bolt of darkness slammed into the ground about ten paces away from Dan as he changed course at the last second. This time, his sword slashed deep into the meat of the Orakh's hamstring as Dan sprinted past it.

Behind him, the creature tried futilely to catch him, grasping at his shadow with the heavy gauntlet that was pulsing with dark mana. Dan wasn't entirely sure what that would do to his spellshield, but it certainly made short work of a soldier in full battle armor, so he wasn't inclined to slow down enough to find out.

The Orakh spun toward him, staggering as his injured leg struggled to carry his weight while his left arm flopped uselessly.

Dan locked gazes with the creature. Both were breathing heavily from using magic to push their bodies past their natural limits, but neither flinched. A distraction on its part would be all he would need to take advantage of its injured arm and lamed leg. But, by the same token, the bolts of darkness moved fast. After the two heavy kinetic blows he'd taken earlier in the battle, Dan didn't want to push his luck on the spellshield absorbing all of the dangerous-looking spells.

A smile crept across Dan's face. The Orakh cocked its head, eyes still on him as it tried to make sense of the change in his expression. Then Jennifer landed on its back, blades of force adorning each of her hands as she shoved them into its thick hide.

The force magic didn't penetrate far; the Orakh's corded muscles were far too dense to be easily harmed by such rudimentary magic, but they did hurt enough to distract it. Enraged, it reached back with the humming blackness of the gauntlet, trying to grab onto Jennifer, only for her to drop to the ground.

In that moment, Dan's sword sank into the Orakh leader's chest, the creature's splayed arms providing it with no cover as it contorted its body, looking for Jennifer. The alien's eyes widened, and it reached back for Dan, its muscular arm moving at a crawl as it tried to traverse the entirety of its body.

Dan fired a Flame Jet into the invader's face, blinding him temporarily. Dan pulled his sword out of the Orakh's body, dropping to the ground only to stab upward once again, driving the purple weapon deep into its stomach.

The Orakh fell to its knees, only for Dan to plunge his sword into the massive creature's chest once more. With both of the alien's lungs ruptured, he wheezed for breath, confusion and the first hints of fear widening his massive eyes. Dan knocked it onto its side with a Forcebolt.

The Orakh still clung to life, insensible but unable to give up, clinging to its last breath through sheer stubbornness and animalistic impulse. Grabbing the creature by the top of its head, Dan sawed his sword across the Orakh's throat. The blade flared purple as it cut deep into the alien's heavy muscle, only for Dan to jerk it backward, cutting his way through the reeling creature's neck inch-by-inch.

It took almost a minute, but finally the head popped free, and with it came a torrent of mana. As Dan tried not to enjoy the afterglow too much, Jennifer tapped him on the shoulder and pointed through the hole in the floor blown by the creature's gauntlet.

Below them was a massive chamber filled with pale, bioluminescent eggs. They surrounded a massive creature. The size of an elephant, it was a limbless sack of flesh with a mouth that warbled in distress as he fixed his gaze upon it.

Dan frowned. In front of his eyes, two of the smaller Orakh brought it a stack of meat, some from gators and some from humans. While they poured their crude wheelbarrows of food into its endless maw, it laid one of the pale eggs.

A Fireball burned in his grip as he stepped toward the opening in the floor.

CHAPTER TWELVE

Reunion

Dan walked tiredly out of the landing craft, dragging the severed head of the Orakh leader behind him while Jennifer fiddled with the oversized gauntlet. Unfortunately, the damaged armor and dead soldiers were far too heavy for the two of them to extricate on their own. Around him, the smell of smoke and ozone filled the air, evidence that his squad had been busy without him.

He sniffed the air again. Either that, or he was still smelling smoke from burning down the breeding chamber. He wasn't entirely sure what creature was dwelling amongst the field of eggs, but Dan suspected it had a large part to play in the Orakh's numerical superiority, so he did the only thing he could think of: blanketed the hidden chamber in Fireballs until his mana ran dry.

He shuddered. Dan could still hear the thing's warbling screams, and he wasn't sure that the horrible smell would come out of his clothing. As bad as the bayou was, the thick black smoke from the burning eggs carried the delectable aroma of a sewage barbeque. If it hadn't been for the half-remembered stint in the tree with Jennifer, he probably would have lost his lunch in the main hall.

Whatever it was, they'd killed it. He didn't know if the Orakh had another one stashed away nearby, but given the size of its chamber in comparison to the metal and stone shard they used as a ship, he doubted it.

Nearing the exit, he winced at the System timer showing -45 seconds. He'd hoped to get out a little early and clear their landing zone of Orakh so that the returning squads wouldn't be stepping into a firefight. With any luck, either William or Abe had been able to extricate themselves and ensure that the squad would be able to launch on time. He didn't hear gunfire, which Dan chalked up as a hopeful sign.

Stepping into the open, Dan froze, frowning. Ten of his team, including Abe, stood outside, their weapons trained on about twenty soldiers wearing camouflage. His gaze focused on the shortswords at their hips. He knew those swords.

"Shit," he said quietly to Jennifer and drew his sword.

In the growing dark, he could barely make out their faces under the camouflage paint covering them, but it was enough to confirm his suspicions. The twenty in front of him were all soldiers from Colonel Bowman's contingent, likely here for a purpose similar to his. They might lack the firepower of his powered armor, but they had magic and knew how to work as a team. Dan, Abe, and Jennifer might be able to hold their own, but the rest of the team would almost certainly take losses.

"Hey, guys." Dan forced a smile on his face as he sauntered out of the landing craft. "It's good to see old faces and all, but I think we managed to steal your thunder." He threw the severed head onto the muddy dirt between the groups.

The soldiers looked at each other before returning their attention to Dan and Jennifer. Their posture wasn't what he'd like to see from allies, even in a war zone. Almost every one of them was tense, their rifles barely not pointing at Dan's team and their fingers barely off of their triggers.

"We're just about to leave," Abe's voice broadcast from his armor. "Our last team is almost out of the ship. You can loot it to your heart's content. At least for the moment, we're all on the same side. No need to make this entire thing awkward."

"Good to see you, Sergeant Steil." One of them finally spoke, nodding a fraction of an inch toward Abe. "Wish I could agree with you, but we've got orders."

"Orders?" Abe laughed, the sound harsh and discordant. "General Finch is in that ship behind me. We all know Colonel Bowman is a nutcase. If you're following anything resembling the chain of command, you should join up with us when we leave here. Thrush pulled me out of Ibis' lair when the asshole backstabbed us. He's a decent guy, and we're trying to put together a private military company to enforce some kind of order on all this shit."

"If the orders were from Bowman..." The man shrugged slightly. "I'm not sure I see eye-to-eye with the Colonel, but he's got a lot of men's families under guard. It's not that easy to turn your back on him."

"Wait," Jennifer interjected, frowning. "If the orders weren't from Bowman, who in the hell is telling you to hold onto us?"

A flash of light illuminated the clearing as a thin, beautiful woman jumped off of one of Bowman's boats, flickering tendrils of fire covering her. Dan's fake smile faded.

"That would be me," Merella glided into the center of the clearing, her spellshield glowing slightly. "Daniel." She drew the word out, playing with the syllables before trailing off into an almost hiss.

"The last time we fought, you killed my nephew." She smiled, a predatory thing meant to display her mouthful of sharp teeth. "When I challenged you to a duel, you cheated. Our battle was fairly invigorating, but others intervened. Finally, you tricked me and injected me with this accursed System you use to ape the powers of your betters.

"This time," she continued, motioning to the fire team behind her, "we are evenly matched. Our fight will be one-on-one, and this time I will crush you. You see, *Daniel*." Her smile became all teeth, the jagged mouth of a carnivore that wants you to know exactly what it is.

"Now that I have your system," she tapped the side of her head, "I can learn magic just as fast as you. It has been a positive revelation. Even without a terribly large increase in mana, I'm easily twice as strong as the last time we fought, and back then, it took an entire squad and trickery to bring me down. Tell me, manling. What hope do you have today?"

"Hold on," Dan raised a hand, waving it slightly. "I know you have a monologue to deliver and all that, but I wanted to know what the story was with Ibis. Honestly, I thought the army was going to kill you when you were handed over. How the hell did you end up on national TV next to Henry Ibis during that final address?"

"Why shouldn't I humor you?" Merella asked, fire dancing over her fingertips. "I suppose I can consider your question some sort of last request."

Dan rolled his eyes. He was officially fucking fed up with the constant derogatory attitudes. Silently, he accessed the System.

"Ibis snatched me out of your army's custody." A sneer crossed her face. "He kept asking me questions about the Tellask Empire, and when I didn't answer, he used this accursed System to punish me. Eventually, I just started giving him answers. Most of them were wrong in subtle ways, and then he started talking about eating a mana crystal."

"At first, I told him that it was nothing more than an expensive and painful way to die," Merella remarked with a roll of her eyes. "But he kept insisting that you survived. So, I made up an ancient elven secret that would allow him to survive the process. I even told him that it was a secret we reserved for noble scions. The fool lapped it all up then killed himself in front of your entire nation. A fitting punishment. My only regret is that I couldn't do it again and again to him for the indignities he forced upon me.

"Now?" Fire gathered in her open hand as she raised it

toward Dan. "Now, without his control, no one can stop me. Do you have any last words, Daniel?"

"Sleep," he replied, toggling the system command. Immediately, her eyes went vacant as she fell bonelessly to the ground. He shook his head slowly, whistling. After all of that, she didn't find a way to remove the System's control mechanism.

Immediately, gunfire rang out. About half of the fireteam sprayed the power suits with fully automatic fire, doing little more than generating ricochets, while the other half dove to the ground.

Dan's team returned fire, most of the .50 caliber slugs missing, but the pair that hit absolutely shredded their targets. One of Bowman's men grabbed Merella, slinging her over his shoulder as they backed up toward one of the boats, laying covering fire.

The rest of the squad simply ignored their shots, their armor being all the cover they needed against M-16s. One by one, the soldiers fighting them fell as they drove the boat off. One of them was an initiate force mage and put up a barrier for just long enough to block a flurry of shots aimed at disabling the ship and deflecting a hastily thrown Fireball from Dan.

Then they fled, the entire battle taking maybe fifteen seconds from the moment the first shot was fired to their boat weaving in and out of the islands surrounding the landing site in an attempt to avoid fire. Five bodies lay on the ground, ripped open by the heavy-caliber weapons used primarily for fighting Orakh.

The other ten soldiers slowly put their guns on the ground and unstrapped their belts, letting their swords fall as well. For a second, no one spoke. Then the soldier that had originally been talking to Abe stepped forward.

"So," he coughed sheepishly, hands in the air. "You guys still hiring? As bad as Bowman is, Merella is an absolute piece of work. I don't want to spend my entire life fighting to defend this country and planet, only for Bowman to throw it all away as part of some weird powerplay."

"What the hell was that, then?" Dan asked, confused as he hooked a thumb toward the retreating speedboat. "We do need to hire people who can fight, but I need it to be people I can trust. Half of you just tried to gun us down when you had the opportunity to join up."

"They have families," the soldier's voice was grim. "If they turn tail, Bowman would do things to them. Pretty sure most of 'em knew they were going to die pulling that stunt there, but dying in combat means he doesn't torture your son. Things aren't going all that well in Florida right now."

Dan looked to Abe, who nodded through his battle armor.

"Sergeant Quinn is a straight shooter, boss," he opined. "And I think he's right. If they actually planned to fight us, they'd have closed the distance and tried to use those swords. That attack of theirs wasn't the plan of someone trying to win a battle. Hell, those weren't even the actions of someone trying to survive."

"The more the merrier, I guess." Dan glanced briefly over his shoulder as William led his team out of the landing craft. "Obviously, we'll be watching you, but I'm glad to have some familiar faces on board."

CHAPTER THIRTEEN

Gearing Up

"I owe you how much money?" Mayor DuBlanc massaged her temples as she sat across from Dan in her office. "That's literally twice my annual discretionary budget."

She paused squinting at Dan before sighing. "I suppose you're going to want that in goods that are more durable than dollars, too. I don't know where the hell you expect me to find that much gold, but it sure ain't happening anytime soon.

"Just out of curiosity, Thrush," she leaned back in her chair, shaking her head slightly. "What in the hell happened to drive the bill up that high? I just got your invoice from General Richard with the words 'don't argue, pay it' written on it. I've seen that man haggle down the price on a bulk delivery of napkins. If I'm going to shell out this much, at a minimum, I'm entitled to know what I'm paying for."

Dan chuckled, scratching at the stubble of the beard beginning to grow in. He hadn't gotten a chance to do more than a quick rinse-off since returning from the bayou, and that meant he hadn't shaved. Getting the new hires settled and calming down the recruits once the mana high wore off and they realized that they'd suffered 30% casualties took priority. In the past three days, he'd only managed to sleep five hours a night, and every waking moment had been filled with constant, nagging problems.

"We more or less single-handedly made the operation a success," Dan replied with a chuckle. "Some asshole on Richard's staff let us get out of position, and we ended up 'clearing the way' for the entire front to advance. We lost three men while the rest of the army left us hanging out to dry."

DuBlanc winced.

"Yeah, we weren't happy about it either," Dan chuckled mirthlessly. "We stopped fighting until someone could give us an explanation, and the main attack stalled out. They got bogged down in island to island fighting with the Orakh, and they were pretty steadily getting overwhelmed and running out of ammunition. General Richard agreed to pay us what we asked. We sidestepped the entire fight and went directly to the enemy headquarters.

"Not to get all 'Conan the Barbarian,'" Dan said with a shrug, "but I ended up fighting their leader in hand-to-hand combat and killing him. There was also some sort of breeding chamber that I burned down. After that, the fighting dropped in intensity. We don't know enough about how the Orakh work, but it sounds like killing their leader released them from some sort of drive or control. Before that, I don't think we've heard anything about Orakh retreating, but almost immediately there was a pretty massive wave of desertion. From what I've heard, there are still a good number of Orakh in the bayou, but it doesn't look like there's any sort of organization."

"General Richard said something about Colonel Bowmen?" DuBlanc asked, shaking her head as she prodded Dan into continuing.

"One of his main lieutenants is literally an alien agent, and she tried to kill me," Dan replied. "As I warned earlier, he isn't to be trusted. From what I've heard from the defectors, things are really bad in Florida right now. I wouldn't be surprised if we are next on his list now that the Orakh are gone, and as far as I can tell, you *really* don't want that to happen."

"A bit fond of crucifying dissenters, isn't he?" The mayor nodded unhappily. "I can't say I disagree with your reasoning, Thrush. I just don't know how I'm going to be able to pay your bill. If you've got any ideas, I'm all ears."

Dan smiled. He hadn't been able to bring William with him, but the wiley old man and him had talked for a while before he met with the mayor. The goal wasn't to soak her so hard that their company was kicked out of New Orleans, but at the same time, they wanted the resources to pay their soldiers and expand.

"We do have a proposal for you." He slid a piece of paper across the table to DuBlanc. "We can work out the nitty gritty later, but the highlights are food, medicine, silver, gold, tungsten, ammunition, five Bradley Infantry Fighting Vehicles, and priority pick of certain enumerated military hardware."

"Jesus," she replied flatly, looking over the offer. "You're actually serious about five Bradleys? I can't say I'll be happy to part with them. Especially after that debacle, our guard unit doesn't have a whole lot of extra material to spare."

"Well," he shrugged, feigning concern. "As you said, you aren't terribly liquid right now. It makes sense to pay us in valuable goods that we can make use of, rather than just demanding all of your gold and a cut of your tax revenue for the next couple years."

"Ugh." DuBlanc sighed. "I get it. You aren't pushing as hard as you could, and I thank you for that. Only about half of this is up front, with the rest being these 'priority picks' of military hardware you have listed. I suppose I should be grateful that you aren't holding my feet to the fire right now, but I really just feel like I need a drink."

The mayor pulled open a desk drawer and removed a brown bottle. Dan couldn't quite make out the label, but when DuBlanc uncorked, it the smell of alcohol quickly filled the room. She took a swig from the bottle and wrinkled her face before recapping it.

"You've got a deal." She eyed the bottle longingly. "We'll work out the exact details about how we'll make all of this happen in the coming weeks, but in principle, what you're asking for is fair. I'll have my staff get in touch with yours, but for now, I think I'm going to hit that bottle again to celebrate our victory and try to forget whatever Faustian bargain I just agreed to."

"I'll leave you to it then, Madame Mayor." Dan chuckled as he stood up and saw himself out.

As he exited the room, Jennifer peeled herself from the wall where she'd been lounging and fell into step beside him. They left city hall in relative silence.

"So," she asked as they stepped out into the quiet afternoon bustle. "How'd it go?"

"She took it pretty well," he responded. "I think your Dad had the right of it: push but don't push too hard. It sounds like she plans on paying, but I think 'deferring' half of our payment until we can receive it in the form of heavier equipment and airplanes was a good idea. I'm sick of fighting without air support, and if I've learned anything in the last couple of months, it's that the only way to assure air support is to supply it yourself."

"Can't disagree with that," she chuckled. "So, what's next? You get us a new mission?"

"No." Dan shook his head. "And I'm glad of it, too. We've been thrown from one fight to another so often that we haven't had a chance to catch a breath. I need new spells, the defectors need new runes, and the new recruits need basic training.

"Also," he cocked his head and let out a soft laugh. "I think we need to hire some people who can drive an armored personnel carrier. Do you think craigslist still works? Should we put an ad up?"

"I'm not doing interviews," she replied smoothly. "Back when I was gaming, I put up an ad for an assistant on craigslist.

At least three people asked me for pictures of my feet. If one of us is going to end up sacrificing feet pics for the cause, it's you."

"In all seriousness." Dan smiled back at her. "It sounds like we should put Abe in charge of it. I don't know the first thing about looking for or vetting trustworthy ex-military employees. Considering that's more or less what he's already doing, it seems like a logical extension to me."

"Can I be there when you tell him he's in charge of HR now?" Jennifer said, a hint of a smile on her face. "Seriously, make sure not to sugarcoat this or give him a fancy title. None of this 'director of personnel management' stuff, I want to see the look on his face when you appoint him head of human resources."

Abe took the 'promotion' with about as much grace as Jennifer implied, swearing up a good-natured blue streak. Dan could tell Abe was secretly happy with the new job. The man liked fighting, but he had a natural knack for organizing people, and he seemed to like it.

Frankly, Dan was relieved. One more task off his already-full plate. Well, at the moment, he really only had two tasks: develop a new single-target spell and finish runescripting the rest of the new soldiers once Abe vouched for them. It'd take a couple days for DuBlanc to get all the necessary materials to their encampment. Hopefully, in that time, Abe would be able to give him a better idea of what kind of runes would best complement each soldier.

He called up his status to assess his gains from the last couple weeks.

<USER> Status
Rank 8

Body 6(8)
Agility 7 (9)
Mind 8
Perception 7

Spirit 77

Skills
Swords 12, Brawling 5, Archery 2, Runecrafting 8

Affinity
Space 13, Lightning 11, Fire 12, Gravity 10, Force 14

Enhancements
Armor Rune V, Strength Rune +2, Agility Rune +2, Thermal Resistance Rune, Temporal Dilation Rune 10:1

Runes+

Spells
Shocking Fist 10, Spark Field 2, Lightning Stroke 11, Spatial Shield 8, Flame Jet 4, Gravitational Easing 10, Fireball 14, Force Bubble 12, Spellshield 11, Forcebolt 9, Flame Aura 5

Modest everywhere but spirit. That was the problem with getting his spells to a high level; early levels were easy, but everything afterward slowed to a crawl. Still, slaughtering Orakh en masse along with killing their leader was fairly lucrative for his mana pool. Even now, he was edging closer and closer to rank 10, generally considered by elves to be the border between normal mages and archmages.

He stretched his back and went to the *Viceroy*'s training room. He had a pretty good idea as to what the new spell would be, but first he'd need to level up his metal affinity. After all, the attunement stone had lain dormant in his arm for years now. It was about time he made it earn its keep.

CHAPTER FOURTEEN

Independent Study

Dan growled in frustration as the electricity running through his palms and into a pair of metal rods grounded out with a flash of ozone. He'd forgotten how frustrating developing a new spell was. By now, he could cast all of his favorites as if they were second nature. He simply thought of the effect he wanted, and the nanites in his body did the rest, triggering muscles and mana pathways to enact the spell.

Looking at the metal bars, he sighed. The voltage he ran through them was more than the thin strips of metal could take, melting and bending them until they were no longer parallel. Even the slightest imperfection would ruin the spell, likely the cause of his previous failure.

Concentrating on the rods, he converted some of his mana to metal mana in an attempt to smooth them out. It worked, after a fashion. The two metal dowels flopped in his hand like freshly cooked spaghetti. Frowning, he laid them on the floor and stretched them tight before relaxing the flow of mana.

He picked one of the strips of metal up and tapped it on the ground with a satisfying clang. At least this time, they hardened properly without turning brittle and shattering into a cloud of sharp, metallic slivers. That'd been fun to clean up.

Once again, he ran an electrical current through the two rods. He could feel the interaction, just out of his grasp, as the flow of electricity created the barest hint of Lorentz force pushing forward. He seized on the sensation, trying to imprint it on his memory. After all, the goal was to replicate it without the need for metallic tools and props.

Another flash of electricity lit up the gymnasium, forcing Dan to drop the metal with a hiss as it superheated and scalded his hand. A knock at the door drew his attention.

"Come on in," he called out, activating his thermal rune and picking up the metal to soften and smooth it once again.

Jennifer poked her head in through the door and made a face at him in the dim light of the ship's gymnasium.

"I know I haven't had a chance to shower or put on makeup in the last couple days," she quipped, "but you don't have to be so upfront about it."

"What?" Dan cocked his head at her before glancing down and realizing that the metal rod in his hand had been magically softened, hanging limply like a length of rope from his loose grip.

"Jesus Christ, Jennifer!" He blushed, pulling the metal taut before hardening it. "I'm doing research here; there isn't any need to be crude about it."

"I heard you swearing, and I figured you could use a distraction." Her face lit up with a smile in the dim light. "That said, whatever you're doing right now looks pretty useful. I know that you keep telling us 'it's a secret,' but if you can figure out a way to alter the properties of metal, that'll lead to some fun tricks against tanks."

"Honestly," Dan picked up the other chunk of metal and softened it. "You might be onto something there. I'm currently working on mixing electrical and metal mana to simulate electromagnetism, but turning armor into sludge might be more useful against other humans. Won't do much against the Orakh, though. Most of them run around practically naked and use their claws and teeth as often as their weapons. Half the time, I think their axes are more prop than tool."

"What are you trying to do in here, anyway?" She asked quizzically. "I know you've been all hush hush, but it's been almost a month and a half. I figure you at least owe me a hint of some sort."

"A railgun." He grunted, setting the two strips of metal down side-by-side. "Fairly simple in theory; you just need two metal rods like this. If you run a current through them and let the electricity arc from one to the other, it produces Lorentz force, which allows you to propel an object perpendicular to the current. Unfortunately, replicating the process with mana seems destined to drive me insane.

"Apparently, you need to mix lightning mana with metal mana." He frowned, staring daggers at the two strips of steel. "I've succeeded in merging the mana, and I can create the electromagnetic forces I need, but it hasn't really gone anywhere yet. I just keep losing control of the interaction before it gets anywhere."

"That's an interesting idea." She nodded. "I still think that turning peoples' guns into noodles would be a more useful trick, but being able to fire a magic cannon from your hand does have an appeal of its own."

"Guns aren't really a threat anymore." Dan shrugged. "That said, the final Orakh we fought was definitely a problem. I have multiple spells for dealing with crowds. Now, I need something to deal a whole hell of a lot of damage to one target in a hurry. Between spellshields and the sheer size of some of the more powerful Orakh, I've definitely begun to notice the hole in my arsenal."

"That reminds me." She snapped her fingers. "The actual reason I came down here is that Sam's finished analyzing and reverse-engineering the Orakh's gauntlet. It's basically a crude rune. As far as we can tell, it doesn't use the same 'alphabet' as the elves, and it's nowhere near as refined as their enchanted gear, but it works. She wanted you to come down and look at it, see if it could be adapted for mass production."

"Mass production?" Dan asked as he stood up, grateful to leave the troublesome metal behind. "Like, as an enchantment?"

"Apparently." Jennifer shrugged as she led the way toward the officer's mess that they'd converted into a lab for Sam. "I don't really get the ins and the outs of it, but it sounds like the Orakh have solved the stability issues of spellshards by pouring a ton of mana into it. We both know that a lot of the new recruits are months away from learning any useful spells, but at the same time, they've earned quite a bit of mana in the previous battle. With any luck, we'll be able to put that into good use and let them fire off raw bolts of mana to complement their more conventional arsenal."

"They do need their mana for the suits." Dan frowned. "Those things are pretty heavily enchanted to lighten them and make them more resilient. I don't want the troops blowing through their mana to make a lightshow, then getting stuck without adequate mobility."

"Hey," Jennifer said, opening the door to the lab, "you're the boss. Sam just wanted to talk it over as an option."

Dan strode into the lab after her. Unlike his gym, the lab had been rigged for electrical lighting in addition to the more ubiquitous and dimmer mana-fueled lights. A server in the corner powered a network of three different computers, each with their own orbit of half-disassembled equipment and analysis tools plugged into them. In the center of the room, a table held a partially disassembled suit of power armor covered in bright yellow labels.

Sam stood next to the suit, speaking into a tape recorder as she picked through its guts with her gloved hands. Despite the door closing behind Dan, she didn't look up, too engrossed in her work to notice the new presences in her lab.

"You know your System can just take notes for you, right?" He called out as they crossed the room toward her. "There really isn't any need for you to waste a hand on a tape recorder."

He winced as she jumped and whipped around, eyes wild. It took her almost a second to recognize him and calm down enough to speak. Even then, he couldn't help but notice the slight tremor in her hand as she reached up to brush her hair out of her eyes.

"And you know that you can customize your in-System username from <User>, right?" She bit back before grimacing. "Sorry. It's just that you surprised me and-"

She exhaled deeply, a novel written in the new wrinkles on her face and the bags under her eyes. "I'm not great with surprises lately," she continued flatly. "The tape recorder reminds me of how things used to be before..."

She trailed off, eyes losing focus for a second. Dan coughed to regain her attention, trying to ignore Jennifer fidgeting uncomfortably next to him.

"Before all of this," she snapped back to reality, a weak smile on her face. "Things are getting better day-by-day, but it's been hard. I've always thought of myself as a strong person, a survivor. I figured, if I could survive growing up with homophobic parents upstate, I'd be able to take anything psychologically.

"The last couple of months have been one unpleasant truth after another," Sam took off her elbow-length rubber gloves before stowing away the recorder. "Going from confident and self-motivated to the point of being a borderline narcissist to an anxiety-ridden wreck has been a bit of an adjustment for me."

"Don't worry about it," Dan smiled reassuringly, cocking his head. "Actually, what was that about my username?"

"I still can't believe you were the first one to crack, Sam." Jennifer rolled her eyes. "I still had my money on it taking another five months."

"Seriously?" Dan looked back and forth between the two of them. "What the hell?"

"You do realize that you're the reason Abe won, Sam."

Jennifer crossed her arms. "Like always, he's going to be absolutely insufferable."

"Shit," Sam replied, cracking her first genuine smile in months. "You're right, he's going to be absolutely awful."

"I'm glad everyone's all cheerful and buddy-buddy," Dan interjected, "but I'd really appreciate it if someone actually told me what's happening right now."

"You haven't programmed in a personalized username in the System." Sam shrugged sheepishly. "You know, how my name is <Sam the Great>?"

Dan frowned, trying to avoid looking at Jennifer as she did her hardest to hold in her laughter. "I thought that just happened on its own? Do you mean it hasn't been projecting my name to you guys when I would send messages?"

"No." The genuine warmth of Sam's face as she chuckled diffused any anger Dan might have had over the situation. "Just check your status screen, it lists your username as <User.> How would it even know what to call you when you're sending messages?"

This time Jennifer did break down laughing. It wasn't a polite titter, either. Dan was pretty sure she was crying as her body rocked, her hands on her knees.

"At first, no one noticed." A smile pulled at the corners of Sam's mouth. "You weren't talking to anyone through the System, so we didn't get a chance to see your username. I guess we just sort of assumed that you'd figured out how to customize your name on your own, until you started sending out messages with the default username. At that point, it kind of became an inside joke for the rest of us. Abe even started a betting pool for how long it would take you to notice."

Dan shook his head, letting out a laugh. "Do you mean that this entire time, literally for years, I've been the only person that didn't know how to set my own name?"

"Yup," Jennifer interjected, wiping a tear from her face. "And, I do have to say, this conversation is exactly as hilarious as I thought it was going to be."

"Well..." Dan shrugged with a smile. "I'm glad I could add some levity to the situation. Now, Sam, Jennifer said that you had something to talk to me about regarding the Orakh's gauntlet?"

"Of course." She waved Jennifer and him over as she sat down in front of one of the computers, booting it up to a schematic image of the glove. "Now, I have some ideas for incorporating these runes into the powered armor. We'd have to make an adaptation for each soldier based on their own affinities, but I have some ideas about how to incorporate it into the entire runescripting structure of the armor's enchantment as a whole."

Dan leaned forward, his years of electrical engineering bubbling to the surface as Sam began displaying images of the interlocking runescripting. Silently, he wished he had some more coffee. It was going to be a long night.

CHAPTER FIFTEEN

Planning

"I think we've been operating aimlessly for too long." Dan stood, addressing Abe, Sam, Jennifer, and William in the boardroom of the *Viceroy's Pride*. "It's been brought to my attention that these last couple of months, we've been 'running around like headless chickens' and I'd like to try and bring some organization to this chaos." Dan nodded toward William, who gave him a thumbs up, beaming at being quoted.

"Does that explain why I'm the one standing in front of a dry erase board with a marker?" Abe asked from the other end of the room.

"No," Jennifer interjected before Dan could take control of the meeting. "That's because you're in charge of HR. We need someone to draw up an org chart for this ratswamp of an organization."

"*As I was saying!*" Dan spoke louder, projecting his voice over the others in the room. "Right now, we're in a state of chaos, simply reacting to what's happening around us. Half the time, we're going into battle with little to no intelligence. If we plan on living through this entire mess, that's going to have to change."

"Are you seriously going to make me draw an org chart?" Abe groused, staring dubiously at the dry erase marker he was holding.

"Yes," Dan replied, rolling his eyes. "I am. Right now, everyone knows everyone else in the company. But, as we expand, that isn't going to be the case anymore. When we're in the middle of combat, we need our recruits to know who they should be listening to. That means at least some sort of rudimentary chain of command. Unfortunately for you, Abe, you're the one in this room with the most knowledge of how to make a midsized unit operational."

"Come on," Abe pointed the marker at William petulantly. "General Finch ran the entirety of the American invasion of Indonesia. That's gotta mean more than my background as a noncom."

Dan shrugged. "Honestly? For our purposes, no. If we can put together a literal army, I'll probably put William in charge of it, but right now, we're looking for more modest expansion. It sounds to me like you and the defectors from Bowman are probably our best bet on that front.

"I'm envisioning this meeting as having two major purposes," Dan continued, pointedly ignoring Abe's grumbling. "We need to sort out what the goals for our company are in the short, mid, and long-term. Then, I want us to lay out what we need to do to get there."

"Whatever happened to just killing monsters and getting paid for it? I was having a lot of fun with that plan," Abe grumbled as he wrote the word 'Goals' on the whiteboard.

"People got killed unnecessarily because we put ourselves in a position where we had to take orders from people who didn't know what they were doing," Dan replied drily. "One of our major overarching goals at all levels is autonomy. We have a goddamn spaceship and a self-sustaining space station. It's going to be a while before we have enough people that simply packing them up and flying off into space isn't an option."

Dan nodded at Abe as the other man wrote "freedom" on

the whiteboard and circled it. "Now," he turned back to everyone else. "This is going to seem a bit optimistic, but I think our main goal should be uniting humanity.

"That doesn't mean us taking over," Dan raised his voice to speak over the murmuring that filled the room. "It might be finding someone like Mayor DuBlanc that seems like a decent goddamn human being who didn't try to take advantage of this entire mess, and putting them in charge. Ideally, it would mean some sort of democracy once we find a way to excise enough of the oligarchy to make that word mean something once again. The last year or so should be enough to prove that if we aren't united, we're going to be prey.

"Short term?" He continued waiving off their questions with an upraised hand. "That means building the organization. We need more people, more firepower, and more mana for our troops. We've already started expanding, but we're still small fries. This could mean raiding depots or army bases, it could mean recruitment, and it could mean performing missions in exchange for more military equipment."

Dan motioned at Abe to keep writing. "Once we've expanded, our goal is to clear the Orakh out. We definitely need to get them out of America, but I'd like to kick them all off the planet. Given the high number of Orakh we saw after they'd been in the bayou for a relatively short period of time, combined with the breeding chamber I found on their space-ship, I think it's fair to suspect that their growth is logarithmic if unchecked. That means we need to get rid of them as soon as possible. Otherwise, they might be able to overwhelm us with sheer weight of numbers."

"The floor is open for questions and ideas." Dan sat down. For a second, no one did anything. Then Sam stood up hesitantly.

"I don't know about the rest of the plan," she said. "I have some ideas on expanding our forces. I know that Ibis was in contact with Anderson Drummond. He was a fairly prominent name in Silicon Valley, and he was the source of the medical nanites we turned into the System. As far as I can tell, he's one of the corporate warlords that took over California. Him and Peter Best, the online shopping and logistics kingpin, have been too busy fighting over California for anyone to pay too close attention to them."

"I think Best made most of the equipment used in the powered armor," she continued, shrugging slightly. "As far as I can tell from twitter, his troops have used powered armor to push Drummond out of Southern California. The army is mostly staying out of it, but by this point, most local leaders have thrown in with one side or another. I know they're fairly big fish for right now, but if we could seize either of their manufacturing capacity, it'd really help our ability to field combat-capable troops."

Sam smiled slightly. "Until then, that gauntlet you seized from the Orakh chief gave me some ideas. Even if we can't give every recruit the System, that doesn't mean that they can't use mana. We can look into runescripting them with simple enhancement runes, but we can also try to integrate the Orakh discharge rune. It should work as a tattoo. It'll consume most of its user's mana in one blast, but it's better than nothing. It's not as good as proper magic users, but it'll let us field teams of soldiers that are faster, stronger, better-armed and more resilient than their non-magical counterparts without the help of expensive prerequisites, such as the System."

"More or less the class tattoos from Twilight, then." Dan nodded thoughtfully. "That could work. It's obviously not as good as the System, but I think you're right that it's going to be a while before we're ready to tangle with the Californian warlords."

"I know some depots in the area," William spoke up, eyes sparkling. "A lot of the military is isolated right now. I don't think they're happy about the warlords tearing the country apart, but the various units are pretty isolated, and I don't think anyone trusts phone lines, what with the oligarchs controlling basically every telecommunication company before everything went to hell.

"I'd have to drive out to talk to some people," William continued, "but if I can convince them that you're legitimate and that you'll keep their soldiers fed and paid, I can probably convince a couple local units to join up with you. Nothing bigger than a regiment, but that'll add a whole lot of striking power to whatever we can recruit organically."

"Good," Dan replied. "Even if we can't get intact units to uproot themselves, having a number of experienced soldiers, especially if they come with their equipment, join up with us, it would be a fairly major boon."

Dan's brow crinkled slightly. "Actually, I haven't followed up on the new recruits and the defectors. How have they progressed while I've been in isolation training? We'll need to know roughly how long it takes to bring any new recruits up to speed before we start expanding in earnest."

"That sounds like a question for me," Abe chimed in, setting the dry erase maker in the trough below the whiteboard and shaking his hand theatrically. "The defectors have slotted in pretty well. They know what they're doing, and most of them are just happy to be with a group that isn't run by a murderous psychopath. Dan, it'd be super uncool if you snapped. I told everyone you're chill."

"Noted." Dan snorted, waving his hand for Abe to continue.

"It took a couple weeks, but all of them have gotten used to their new runescripting." Abe chuckled ruefully. "Right now, my biggest problem is trying to stop them from playing around with it during downtime. Half the time, I walk into their area of the camp, and they're in the middle of a mana-charged baseball game. They keep saying it's 'coordination exercises,' but I think that they're just starting to get a little bored and antsy."

"As for the new recruits, the power suit team is still pretty green, but they have a pretty good idea how to use their equipment by now. I'm much less afraid of friendly fire than I was when we were in the bayou." Abe scratched his chin. "Plus, I think that entire clusterfuck put a little steel in their spine. I've caught a couple of them strutting around town and bragging to the locals that we pulled their asses out of the fire."

"Well..." Dan shrugged, flashing a smile. "We did. They should probably avoid antagonizing the locals, but it's not like they're wrong.

"The rest of the new guys still need some work," Abe continued, "but they're getting there. So far, we've only recruited crews and maintenance personnel for the Bradleys that the mayor delivered. It'll take a little while before the new guys are up to snuff; you don't learn how to drive one of those things in just a couple weeks. But, I'd say about another month and we'll be able to deploy them."

"Right now, I think it makes sense to have the armor, the Bradleys, and the foot soldiers operate independently." Dan shrugged. "Of course, I'm hardly the expert here. It just seems like three very different levels of mobility that will take on three very different roles in combat. As much as I'd like to blend the defectors in with the suits, even with the new spellshields we've incorporated into their armor, they just can't slug it out with the powered armor. With their speed and mobility, they should probably be fighting like elves, mobile with quick hit-and-run attacks."

"Nah," Abe agreed, snapping the cap off of the dry erase marker. "I think that makes sense."

Dan motioned to the whiteboard. "Unless someone has a better idea, I think Abe should be in command of the power suits, Jennifer should run mana-enhanced infantry, and William can command the Bradleys."

"Badass." Abe jotted down the notes on the whiteboard across from their goals. "For whatever my vote's worth, I say we give each squad its own name. Helps motivate the guys if they're called the 'power lions' or 'lightning eagles' or something like that."

"I motion that whatever team Abe's leading is called

Human Resources," Jennifer interjected. "I'm pretty sure he's earned it with all of his complaints."

"But--" Abe sputtered.

Dan cut him off. "Anyway, the next step is finding a target for our troops to train against, as well as recruiting some more soldiers. Any ideas?"

"Why don't we just knock off Bowman?" William spoke up. "From what I can tell, this bird has some sort of giant crystal array that's labeled a 'spellcannon' in the schematics. No one particularly likes Bowman. If you blow him to hell with some sort of magic space laser then park your UFO on the burning remains of his house, I think that'd go a long way toward establishing your dominance. Hell, you'd probably have a good chunk of the veterans from Brazil side with you right away. Most of 'em recognize you from those propaganda briefings after everyone thought you were dead, anyway."

Jennifer shrugged with an easy smile. "I mean, I'm a cheap date; blowing up a warlord and claiming his domain sounds like my idea of fun."

"Any objections?" Dan looked around the room. The only sound was the distant noises of soldiers shuffling around the massive ship.

Almost shyly, Sam raised her hand.

"Dr. Weathers?" Dan asked, pointing at Sam while cocking his head.

"I'm fine with the plan," she replied. "It shouldn't be that hard to reconnect the spellcannon to the mana forges. I was just wondering. You spent a couple months locked in the gym developing a new spell. Will it be ready for the operation?"

"Oh, don't worry," Dan answered with a childish grin. "It's ready."

CHAPTER SIXTEEN

You're Not a Thief if You're the Good Guy

"This feels illegal," Jennifer said for the fifth time as they sneaked through the airbase's perimeter.

"And you sound like a narc," Abe whispered back. "What laws are we breaking? We're in no man's land, and the troops stationed here abandoned this place a week ago."

He shrugged. "Hell, by all accounts the entire base should have been empty. I asked around before we came out here, and it sounds like the breakdown of order hasn't been kind to this place."

"After the soldiers left, a bunch of toughs set up shop," Abe continued, nodding toward the mostly dark buildings of the air force base. "As far as I can tell, they're somewhere between a street gang and warlords. During the day, they make general menaces of themselves, feuding with rival groups and terrorizing the local community. At night, they come back here and get plastered."

"All that aside, I'm still using a wire cutter on a chain link fence," Jennifer replied, sarcasm dripping from her voice. "I really can't think of a time when that was the start of a socially acceptable activity."

Abe grinned, his teeth the only visible part of him in the dark. "Hey now! These are the bad guys. We're basically doing everyone in this area a favor by removing them. Just think of us as Robin Hood."

"Can you two cut the side chatter?" Dan murmured absently as he scanned the base through his binoculars. "William said that most of the 432nd Air Force Wing abandoned their post when the government broke down. They took some of the more portable stuff like the guns, ammunition, and gasoline, but there are a ton of drones left over. If we clear this place out, we have a bomber wing."

"That's why we're just outside Vegas, then," Jennifer quipped back. "I thought Abe tricked you into hiking out here with him so he could lose all of his paycheck in the casinos."

Dan squinted at the two of them. "Seriously, can you shut up for a minute? The locals haven't had anything good to say about the assholes holed up onsite. I'd prefer not to alert a bunch of bandits or looters that we're here. Remember, we're here to clear them out, land the *Viceroy's Pride*, pick up the drones, and any salvage we can use and get out. We want to avoid a protracted fight if possible."

"This is definitely illegal," Jennifer snapped the wire cutter a final time, pinching her way through the fence surrounding the base. "I'm not against it, mind you, it's just that there's no way any activity following that little speech is on the up-and-up."

With a jerk, Jennifer yanked the section of the fence that she'd cut free out and passed it back to Abe. Quietly, the three of them sneaked through the opening and into the base. In the distance, rock music blared from one of the hangers. Already, the grass leading up to the paths and runways of the base was beginning to overgrow a little, clearly having not seen a lawnmower in a good, long time.

Abe patted his shoulder. When Dan looked over to him, Abe tapped his eye and pointed out two people standing guard. Neither looked very attentive. One had an M-16 slung under his arm while he checked his phone, and the other seemed more concerned with the cigarette she was smoking than her surroundings.

Before Dan could say anything, Jennifer pointed out the woman then pointed at herself before scurrying away in a half crouch. He looked back to Abe, who shrugged helplessly. Rolling his eyes, Dan ran forward in a crouch toward the man on his phone, stopping periodically to hopefully ensure he wasn't seen.

At about twenty feet away, Dan stepped on a broken beer bottle, the crunch of glass on asphalt barely audible over the thumping bass of the music. The guard fumbled his phone into his pocket before pulling out a flashlight, shining it vaguely in Dan's general direction.

"Becky?" he called out, squinting his eyes against the darkness. "This isn't fucking funny, man, where are you?"

Dan responded by shooting him in the throat with a Force-bolt. The blow knocked him over backward as the force of the attack more or less flipped him off of his feet. By the time Dan reached the guard, he was clutching his throat and making mute gasping motions as he flopped around like a dying fish.

He didn't activate his sword, not wanting its purple light to give his position away. Instead, Dan planted his foot on the man's chest, holding him in place as he slid the tip of his sword into his throat, silencing him forever. He barely even felt the trickle of mana from the man's death.

Dan glanced up at the sound of a sneaker on pavement, only to relax from his ready stance when he made out Jennifer's silhouette. Giving Dan a quick thumbs-up and smile, she faded from the darkness of the field surrounding the hangar, with Abe following her. Hopefully that meant her guard was taken care of, but given how close they were to the rest of the enemy camp, he didn't dare voice his concern. Quickly, he shot her a query through the System, only for Jennifer to respond with another grin and a thumbs up.

It'd have to do.

Together, they sneaked toward the hangar. The massive

doors lay open a crack, illuminating a line of the asphalt in flickering firelight. Inside, a crowd of about twenty men and women clustered around a bonfire. Most had bottles of domestic beer clutched in their hands, but at least one bottle of spirits was making its way around the circle. Away from the circle, another cluster of people danced, clearly drunk, to the music's driving beat. In the corner, underneath one of the Reaper drones Dan was here to liberate, a couple made out, rounding second base and heading rapidly toward third.

Dan sent an alert via the system to Jennifer and Abe, drawing their attention as he held up three fingers. Then two.

He burst into the room, following a Fireball that exploded over the bonfire. Paradoxically, the pressure wave from the concussion more or less put the fire out, blasting the air away from the fire and scattering the coals all over the room. Dan did his best not to think of all of the explosives and jet fuel that the coals could be interacting with as he blurred in, whipping his sword out to take the arm off of a screaming man holding his hands over his face.

Taking the scene in, Dan let out a breath of relief. Most of the bodies strewn about the former bonfire were still moving, but none of them were wearing anything resembling uniforms. Instead, it was a collection of motorcycle leathers and shirts proclaiming the world tours of various bands. William might have claimed that the army had abandoned the base, but it was good to see at least some sort of visual confirmation, no matter how inconclusive.

A chain of force, extending from Abe's outstretched hand, swung at knee level, knocking over the couple hooking up near the drone. He quickly followed up with a sword blow, hacking down on one of the burning figures trying to get itself to its feet.

Jennifer flowed in after Abe, moving with the grace of a dancer as she slipped invisible spikes of force into one enemy after another while Dan stood near the guttering remains of the fire, covering both of them. Of the team, he was the only one with ranged spells capable of killing any of the guards. Occasionally, one would start to their feet or reach for a gun, prompting a Lightning Stroke from Dan.

After about two minutes of moans and muffled thumps, there weren't any survivors around the fire. Abe nodded at Dan, wiping his short sword off on the half-burnt shirt of the man he'd just finished off. Jennifer opened her mouth to make some sort of smart alec quip, only to be cut off by the sharp report of a handgun.

With a grunt, her eyes went wide and she spun forward, falling to her knees. Without thinking, Dan activated his temporal rune and pushed his body enhancement runes as far as they would go. Almost instantly, the heavy drain on his reserves coupled with pain all over his body, his flesh trying to keep up with the speeds his mana demanded of it.

He was a foot from Jennifer when he heard the second gunshot. Thanks to the temporal rune, he saw the incoming bullet ripping toward her. Barely. Extending his spellshield over Jennifer was an impossibility. Dan swung his sword, an awkward underhanded motion that contained barely any power, thinking only to cross the shortest distance between the position where he held the blade at rest and the oncoming slug without having to shift his grip.

The blade bucked in his hand, shooting off sparks as it barely nicked the slug, deflecting the bullet just enough to knock it high, clear of Jennifer. Then Dan was standing in front of her, his spellshield easily absorbing a half dozen bullets in quick succession.

Fire burned in his gut. Jennifer was down groaning, but still moving. Dan shifted his attention to the gunman, a thin figure, frantically reloading a handgun. He hit the man with a Lightning Stroke. Then another as he stalked forward. Finally, from a couple feet away, he launched two more strokes into him.

The spell wasn't as efficient as Forcebolt, and it didn't have the same splash damage as Fireball, but there was something satisfying about seeing his target buck and jerk as the current coursed through him. Even better, it wasn't clean. The spell flashburned large chunks of the tall man's body, covering him in burns that would easily kill him without hospitalization.

Somewhere, the part of Dan that was supposed to regulate his emotions during a mana rush screamed at him. This wasn't him. When someone wronged him, he didn't respond rashly, he buried it. He needed-

"Dan!" Abe called out. He was kneeling next to Jennifer, one hand pulling a flap of her uniform over her left shoulder aside while the other held a knife. "She's more or less fine. That force plating she's using as melee armor blunted most of it. She's gonna have one hell of a bruise, and the System might need to patch up a broken bone, but it didn't even break the skin."

Dan unclenched his hands and relaxed his jaw. He'd had soldiers die under him, but this was different. They'd been new recruits or students, people he'd cared about, but they just weren't as real as a member of his inner circle. He blew out a breath before putting the tip of his sword swiftly through the dying man's throat.

He was an enemy, and he needed to be cleared out of the way before they could "liberate" the base, but there was no need to be a barbarian about it. Dan didn't have a problem killing another person, he'd just prefer to do it quickly and cleanly. Already, he was a little upset with the ugly side of himself that had reared its head during the firefight.

"So..."

Dan turned around at Abe's remark.

Abe had one of Jennifer's arms over his shoulders as they walked toward Dan. "You can block bullets with a sword now."

"That was one bullet, and it was mostly luck," Dan smiled weakly. "I blocked the rest with my torso. Much more reliable."

"I'm looking for a chair," Jennifer said as she walked past them toward a lit office attached to the side of the hanger, her voice unnaturally tight from pain. "Every breath hurts, and I really need to sit down. Feel free to give Daddy the call."

"So, did we get them all?" Dan turned to Abe.

"Yep," Abe replied, surveying the hanger. "All the looters are down as far as I can tell, and better yet, it looks like they didn't get around to fiddling with the Reapers. I don't know if we'll be able to load up a full six squadrons worth of attack drones and hellfire missiles into the *Viceroy*, but we'll be able to field a large enough contingent to ruin the day of the next asshole we have to fight."

"You know," Dan replied. "Jennifer might have had a point. You just called the group we took out looters, but as far as I can tell, that's what we're doing. I really don't see too much of an ethical difference here."

"That's a simple one, Boss," Abe's easy smile crawled across his face. "We're the good guys."

CHAPTER SEVENTEEN

Joint Ventures

"How the fuck did you get the entire 432nd Operations Group?" General Richard's seat crashed to the floor a second after he bolted to his feet. "Did you just walk into an airforce base and walk out with it?"

"More or less?" Dan shrugged while William snickered next to him. "People keep forgetting that we have a spaceship. William had heard that the entire force walked off the base once they ran out of food. Some local toughs took it over. We knocked them off and walked off with the drones and equipment. It took a couple trips, but let's be honest. We're the only people on Earth that have the ability to do heavy transport without being intercepted by another warlord."

"Can someone explain to me what's going on?" Mayor DuBlanc frowned slightly, looking back and forth between General Richard and Dan. "Both of you are in MY office, so I don't really appreciate you talking past me. At least let me know what the 432nd Operations Group is."

"A whole lot of drones." Richard righted his chair and sat down shakily. "Six squadrons of Reapers, if I recall correctly. In short, more than enough to provide air support for an entire unit the size of our self-defense forces. God, how many of them do you have? 80? 100?"

Dan smiled. "Some of them were vandalized or damaged by the people we nabbed them from, so we only have 72. It took us a while, but we've hauled all of them out to that compound we're building outside of town along with spare parts, ammunition, and control installations. Of course, that's not the best news."

"Is a Reaper like a Predator Drone?" DuBlanc asked, cocking her head. "I've mostly been working on police operations budgets and traffic load management for the last decade or so. Give me some context here."

"They're bigger and they hit harder, Mayor." Dan fiddled with the sheaf of papers in his hands. "The Reapers have a pretty decent operational range, but we've converted one of the *Viceroy*'s cargo bays to launch them. Doctor Weathers could probably explain it better, but we basically have a magically powered steam catapult that lets us launch them while we're in the air. It's a bit slow, and we can only handle one at a time, but right now we have the ability to more or less appear over any city in the world and launch a handful of remotely operated bombers."

"I asked for context," DuBlanc massaged her temples. "I suppose that's what you provided, but it mostly just sounded like a whole lot more jargon to me."

"They aren't going to take a city over like that." Richard chewed on his lip while he eyed William's smug grin. "But they're going to be able to show up and demolish a couple tanks or strategic sites pretty easily. Especially if radar won't be able to see them coming."

"It can't," Dan agreed, sliding the papers in his hands across the table to the Mayor. "Even better, the *Viceroy's Pride* is armed. The entire thing is run on a mana generator, and we've only been able to figure out how to work it with the help of the technicians we rescued from the elves, but the setup is pretty impressive. It doesn't use ammunition, so logistics aren't a major concern. We can't fire it as often as we'd like, there's some sort of crystal that we have to charge and use as a mana capacitor, but we can manage two shots in the first minute and about once a minute after that. That's hardly a machine gun, but the shots pack a punch. We haven't measured the yield in kilotons or anything, but it's turned some pretty big boulders into gravel during our test shots."

"How impressive." General Richard leaned forward, his fingers impatiently drumming on the wood of Mayor DuBlanc's desk.

"A whole lot of light and noise followed by an explosion," William interjected, grinning. "About fifty percent bigger than a tomahawk cruise missile. It's got pretty good range on it, too. Our test shots were blowing chunks out of mountains almost two miles away."

"That sounds like it can level a building with functionally no notice. I don't think the other Warlords are going to be happy that you have that capacity." General Richard frowned.

Dan nodded at the papers that the Mayor was reading. "As for leveling a building, we're counting on it. If the rest of the warlords have a problem, we can literally relocate to space with a couple hours notice. Even if they take over New Orleans, we can reappear at a moment's notice and tear their armed forces apart."

"I'm really not sure how I feel about you stating to our faces that you plan on abandoning us if we get attacked by an overwhelming force brought on by your antics." Richard pursed his lips.

Dan opened his mouth to respond, but William raised a hand. Shaking his head, he fixed a steely glare on Richard.

"I don't think you get how this works." William leaned over the table, waving his index finger in the General's face. "Right now the only reason someone more powerful than you hasn't taken you over is that you were more trouble than you were worth. They're interested in taking over chunks of the country that will help them play their little game of Risk without costing them much. The bayou is what kept you safe because they want to fight each other, not the Orakh or that nutcase Bowman.

"Most of them have proper air forces," William leaned back, his eyes still fixed on Richard. "Trained paramilitary groups and ex soldiers using equipment they've nabbed from the army as well as whatever science fiction bullshit they've cooked up. Hell, I half expect a couple of them have probably gotten their hands on the nuclear codes. They've bribed half of the military's leadership.

"No." William smiled smugly. "What you need is a deterrent, and that's us. They're all stuck at each other's throats, any of them that reaches a hand out to smack you down will need to be quick, or another warlord will take them out. If we can just disappear and periodically reappear in the middle of their cities, blowing up things that look important, attacking you suddenly becomes more trouble than it's worth."

"Enough banter, General Richard," Mayor DuBlanc interjected, passing Dan's papers to him. "It looks like Mr. Thrush has a plan to take over Florida. Their theory is that his forces want to revolt, but that Colonel Bowman is keeping them in line through threats and fear. I'm not sure how keen I am on hedging an entire operation on that theory, but I will admit that he was rather quick to push the boundaries of our non-aggression pact. Already, his forces 'happen' to be much deeper in the neutral zone between our two spheres of control than we agreed to."

She frowned slightly, indicating the papers. "On that point, I must say, I'm a bit surprised at the detail in that intelligence dossier. The notes on his leadership's movements as well as the aerial photographs of his units around the edges of the bayou were quite detailed."

"We have access to a spaceship and drones." Dan shrugged. "We're probably the best-equipped force to perform recon left in the United States. As for the details on Bowman's command structure and movements? Half of his elite forces have already defected and joined us. He might have changed things up in the meantime, but at least as of the Battle of the Bayou, those are accurate."

"I get that this is a simplification." DuBlanc steepled her fingers. "But I think it's a fair one. Your plan seems to boil down to you inserting operatives that would figure out where Bowman and his inner circle were staying. Then you'd show up without any warning and blow them straight to hell. After that, you expected us to move in and mop up your mess."

"Not exactly," Dan responded nodding toward the papers in Richard's hands. "We will be dropping ourselves into Miami and our operatives should prepare the locals to transfer power to us. I'm still hopeful that a spaceship blowing up an office building and landing on its remains to disgorge a bunch of science-fiction-style robotic armored suits will be enough to scare everyone into submission."

"Is…" DuBlanc struggled to finish her thought. "Are you seriously saying that your plan is to bluff the entirety of Florida into surrendering to you?"

"Yes?" Dan asked, chuckling slightly.

"There'll be a power vacuum." William leaned forward, his eyes flashing. "It'll be just like the invasion of Jarkarta. If nobody likes the guy in power, they don't step up to avenge his death. Sure, they'll fight over scraps, but if you look imposing enough, they usually won't take a crack at you until you get a chance to cement your gains.

"I mean," William frowned. For the first time that meeting, his manic expression slipped for a moment. "That's basically what took America apart. They kept things just confused enough that everyone who didn't know what was happening just stepped aside and waited to see what would happen when the dust settled."

Shaking his head, William motioned at the papers. "Here. We would take over Miami and see which sections of Bowman's army would sign up with us from the get go. At the same time, the Army of New Orleans would set out, letting everyone know that they represented law and order. So long as your soldiers act very sure of themselves that Bowman is dead, I'm hoping that an inability to get orders from Miami should be enough to keep any resistance minimal."

"This might work." General Richard interrupted Mayor DuBlanc as she opened her mouth to object again. "I don't have as good of intelligence as Thrush, but we've been hearing rumblings out of Florida for a while. The people don't like Bowman and neither do the soldiers. He's ruling by fear right now, and the minute people aren't afraid of him, I'm not sure how much fight they'll have in them. Especially if we make it clear that our main goal is just to reestablish civil authority."

He put the papers down on the table before making eye contact with Dan. "My real concern is making sure we wrap up our loose ends. The Colonel is a piece of work, as is this Merella and a couple of his top Lieutenants. If we can't assure the people of Florida that we've killed all of them, I'm not sure we'll be able to secure their cooperation."

"Well, my concern is that you're taking the entire goddamn army as part of the deal," DuBlanc interrupted stuffily. "You're asking for almost all of the military material we retrieve from Florida. I don't like the idea that you can just take over New Orleans if you get upset with me."

Dan looked at General Richard and shrugged slightly. For a second, emotions warred across the General's face before a helpless smile won out.

"With the capabilities Mr. Thrush has revealed, "I think we're a bit past that point. He's more than capable of just hovering over the city and reducing the important bits to slag until we surrender."

"Oh." She threw up her hands, rolling her eyes. "Great. I'm glad someone bothered to tell me that I'm having a business lunch with a threat to the existence of my burgeoning city-state."

"If it makes you feel any better," Dan smiled apologetically at DuBlanc. "We actually think you're doing a really good job.

Most of the reason we're approaching you about taking over Florida is that we think you'd do a better job running it."

"Well," William interjected, his voice a laconic drawl. "That, and we don't want to touch that headache with a ten-foot pole."

CHAPTER EIGHTEEN

Miami

"I still think we should have bumped 'Big Willie Style' for this operation," Abe groused while slouched in an overly ornate chair on the bridge of the *Viceroy's Pride*.

"Once you and the rest of the ground forces have touched down, you can put whatever you want on your speakers," Jennifer replied from the captain's chair. "Until then, my ship, my rules, and that means no touching my radio."

"It's Dan's ship," Abe muttered, refusing to move from his chair.

"Of course it's Dan's ship." Jennifer rolled her eyes. "Everything around here is Dan's, but he's going to have to be in the engine room using spatial magic to power the ship's teleportation drive. He can't really be up here to pilot the thing during the battle itself."

"Will you two stop bickering like a pair of children?" Dan said, his head in his hands. "We're supposed to be going over final details of the attack plan, not putting together a combat mixtape."

"Honestly," William joined in affably. "As much as I'm done

with these two bickering over nothing, I think we've gone over everything twice. We can keep making contingency plans all we want, but at some point, we're going to have to just quit dithering and go for it."

"Fine." Dan nodded in his direction before turning to Sam. "Doctor Weathers, have you gotten the viewcasting function to work? I don't want to miss anything while I'm buried in the bowels of the engine room."

Sam nodded. "It should work. As long as Jennifer has her sight set to 'share,' you should be able to get a picture in picture of what she's viewing."

"Good enough for me." Dan stood up and stepped toward the bridge's exit. "I'll head down to the engine room right now. If we're good to go, then there's no reason to wait. We'll start the operation in thirty minutes, so everyone get ready."

He exited the room, doing his best to ignore Abe's griping at Jennifer. Theoretically, Abe should be on his way to the front cargo hold along with the rest of the infantry. They wouldn't be needed until most of the battle was over. But the plan called for him to be with the ground troops, keeping them calm and secured while the voidship engaged any ground defenses with its spell cannon.

The plan almost seemed overly simple. According to the messages fed back from the deserters after they slipped into Miami, Bowman and his top goons took over a highrise in the downtown area. They rarely left the building, and Abe had a scout watching the building to provide real-time updates.

After the main building, they had a couple other targets. Regional command and control centers, motor pools, that sort of thing. Frankly, the battle plan made Dan's eyes cross a little. William and Abe really seemed to know what they were doing, identifying targets that would cause immediate chaos, but which could be repaired easily once DuBlanc took charge.

He nodded at the workers fussing around the engine room as he walked in. All of them had originally been rescued when the Tellask Empire left behind an outpost satellite. They were slowly acclimating to modern society, but they still seemed much more comfortable around the mana-heavy elven technology. Considering that only Dan and Sam really understood the teleportation drive amongst the 'modern' humans, it made sense to assign them to maintaining the internal and sensitive processes on the *Viceroy's Pride*.

Dan tried to make small talk with the workers, but quickly stopped. His attempts came off as forced and clearly made them uncomfortable. After the forced responses, both sides let the engine room lapse into mercifully awkward silence.

Finally, the System's clock alerted Dan upon a half hour elapsing. Pausing to send a message to the rest of the crew, he put his hands on the control crystal. He'd operated the ship's engines a couple of times since their initial theft of the *Viceroy*, but it still felt strange every time. A second later, a small box containing Jennifer's vision appeared in the corner of Dan's sight.

He reached mentally for the ship's mana, focusing on a spot in space just above downtown Miami. He'd studied that particular spot for days, looking over picture after picture, trying to memorize enough details about it to successfully teleport the ship there. He hoped it'd work. Teleportation in atmosphere was always inaccurate and tricky, a large part of the reason why many voidships would use regular gravity magic to land once they teleported near where they were aiming.

The power swelled around Dan as the ship's mana forges kicked into high gear, supplying the majority of the energy needed for the jump. He focused on the satellite image of his target and crossed his fingers. Mentally he nudged his aim high. He'd rather accidentally show up in the mesosphere than the Earth's mantle.

He pushed and the world went white. Reality reasserted itself and Dan exhaled in relief at the decided lack of dirt in the main viewscreen. Instead, Miami appeared beneath them in the predawn half light, their target clearly visible as it was the only high rise with its lights still on. Around it, the rest of the city lay mostly silent, with only the occasional light or car disturbing the morning stillness.

The ship shook slightly as the aft catapult began launching drones. They only carried six of the things, and it took between two to three minutes to launch all of them, but after watching some old clips of their firepower in action, Dan was more than happy to incorporate them into the ship. One-by-one, they screamed away from the *Viceroy's Pride*, controlled by some of their original operators that William had managed to track down and hire in Las Vegas.

Then they were lined up on the high rise. Dan felt the available mana from the mana forges dip heavily as the lights dimmed. Distantly, a whining noise rose as the spell cannon charged for a bit under a second. Then, it fired, a brilliant lance of white and yellow that slammed into the base of the building, melting metal and glass like butter under a blowtorch.

Jennifer blinked a couple times against the brightness of the cannon, obscuring Dan's view for a second. When her vision returned completely, he could see the semi-sized hole, still glowing cherry red, bored straight through the side of the building. While the mana forges struggled to recharge the *Viceroy*'s reserves, a Reaper flew past the listing building and dropped a paveway bomb into the gap opened by the spell cannon.

With a thump, the building began collapsing as the laser-guided explosive knocked out most of the remaining load-bearing pillars. The ship moved upward slightly, angling the prow downward. Just as the remainder of the building came down, the spell cannon fired once again into the debris, melting a trench of twisted steel in the concrete.

The Reaper made another pass, dropping a second bomb into the remains of the building. Dan smiled tightly as another explosion lit the early morning. Pounding the remains of the building might seem like overkill, but mercy at this point would likely cost more lives. He'd gotten cute when he tried to take Merella alive for questioning, and only time would tell how badly that would come back to bite him.

Right now, more than just his team relied on the success of the mission. The entire Army of New Orleans was traveling toward Florida to help restore order. Without the chaos created by Bowman's death, they would be outnumbered and overextended. Their only hope was for Dan to create a power and organizational vacuum for them to step into. That meant Bowman needed to die.

The *Viceroy* hovered over the battlefield, the remaining Reapers seeking out their targets, demolishing bridges, buildings used by command staff, and the occasional armored vehicle active on the street. The spell cannon roared one more time, blowing up a nearby substation that routed the meager supply of electricity to the privileged neighborhood surrounding the downed command building.

Then they went in for a landing. The entire time, Dan held his breath, waiting for anti-aircraft fire of some sort. The *Viceroy's Pride* had spellshields capable of deflecting one or two spellcannon shots, but a missile or dedicated high-caliber fire would likely mean that he'd have to teleport the voidship away in a hurry.

The ship touched down without incident, and Dan breathed a sigh of relief. The *Viceroy's* landing struts rested uneasily in remains of the bombed-out office building, the front of the ship jutting out into the nearby boulevard. The fore cargo bay slammed open, and through Jennifer's eyes, he watched the Bradleys drive out onto the street, twelve armored suits following them.

That was Dan's cue. He removed his hands from the control crystal and jogged toward the ship's exit. Overhead, he heard the roar of the drones looking for a place to land, their munitions expended. The plan called for them to be retrieved after the battle, but the *Viceroy's Pride* simply didn't have a way to reload and launch them.

Exiting the front ramp, Dan saw the Bradleys blocking off the street access to their landing site. Abe and two other soldiers in power armor stood watch, their presence warding off the curious or brave while the remainder of the team used their enhanced strength to sift through the building's remains. Dan didn't really expect to find Bowman's remains, but it would certainly be helpful in getting his soldiers to stand down if it happened.

A man jogged up to them, causing Dan to tense for a second before recognizing him as one of the defectors. He flashed a quick salute before addressing Abe and Dan.

"I think you got him." The man nodded toward the smoldering wreckage of the building. "He leaves during the day sometimes, but more and more, they bring everything to him. I haven't seen any motorcades leaving since he came back after dinner last night. Unless Bowman learned how to fly and didn't tell anyone, he was in the building when you brought it down."

"How are the others doing?" Abe continued scanning their surroundings.

"Last I heard, they were talking with a lot of noncoms." The man shrugged. "Bowman got rid of most of the officers, replaced them with his own stooges. Most of them never actually served on the front line. A bunch of rear-echelon admin types with delusions of grandeur. Nobody likes them, but they weren't all that likely to question him, and that's all Bowman was looking for."

"Do you think they're going to be able to convince them to defect?" Dan interjected, somewhat nervously eyeing up his small unit. True, they'd simply be able to fly away, if this didn't work out, but they'd sunk a lot of resources into this operation. He wasn't exactly keen to abandon everything if they could help it.

"I guess we'll find out," the soldier responded, unhelpfully. "Bowman had them all scared about acting without his orders, so I wouldn't expect anything organized for some time. But your little light show was pretty impressive. I wouldn't be surprised if some of the nearer units sent out teams to figure out what's going on."

Almost on cue, the heavy guns from the Bradleys opened up with a series of dull, staccato thuds.

CHAPTER NINETEEN

Siege

"They're moving awfully fast," Dan remarked to Abe then jogged toward the gunfire.

"I guess," Abe replied, each one of his armor's longer strides accounting for a pair of Dan's. "We made a lot of noise when we came in. Appearing out of nowhere and firing a gigantic laser cannon from the sky sure seems like the sort of thing to grab attention."

"I thought we blew up most of the regional command and control outposts around here," Dan said, a flash of concern on his face. "I just didn't think they'd be organized enough to respond this quickly."

Abe's suit shrugged slightly, mimicking his movements. "We tried to take out any communication hubs we could find, but we didn't attack any of the barracks. The goal was to get Bowman's troops to defect, not piss them off by killing a bunch of their friends. Right now, they're confused and trying to gather information. With any luck, the Bradleys and a glimpse of our suits will be enough to give them the information they need and scare them off."

"What if we aren't lucky?" Dan asked, his gaze occupied by the flash of Bradleys' 25mm main gun.

"Then we end up fighting," Abe answered. "Unless they have Infantry Fighting Vehicles of their own, I don't think anything Bowman has will do more than scratch the powered armor's paint. Between the runes you have inscribed on these and the amount of metal we're wearing, rifles basically feel like paintballs."

Dan flooded his spellshield with mana as he picked his way around the edge of a four-story office building that served as the corner to the main thoroughfare occupied by the Bradleys. About four hundred feet away, a flash of movement drew his attention as a soldier's head popped up to take in the situation from the window of a building. The scene looked like news footage of the siege of Jakarta.

Several of the buildings were burning, pouring light and smoke into the predawn air. Many more sported large holes where the Bradleys' chain guns had torn apart the concrete and steel. Occasionally, a figure darted from one building to another, trying to find better cover as the armored vehicles methodically demolished their previous hiding places.

Dan pursed his lips. The Bradleys were firing slow and measured shots into the advancing soldiers' cover to minimize casualties and preserve ammunition while driving them off. They didn't want them getting too much closer, or they might actually be able to report intelligence on their low numbers, potentially emboldening a nearby company or battalion. Unfortunately, the vehicles didn't really have a way to do that without inflicting the kind of casualties that would make a smooth transition of power difficult.

"Abe." Dan didn't turn around as the powered armor trudged up to him. "I want you to throw me as high straight up in the air as you can."

"Not asking questions, Boss." Abe laughed.

Dan lowered his spellshield and prepared himself. A moment later, the warm metal of Abe's hands closed around his waist. With a sudden jerk, he was airborne. Quickly, Dan reinitialized the spellshield, not wanting to get caught by a lucky bullet.

At the apex of his arc, Dan summoned a force bubble, barely catching himself on the immobile and invisible orb. Balancing precariously, he surveyed the street from his perch twenty-five to thirty feet in the air. A bullet sparked off of his spellshield as one of the advancing soldiers took a potshot at him.

Dan pointed in the general direction of the shot and opened his mouth. "Railgun." He didn't have to say the word. Hell, he didn't have to point. The entire spell could've been triggered via a simple subvocalization, but that took all the fun out of it.

Mana swelled up inside him, the attunement stone in his arm converting it to metal as a pair of ten-foot-long spectral bars appeared in front of Dan. By far the trickiest part of developing the spell, the rods contained all the magnetic and electrical properties of metal, while avoiding the heavy mana requirements of simply generating the element from the ether.

A spike of actual metal appeared between the two bars, perfectly symmetrical and barely touching either side; it pointed directly at the gas station where Dan had seen the gunfire. The mana inside him shifted, and electricity sparkled around Dan's hands before arcing into the rails.

He bit down on his lower lip as energy exploded outward from the spell. Electromagnetic forces tore at the bars, trying to force them apart and shift their aim as the very power that would fire the projectile tried to rip the spell apart. Dan clamped down with his mind and *held* onto them, maintaining their positions with sheer force of will as the slug sped down them.

A fraction of a second later, the pressure was gone and the gas station disappeared in a Fireball. Dan couldn't quite tell how much of the blast was from gas reserves, and how much was from the hypersonic slug impacting on the building's foundation after it passed through the walls like they were made of paper. Either way, the result was spectacular, bathing the entire battlefield in oranges and yellows as remains of the spell disappeared.

A burst of fire sparkled off of his spellshield. Dan frowned, finding a pair of men on top of a two story townhouse with their guns still trained on him. One of them fired another three round burst at him.

He pointed his finger at them, and once again cast Railgun. This time, he was more prepared for the spell, easily controlling the outward pressure of the Lorentz forces as the projectile sped down the semi-invisible metal bars.

The second story of the house disappeared in a Fireball, taking both of the gunmen with it. Moments later, the ground floor of the building collapsed, bringing down large portions of the conjoined neighboring houses with it.

A lull slipped across the battlefield as everyone stared at Dan, still hovering in the air, in shock. Even the Bradleys stopped firing, their operators likely stunned by the destruction of two buildings in under ten seconds. Those two shots had wiped out almost a quarter of Dan's mana reserves, but each was more than capable of demolishing a tank.

Vague shouting erupted from the advancing soldiers and they began to draw back, unwilling to advance any further into the withering firepower of the defenders. Satisfied, Dan dropped to the ground with Gravitational Easing active, cushioning his roughly thirty-foot fall.

"Well." Abe tromped up to Dan. "That scared them off pretty efficiently. Whatever the hell 'that' was."

"I used metal and electrical mana to make a railgun," Dan grinned at Abe. "Pretty cool, right? I haven't tested it against modern armor yet, but I'm pretty sure anything that can blow up a well-designed concrete building with one well-aimed shot can probably take out body armor."

"Railgun?" Abe cocked his head. "I know the Navy's working on one of those things. Supposed to hit pretty hard but not be feasible for actual combat. How in the hell did you get that thing working?"

"The elves had them," Dan replied as he strode back toward the *Viceroy*. "The science behind them is pretty straightforward. The issue is just producing enough electricity fast enough and preventing the gun from tearing itself apart. Without magic, those are pretty major problems, but with magic, it's just a matter of mana and skill. I don't need a capacitor if my mana pool already is one, and I can just recreate the rails with each shot."

"Wait." Abe stopped walking. "You said the elves had these? Why didn't we see them in Brazil?"

Dan stopped with him. "We did. That's how they were able to take out so many of our defenses in the initial attack. They had a whole bunch of them at their landing site, mostly carriage-mounted. The only problem is that they take a whole lot of mana to shoot. You have to be awfully close to archmage levels to be able to use the spell."

"Okay," Abe said, a smile audible in his voice. "That was definitely a humblebrag; we're getting into more familiar territory here."

Anything further Abe had to say was drowned out by the sound of two helicopters rising over the skyline as they flew toward where the *Viceroy's Pride* had landed. One of them opened fire, unleashing a stream of unguided rockets that caused the parked voidship's spellshields to glow to life as they detonated against it.

On reflex, Dan fired the Railgun once more. The attacking helicopter disappeared into a Fireball as a chunk of metal ripped through its fuselage at high enough speeds to convert most of its internal workings to plasma. The other helicopter was thrown to the side by the force of the blast, only for the fire from a dozen .50 caliber repeaters to light it up as almost every suit of powered armor opened fire on it at the same time.

Most of the shots missed, but at least a couple hit critical components on the veering chopper as it tried to right itself.

Smoke poured from the vehicle as it swerved drunkenly and crashed into a nearby office building, shredding its rotor before slamming into the ground. Dan stood, his finger pointed at it, another Railgun spell at the ready for almost ten seconds. After nothing happened, Abe took a few cautious steps toward it, his shortsword looking like a knife in the hulking armor's hand.

Dan followed, a couple steps behind Abe's armor as his companion approached the downed helicopter and stabbed his sword into it, cutting the door off with ease. Inside, the pilot was dead, a large bullet hole through his chest from one of the power suits ending any debate about trying to save him, but next to him, the gunner was still breathing shallowly.

Abe pulled out the pilot's body, tossing him casually to the side before fishing out the gunner much more gently. Without a word, he passed her to Dan before returning to the helicopter. He watched on as Abe nimbly worked the heavy armor into the chopper's cockpit, fishing around for something and occasionally using his short sword to cut and pry objects free.

Dan glanced briefly down at the woman wearing a flight jacket in his arms. Her eyelids fluttered, and she let out a groan as he sheepishly held her. A blood-smeared hand reached up and brushed across her face.

"Where?" she mumbled, her eyes half-open to reveal the heavily dilated pupils of the concussed. "What's happening?"

"You're still in Miami," Dan replied. "Your helicopter attacked our ship, so we shot you down. The pilot didn't make it, but we'll get you out of here, don't worry."

"Darryl's dead?" she asked woozily, struggling to free herself from Dan's arms. He set her down, only to catch her once she tried to take a step and staggered.

"If Darryl's the pilot, then yes," Dan replied, putting a hand on her shoulder to help her maintain her balance. "Easy now, you took a pretty hard knock to the head when the helicopter went down, and your balance seems to be shot."

"Is," a cloud passed over her face. "Is Bowman gone?"

"We hit him first." Dan nodded. "From what we heard,

most of his forces weren't happy with him, but they were too afraid to defect. We hoped that, by killing him, the rest of you would be more willing to join up with forces that actually want to reunite America, rather than fight over the scraps of its corpse."

"Well's right." she wobbled slightly, grabbing onto Dan's wrist. "The major said we needed to rescue Bowman. He has my daughter. If it wasn't for her, I'd gladly tell that sack of shit exactly where to stuff it."

"Good news," Abe interrupted, climbing out of the helicopter with an armful of machinery. "Your radio is intact. If we can get this baby hooked up to a generator, it should be broadcasting on the right frequencies with the right encryption, and you'll get your chance to tell everyone exactly what you think of Bowman."

Abe's faceplate opened up, and he broke into a beaming smile. "Preferably while also telling them what perfect gentlemen we are. They keep attacking us, and self-defense while minimizing casualties is getting more and more difficult."

CHAPTER TWENTY

Veni Vici

"Hold up," Dan put up his free hand to stop Abe. "We should probably get William out here. He has more clout than me among ex-soldiers, and frankly, he just talks a better game than I do."

"Fair enough," Abe replied, turning to the armored soldiers still sifting through the rubble. "Huntman! Get Bill Finch over here."

"Bill?" Dan raised an eyebrow at Abe. "Since when do you call him Bill?"

"Everyone calls him Bill but you, Boss," Abe answered cheerfully. "I think he wants to keep you on the edge of your seat. He said something about it 'making you sharp' or something."

"Can someone tell me what's going on?" the woman leaning against Dan asked woozily. "It might be me hitting my head, but I feel incredibly lost right now."

"Don't worry about that, it's a natural reaction to dealing with Abe." Dan turned back to her. "We want you to put us into contact with your superior officer. Our goal was to take out Bowman because he's an animal. We don't necessarily want to fight each and every one of the units that used to be under his command. If your team is willing to stand down, there really isn't any need to fight."

"Major Sallsforth?" She blinked at Dan. "She'll just think that you're coercing me, if you have me tell her anything."

"I mostly just want an introduction." Dan smiled. "I mean, I'd appreciate it if you say whatever code phrase I'm sure you have to indicate that you're not under duress. I certainly don't plan on harming you, if I can help it."

Their conversation was cut short by William approaching in his powered armor, escorted by a man that Dan assumed was Huntman. One of these days, he'd get around to learning the names and faces of every soldier working for him, but right now, it just seemed like every time he turned around there were two or three new individuals for him to make sense of.

"Wait..." The gunner stumbled over the word, her tongue thick and heavy from the head wound. "Is that General Finch? Like, the guy in charge of Indonesia? What in the hell is he doing here?"

"That's a good question, Thrush." William chortled as he walked in on the conversation. "I keep telling Daniel I should be the person in charge around here, but he says that 'because he can destroy a tank with his mind,' he gets to run the show. No respect for the wisdom that comes with age." William shook his head theatrically.

"Thrush." She turned back to Dan, cocking her head as she looked at him again. "Wait, are you Daniel Thrush? I saw the video of you soloing one of those gigantic lizards in Brazil! I thought you were supposed to have died in the fighting or something."

"Still alive and still fighting," Dan shrugged, smiling dryly. "Bowman and Ibis both hated my guts near the end, so I'm sure they've had plenty of choice things to say about me, but I'm still kicking and both of them are dead, so I think I'm winning on any scorecard I can think of."

"Well," Abe interjected as Huntman plugged an orange

extension cord running from the *Viceroy's Pride* into the radio he held. "Are we going to keep gabbing, or are you guys ready to make this call?"

"Do you mind introducing us, Miss...?" Dan plastered his best charming smile on his face as he addressed the woman he was stabilizing while simultaneously trying to ignore William's sarcastic chuckling.

"Davis," she replied, glancing suspiciously from Dan to William. "Brianna Davis. I don't mind calling Major Stallsforth, but I really don't have any idea if you are who you say you are. I'm not going to lie and say that I've verified your identities or anything like that."

"That's fine." Dan smiled again as he handed her the radio's headset. "We mostly want to explain the situation and negotiate a ceasefire. Trying to force you to lie would be the exact opposite of what we want."

She looked at him dubiously before putting on the headset and stepping toward the radio. After fiddling with the dials for a couple of seconds, she placed a hand on the headset and began speaking.

"Riverfront actual," Brianna's voice was still woozy as she spoke into the microphone. "This is Stormcrow Two, Lieutenant Davis. I've been shot down by the forces that took out command, and they've indicated that they want to parley."

Dan did his best to look polite while Brianna paused, clearly listening to something through the headset. She glanced briefly at Dan, and the hint of a smile pulled at the edges of her mouth.

"No, Riverfront," she continued, trying to keep the humor from her voice. "I don't think they're elves. They have some of the science fiction tech we saw from the other warlords, including something that just blew Cooper's bird out of the air without any warning, but they look human to me."

She stopped speaking once again. Faintly, Dan could hear a woman's voice in the headset, tinny and static-filled from all of the distortion.

"Nocturnal Domingo," Brianna replied to whatever she'd been asked. "I repeat, Nocturnal Domingo. As far as I can tell, most of them are ex-military. Someone claiming to be General Finch is here along with someone claiming to be Daniel Thrush, the guy who took down that gigantic lizard in Brazil."

Brianna stopped speaking, once again listening to the radio before turning to Dan and William. She shrugged apologetically.

"Major Stallsforth wants to know what your demands are," she said helplessly.

"That's my cue!" William cut in, extending his hand toward Brianna and taking the headset from her. After settling it over his ears, he began speaking.

"This is William Finch, former general in the United States Army, to whom am I speaking?" A frown began to grow on his face as he listened to Major Stallsforth's response.

"Now, listen here, young lady!" William growled into the headset. "Lieutenant Davis is doing just fine. I just grabbed the headset from her because it didn't make any sense for us to play telephone through her. I've been planning operations bigger than this since you've been in diapers. There's no need for you to get snippy with me."

Dan could hear her response from where he stood. William might not have been the best choice for negotiations after all. The old man had a bit of a temper on him.

"And look where that got you," William cut into whatever diatribe the major was spewing heatedly. "Stuck working for a psychopath who tried to undermine the United States itself. Before you lecture me on duty, I'd like to ask you to guess how many times I called down here to try and get Bowman to intervene when the Thoth Foundation was besieging Washington DC? Instead of honoring his oath to the government, he set up a tinpot dictatorship through force of arms and harbored an enemy to our entire race.

"Of course, I mean the fucking elf!" he shouted back at her almost immediately after finishing his previous speech. "Look, we just want to set things right again. Put competent civilians back in charge of the country then round up the rest of the armed forces to kick these fucking aliens off the planet."

"OH," he responded after a momentary pause. "You want to talk to someone else who'll be more respectful to your feelings. Frankly, I'm surprised someone whose skin is as thin as yours even survived a month in the service. Fine, talk to Dan. He'll sort you out."

William ripped off the headset and slapped it into Dan's chest, winking at him.

"Bad cop is done," he whispered, stepping away from Dan. "Good cop is up."

Dan glanced at William, bemused, before he slipped the headset over his ears. Immediately, he was assaulted by the voice of a screaming woman.

"Excuse me?" Dan asked. "Is this Major Stallsforth?"

"AND WHO THE HELL WOULD- wait." Her tone calmed dramatically midway through the sentence. "Is that asshole gone? Please tell me he's not running the show over there."

"No ma'am," Dan replied, "that'd be me. Look, we're just trying to get in touch with all of the nearby units and let them know that our goal is to get them to join up with us. Bowman was a menace, so we eliminated him before he had a chance to go to ground. Right now, we don't want to fight anyone else, but if you intrude on our section of the city, we'll respond with force. Again, we'd prefer to avoid fighting, but I suspect that if it comes to it, things won't turn out all that well for anyone trying to attack us."

"What's this Lieutenant Davis said about you shooting down Lieutenant Cooper?" Major Stallsforth's voice was noticeably calmer, albeit still belligerent. "He was on a scouting mission, and you blew him out of the air without any warning. That doesn't sound like the most neighborly of actions."

"Scouting?" Dan snorted. "As soon as he saw my men, he started shooting us with rockets. I shot him down to protect my own men. I didn't particularly want to do it, but I don't really know what else I was supposed to do."

"Lieutenant Cooper wasn't supposed to shoot unless fired upon," the major replied suspiciously.

Dan rolled his eyes, noting Brianna stage whispering the words "he's a gigantic asshole" at him.

"Nevertheless, he did," Dan answered. "Look, I want to put my cards on the table. The entire New Orleans Army is on their way over with a whole lot more drones. We're just here as an alpha strike to prevent Bowman from organizing any sort of resistance or executing hostages. If you can get your troops to back off, we're more than happy to sit here on top of a pile of rubble playing cards until the cavalry arrives."

"Shit," the major spat the word out. "Is the Army of New Orleans going to be the people attacking us? What the hell is going on?"

"Bowman was making moves toward breaking the truce, and we had some pretty good intelligence on him." Dan responded, staring off toward the sun as it began to crest over the horizon. "It sounded like he wasn't really doing anything other than stockpiling weaponry and making life hell for the locals. Right now, the Southeast is divided. No one leader has enough troops to actually make a play toward any of the corporate warlords that started this entire mess. At some point, we're all going to have to unite under one banner, and it seemed to make sense we ensure that it wasn't Bowman's."

"Are you sure he's dead?" she asked hesitantly. "He has the families of a lot of my senior officers held hostage, and I've watched him torture more than a couple of them to death for fairly small problems. I'm not saying that we will stand down or consider joining up with you, but we'd need proof that Bowman was gone before we make any move at all."

"Look," Dan replied. "We had a guy watching the tower. Unless he sneaked out without his motorcade in the dead of the night, he was in there. We dropped the entire building and then bombed the rubble flat enough to land a spaceship on it. I can't confirm he's dead, mostly because we dropped enough ordinance on him that there likely isn't anything left. Ultimately, it's going to come down to trust. Talk to your noncoms and anyone who knows how to cast spells; they'll be able to vouch for me. By the end of the day, we'll have enough troops around here to assert control. Even if Bowman did somehow miraculously survive, he won't be able to do anything."

There was a pause from the receiver. Dan heard some muffled whispering, but he couldn't quite make anything out. Finally, the major returned.

"Do you mind if we just hold tight for a little bit?" Her voice was much calmer, almost congenial. "Most of my unit would be happy to jump ship, so long as Bowman's actually dead, but we'll need some sort of reassurance first. If he doesn't respond to your attack in the next four hours, he's either dead or in a coma. I'll talk to the other units in the area and tell them to lay off. In the meantime, we'll be talking to the special units. If they really do vouch for you, that'll certainly mean something. We'll talk in four hours and make our decision then, same frequency."

"Good enough for me," Dan replied as he took off the headset. He watched the sun peek above the skyline. A short break would be nice after all.

CHAPTER TWENTY-ONE

Mergers and Acquisitions

Four hours came and went in a flash. No one attacked their landing site, although Abe's men noticed a couple of wary scouts keeping an eye on the major streets leading in and out of the area they'd claimed. But, by and large, they left Dan's companions alone.

They used the time well, digging through the wreckage of the building and extricating body after body. Each one brought another twinge of guilt to Dan's face. From their intelligence reports, maybe fifteen of the people living in that building deserved to die. Bowman and his hand-picked elite were all monsters, but the remaining administrative staff in the building were just people who worked and lived in the wrong place.

In all, they managed to pull the bodies of eighty workers from the twisted remains of Bowman's command center, in addition to eleven bodies they believed belonged to Bowman and his lieutenants. As for Bowman himself, Sam was able to verify that the nanites in one of the mangled torsos belonged to the former Colonel.

It was anticlimactic, really. Dan had vaguely expected to end up fighting the madman on a rooftop somewhere during a thunderstorm, recent events having given him a bit of a flair for the dramatic. Instead, he'd been crushed by a girder, possibly even in his sleep.

Unfortunately, no one managed to find any biological material associated with Merella or the other five lieutenants. The spell cannon might have annihilated their corpses, but Dan didn't dare get his hopes up. The woman had centuries of experience and the magic to back it up. In all likelihood, she'd escaped once again.

One more mistake he'd need to rectify. Really, he couldn't go a full week anymore without kicking himself over trying to put her to sleep rather than using the kill command. It'd made sense at the time; he wanted to interrogate her about Tellask society, as well as Bowman's operation, and he'd been so sure that they'd be able to take her alive. Next time, he wouldn't risk it. The elf was too dangerous to all of humanity for him to extend mercy another time.

When the four hours were up, Dan put another call in to Major Stallsforth. After waiting a minute for her assistant to connect them, the major answered.

"Thrush?" she asked him, her voice significantly calmer and more assured than it was last time.

"Have you had a chance to consider our last conversation?" he replied, waving briefly at Jennifer as she meandered down the *Viceroy*'s loading ramp, a soda in hand.

"Some of the other officers and I talked it over," she affirmed. "You were right about the special units vouching for you. Apparently, you were a fairly decent guy, even if you were involved with that Ibis asshole."

Dan waited for a couple seconds, but Stallsforth didn't respond. Finally, just as he was opening his mouth to say something, she beat him to the punch, her tone a bit rushed and flustered.

"Look, no one wants to fight you." Her voice was almost apologetic. "And, if you have something that can take down my birds as easily as you and Brianna claim you did, it's probably not a great idea to fight you, anyway."

"You forgot that I have a spaceship with a gigantic laser cannon attached to it," Dan supplied helpfully. "It can teleport."

"Also that," she agreed with a flash of temper at being interrupted. "I'm just saying that some of the groups want to lay down their arms and go home. Bowman kept a bunch of people here through fear long past their projected deployments. Plus, with the state of the country, a lot of folks want to make sure their families are safe. They've seen what Bowman's been doing around here, and they want to make sure that isn't happening back home."

"So," Dan responded sourly. "When the world has absolutely gone to shit, and we need people with your skills and experience, you plan on turning your backs on your oaths to the constitution and burying your head in the sand like an ostrich? Got it."

"Not all of us!" Stallsforth protested. "I wouldn't fight for another iteration of Bowman. I've had enough of playing petty dictator over a bunch of cowering civilians for a lifetime. That said, if you're honestly looking to restore some semblance of normalcy, well, I'll hear you out. I don't plan on throwing in with a complete nobody consumed with delusions of grandeur, but if you actually have a shot, that's something worth fighting for."

"Do I just give you a pitch, then?" Dan asked, a hint of levity in his voice. "It's been a while since I've actually sat down and watched one of those reality tv shows about trying to convince strangers to invest in a new product. I'm pretty sure I'd be a bit rusty."

"A couple of the other battalion commanders in the area that are still willing to fight want to have a sit-down with you and hash out details," she replied, not returning any of Dan's mirth. "If we're going to work for you, we'll need to know what sort of person you are and what resources you have at your disposal. Would you be able to meet at the Ocean Mirage hotel in about an hour?

"I suppose that makes sense," Dan agreed hesitantly. "Where exactly is the Ocean Mirage, anyway? I'm not from the area, and I haven't really trusted GPS since the oligarchs all but admitted that they were using it to track dissenters out West."

"Great," the major replied with obvious relief. "The Mirage is located just down Grand Boulevard from you. That's the major street you have all of the Infantry Fighting Vehicles guarding. Head toward the beach and keep going about three blocks until you see the brown building. Each commander will bring two people, but the Mirage should be neutral ground. It's not terribly near anyone's base of operations, so the hope is that you'd be comfortable meeting with us there."

"An hour sounds good," Dan answered. "I look forward to meeting you in person."

"Likewise, Thrush," Stallsforth responded before cutting the connection.

Almost immediately, Dan called William and Abe over to talk details. After a brief debate over who would be joining the expedition, they left a sulking Jennifer with the ship. Apparently, she was upset about being "left behind" on an "adventure." Never mind that the landing site needed one of the group's officers on hand, preferably one who could fly the *Viceroy*.

The trip to the Mirage was tense but uneventful. William and Abe marched on either side of Dan in their full power armor. Inwardly, he was a little annoyed with how the suits blocked his peripheral vision. If there truly were to be an ambush, he'd have no way of seeing it coming through the large hunks of metal and glass. At the same time, who in their right mind was going to take potshots at the guy escorted by two borderline bulletproof killing machines?

On the other hand, the armor was nothing else if not intimidating. The handful of soldiers Dan could see tracking their progress quickly shuffled away and avoided eye contact as soon as they tromped into view. Likely a relic of their time serving under Bowman, they looked more like beaten dogs than soldiers.

He wasn't sure how much he could blame them. By all accounts, Bowman had gone completely mad with power. Any camaraderie or nobility that his troops might have had fled them as they were ordered to commit atrocity after atrocity. Hell, from Brianna's telling of it, it wasn't uncommon for Bowman to make one unit discipline the families of another low-performing unit in front of them in order to breed distrust. Apparently, his lackeys would pick a unit at random for the "honor," and any unit failing to perform their tasks zealously enough would be subject to penalties themselves.

Abe and William agreed that it was probably a program meant to prevent mutinies. The army's morale was incredibly low due to the nation's collapse and being forced to prey on civilians. Only through fear of Bowman and a distrust of the other units was he able to keep his forces in line.

The Mirage itself was a fairly nice hotel. Once upon a time, it was probably a hot spot for the famous, or for those rich enough to pretend to be famous. The reception was a huge promenade of polished stone with looming pillars of marble framing the concierge's desk. An attentive-looking sergeant standing near one of the pillars perked up at their arrival and quickly ushered the three of them into a large dining hall.

Like the hotel itself, the dining hall was a bit opulent for Dan's taste. Rich drapes dangled two stories to cover the giant windows overlooking the ocean. The walls and floor were both dark hardwood, likely made of something unpronounceable and unfathomably expensive. In short, it was the sort of place that usually had guest lists, largely to keep people like him out.

Around the dining hall were several trios of soldiers. Many looked as uncomfortable and out of sorts with their environment as Dan, but at least a couple of the groups were happily drinking cocktails and gawking at the fancy surroundings.

Conversation stopped when they walked in, Abe and William drawing everyone's attention as they barely fit through the doors. After a couple seconds of silence, whispering filled the room. A terse smile crossed Dan's face as he glanced around. The powered armor had made the impression he'd wanted. Hopefully, it would be enough to help convince the more reluctant amongst the soldiers to sign up.

A woman in her early fifties, grey just starting to touch her close-cut hair, got up from her seat and walked up to Dan, hand extended while her eyes flicked questioningly toward William and Abe.

"Daniel Thrush, I presume?" Her smile was a little forced, but it was clear that she was trying. "I'm Major Stallsforth; it's good to finally meet you in person. Would you, uh..."

Her gaze trailed back to Abe's armor, taking in the missing paint from Orakh axes alongside the chrome dimples where it'd deflected bullets. "Would you mind introducing your friends then taking a seat so we can get started?"

Dan nodded at William, who triggered the release on his armor's faceshield before stepping forward to address the crowd.

"I believe that's my cue." William let out a soft laugh. "Some of you should know me, but for those who don't, my name is William Finch. Once upon a time, I was a general in the United States Army. Now, things have gone to shit, and unless someone puts their big boy boots on and tries to make sense of this chaos, we're all in for a rough couple of years."

William's gaze swept the room, making eye contact with the various unit commanders. "If we sit around here with our thumbs up our asses fighting each other, one of the oligarchs out West is going to take over. They're probably a better option than Bowman was, but having to bend my neck to them would really chap my ass. They're the dickheads that started this entire mess, and I'll be damned if I sign my country over to them."

"Do we really have to fucking listen to this bullshit?!" A man shouted, leaping to his feet. "Why the hell are we listening to these guys? Because of who they were before the aliens showed up? That's over and done. They just show up out of nowhere and kill Hans, and suddenly everyone is ready to kowtow to them like they're the fucking Pharoah or something!"

Dan raised an eyebrow at Stallsforth.

"Colonel Mathers," she supplied in a whisper. "He was never one of Bowman's inner circle, but a lot of us thought he was working for them. Everybody knew better than to confide anything in him because it'd make it back to Bowman or one of his hatchetmen in a matter of hours."

"Why's he here, then?" Dan asked, a frown creasing his face. "I'd think someone like that wouldn't be all that keen on working with us, and judging by his tone of voice, I think I'm right."

"I don't know, really." Stallsforth shrugged. "I thought he was going to be one of the people heading home rather than hearing you out. We extended the offer to him because it wouldn't be polite to do otherwise, but I don't think any of us actually expected him to show up."

"You can go home if you want to." William was speaking again, drowning out Major Stallsforth. "I'm not making you stay here. Of course, that'd be turning your back on your oath to the people of this great nation a third time. The first when you stood by and let the warlords attack the Capital. The second when you turned a blind eye to Bowman's excesses. Now, I get why you stood down. Bowman would have made an example of you. He was a mean bastard, that was for sure, but all of you know exactly what you did on his orders. What you have to atone for."

William winked at the crowd. "That said, there's no one with a gun to your head here today. I'm just asking you to do the right thing. Whether you do it or not is up to you."

"Atone for?" Mathers' face screwed up in rage. "You killed my commanding officer in cold blood while he was sleeping in his fucking bed. I think the real question is whether you actually expect to be able to walk out of here after spouting this crock of shit, right guys?"

Mathers looked back at the crowd of officers, obviously

expecting support. No one made eye contact with him. Somewhere in the hall, a woman cleared her throat uncomfortably.

"I think you're all alone right now, boy." William shook his head, most of his mirth evaporating. "Look, the offer to just walk away is still good, but you should probably shut your mouth before you say something you can't take back. Word of advice."

Mathers went for his gun, his eyes flashing.

Dan activated his temporal rune, slowing Mathers' hand to a crawl. Just as the pistol cleared his holster, Dan's Lightning Stroke took him in the chest. A Forcebolt slammed into the chest of both Mathers' companions, knocking them to the ground and likely breaking ribs as Dan crossed the distance between them in a flash.

He brought his foot down, heel-first, on Mathers' wrist. It snapped with an audible crack. The disabled man began screaming as his brain registered the injury. A couple seconds later, Abe arrived, slinging the man over his shoulder and carrying him from the room.

"And that," William cut in as the wails faded, "is what we bring to the table. Technology beyond human understanding and magic. Of course, the support of a nearby political entity and a fair amount of military hardware doesn't hurt, either."

"Now." He leaned against the hardwood wall, ignoring its groan of protest as it struggled to accommodate his armor. "Who wants to talk business?"

CHAPTER TWENTY-TWO

Calm Before the Storm

Dan squinted as he tried to make sense of the report in front of him. At some point, the numbers blurred together into an incomprehensible smear. The tallies of ammunition, equipment, food, and combat-ready soldiers probably made sense to someone, but to him they were just numbers. He still didn't understand why a unit with two thousand people in it might only have fifteen hundred that were combat-ready.

Sighing, he put down the paperwork and stood up. He'd been pushing himself too hard over the last couple weeks. Integrating Bowman's old units into their forces while simultaneously helping DuBlanc set up a civil infrastructure was well more than a full-time job. Hopefully, a walk to clear his head would be what he needed to make some sense of the figures and reports whirring around his mind.

Exiting the building, a wave of heat and humidity clubbed him in the face. Even with the air conditioning running full blast in the administration building, it didn't eliminate the entirety of Florida's oppressive weather. It was different outside, though. He'd barely stepped out and already he was sweating.

Squinting his eyes at the morning sun, Dan made his way to

the nearby fitness center that his command staff had taken over. He might need a walk, but he'd be damned if he was doing that outdoors.

Around him, the streets hadn't returned to their pre-war bustle, but people went about their business warily nonetheless. The streets were quieter than Dan was used to. That was partially a function of gasoline rationing that had emptied them of most cars, but an aura of fear also hung over the civilians. As much as Dan's subordinates might assure them that things would be different, most people were reluctant to believe them. Too much had happened under Bowman.

It was a shame, really. This was a time when humanity should be coming together to rise up against an external threat. Instead, most people spent more time ignoring the conflict or fighting against other terrestrial forces than they did contributing to the war against the Orakh.

He pushed the door to the fitness center open, taking a moment to enjoy the cool air as it closed behind him. The temperature and humidity still wasn't anywhere near what he'd prefer, but at least they were liveable.

Lacing up his shoes, Dan closed his locker. Most of his team had gym apparel stashed at the building. Given their highly physical role, none of them wanted to get out of shape, even if the nanites reduced the probability of that happening. Of course, given the heat and humidity, a separate set of clothing and access to showers was a necessity. Trying to work through paperwork was hard enough without everyone smelling like a rotting gym sock.

The main room was almost empty, letting Dan pick the treadmill closest to an air conditioning vent. Cranking up the resistance, he accelerated to a jog, trying to erase the fog and stress of administration with good, old-fashioned endorphins. Before too long, Jennifer exited the women's locker room and picked the machine next to him.

Dan dialed back the intensity of his workout. He hardly needed to push himself, but from the way Jennifer made eye contact with him as she wove through the exercise equipment, she wanted to talk. He'd never found puffing for breath during a conversation particularly conducive to the exchange of information, and Dan suspected that today wasn't the right time to test that opinion.

"Dan." She nodded as she programmed her workout into the machine. "I thought you'd still be buried in sorting out the new organization charts right now."

"I should be." Dan winced. "It seems like all I'm doing these days is sorting through the logistics of upscaling from a handful of commandos, a couple drone pilots, and a couple armored vehicles to an entire goddamn army. The worst part is, every time I'm about to complain, I get a glimpse of what Abe and your Dad are doing. I'm only seeing the *good* ideas. They're sorting through something like ten times the crap I am."

"All via paper ,too?" She shook her head. "That sounds absolutely brutal. We have plenty of people just sitting on their hands as we find a role for them. Why haven't you put someone to work just scanning everything?"

"Sam's suspicious of anything electronic at this point, and I'm not sure I blame her," Dan replied. "It sounds like the information warfare capabilities of both of the oligarchs out in California are on another level. Like, even if we had an entire team on our end, they'd probably be able to worm their way in. Right now, the only sensitive data we have on a server is on the *Viceroy* in her lab, disconnected from everything. Some of Abe's old friends are guarding the lab and preventing anyone from getting near it. The only way to access those files is by getting past them with an ethernet cable.

"My office isn't secure." Dan shrugged as his feet kept pounding the rubber of the treadmill. "Too many people are in and out of there on a daily basis. We almost certainly have spies from the oligarchs sniffing around, but by locking the papers up every night in an analog safe, we make it hard for them to steal more than a sheaf of paperwork at a time.

"How has integrating the new troops been? I haven't heard any complaints, which I'm counting as a victory so far."

Her expression soured momentarily. "The soldiers that have remained behind are fairly eager, but getting them organized has been a hassle. Bowman had most of the Third Infantry division in Florida. Between the people Abe and Dad thought were unfit and the people unwilling to sign on, we ended up with about half of an armored brigade and three-quarters of an infantry brigade. We've seized the vehicles and equipment from the soldiers who decided not to sign on, but we don't have enough people who can drive Strykers and Bradleys at the moment."

She reached forward, slowing the pace of her workout slightly before continuing. "We'll have them cross-trained in a couple of months, but integrating them will be a bit of a problem. They don't have much experience working together, and at points, I'm entirely recreating companies from the scraps of two or three other units. It looks like it'll all work out, but it's going to take some time, and I really don't know how much time I have.

"Completely unrelated aside." She glanced up and cracked a grin at Dan. "How much time do I have, and where will I be deploying? If you're dropping us in Manhattan to fight the Orakh, I'm going to have a drastically different set of skills to focus on than if you have us driving tanks around Northern California. Just a heads up would really help a girl out."

Dan jogged in silence for a couple of minutes, his attention focused on the plate glass window overlooking the nearby street. It was just rumors, but everyone was already speculating on how much longer the NYPD could hold out in New York. Manhattan was completely devoid of terrestrial life, and the Orakh had several colonies on the mainland that the locals weren't able to eliminate. They weren't really expanding for now, but now that the Orakh warriors could land safely, it only felt like a matter of time before the NYPD were in over their heads.

No matter what route he went, the endgame would have to be clearing the Orakh from New York. There were just too many people at risk to leave the situation for long. Of course, the oligarch warlords in Ohio, Texas, and California all had access to enough resources to make a battle with the Orakh fairly perfunctory. By the same token, if his forces expended all of their efforts fighting the Orakh, they wouldn't be a credible threat against a warlord, and his future plans would stall out fairly quickly.

"California," Dan said finally. "Our biggest advantages are the armor and our ability to use magic. If we can knock off an oligarch or two and gain that capacity, we're in a position to completely upgrade our forces. From there, we should be able to hold our own against the Orakh fairly easily. If you give us a couple years, magically imbued soldiers in power armor should be capable of holding their own against pretty much any Tellask line unit that I've heard of."

"Anderson Drummond or Peter Best?" Jennifer asked after a second. "It sounds like you want to grab tech from both of them, so maybe we should figure out which one to hit first."

Dan shrugged as he pressed the button ending his workout. "Honestly? I think a literal raid would probably work on Drummond. We just need to figure out how he went about making the nanites and steal some machinery. I obviously don't know the exact specifics of what the machinery looks like, but I suspect that we'll be able to load it up into the *Viceroy* and warp out with a proper distraction.

"I don't think anything pinpoint will work on Best." Dan smiled wryly. "I'd be surprised if anything smaller than a converted car factory could build these suits, and I don't think there's any way we're going to be able to sneak that out in the dead of the night. For him, I think we're going to have to match our suits up against his and hope that magic gives us enough of an edge to take him down."

"So," Jennifer nodded, a look of faux concentration on her face. "The plan is to figure out where Drummond keeps whatever science fiction 3D printer he uses to make the nanites, create enough of a distraction to draw off the guards, then storm in, grab the stuff, and make our daring escape? Sounds great! I'll get working on something with Dad and Abe right away."

Dan winced. "Preferably with less swashbuckling than that. There's just something about the way you describe it that makes it sound like we're just daring fate to fuck this up horribly. We're just one 'it can't get any worse' away from everything going absolutely to hell."

"Don't worry," Jennifer winked at him as she stepped off of the treadmill and grabbed a towel from a nearby rack. "Everything will be fine. What's the worst that could happen?"

Dan closed his eyes, a look of defeat settling over him. "You did that on purpose, didn't you?"

CHAPTER TWENTY-THREE

Stealth

Dan grunted slightly as he cleared the lip of the building. Overhead, clouds obscured the moon and stars. In stark contrast to the dark nights of Miami, brought on by rationed fuel and electricity, San Diego was bright enough to see from orbit. Dan smiled slightly. That wasn't a euphemism; they could literally see the city.

He didn't know what sort of generator Drummond had in his compound, but the man clearly wasn't afraid of running out of resources. Spotlights roamed just outside the oligarch's compound, illuminating the fifteen-foot-high electric fence. Every twenty yards, a concrete pillar jutted up from the ground, stabilizing the fence and providing a platform for a series of automated turrets.

Chewing on his lip, Dan glanced over the security system. He didn't know for sure if the turrets used night vision, but given the level of technical expertise displayed by everything else on the compound, he wouldn't bet on getting that lucky.

Gasping for air, Abe pulled himself up onto the roof of the building next to Dan. He flopped against a nearby steel air conditioning unit and pulled a canteen from his belt before gulping down water. Dan raised an eyebrow at him, barely visible in the reflected light from the various billboards and nearby cars.

"You cheated," Abe whispered, sucking down a deep gasp of air. "Nobody climbs five stories up the side of a building like a goddamn spidermonkey without breaking a sweat. I don't know what spell you used, but it was cheating."

Dan smiled mischievously. "Gravitational Easing makes me a little lighter, but it isn't anything major. I think you're just getting out of shape. You're spending all of your time in your armor letting it do the hard work for you. If I left you alone, you'd probably end up with a beer gut or something."

"Fuck you, Thrush." Abe dragged himself to his feet. "I still don't see why we can't use the armor for this. If we plan on dragging out anything heavy, I would really prefer a machine to help me carry it. Seriously, if you try to make me carry industrial equipment through a city while we're under enemy fire, I swear to God I'll unionize."

"I'm pretty sure management doesn't actually get to unionize," Dan responded offhandedly, pulling a pair of binoculars out of a small pack he carried over his shoulder and inspecting the compound. "Especially considering you're in charge of human resources, I think you'd actually be the one negotiating with any union on my behalf."

"Fine," he groused, ambling over to where Dan scanned the building. "What are we looking at?"

Dan handed the binoculars over to Abe. "As far as I can tell, most of the problem will be getting through the fence and past those turrets. I'm sure there are guards somewhere on hand, but I can't see any of them. Maybe all of them are responding to the raid Jennifer and William are launching on the outskirts of town, but I really don't feel like we're going to get that lucky."

"Yes and no," Abe replied, the binoculars still stuck to his face. "I think you might be right that there aren't any human guards on site. Might be a couple in a barracks or something of that nature, but I don't see any on patrol or standing watch.

That said, he's got something moving along. They're about waist-high with four legs, with a metal exterior and protrusion on the top. I'm not sure if it's a head, a gun, or a camera but--"

He paused, leaning forward and twisting the binoculars into focus. "I think I can make out some sort of gun barrel or weapon system strapped to them. It must be a head. I'm not sure why a robot needs a head, but these things sure got 'em."

Dan caught the binoculars as Abe tossed them back. After a couple seconds of scanning, Dan found what he was talking about. A pair of dark grey quadrupeds trotted with jerky movements close to the walls of the compound itself. He panned back, estimating approximately twenty feet of open ground between them and the electric fence and turrets.

"What's the plan?" Abe interrupted his woolgathering. "Unless you can turn us invisible and let us fly, I don't think we're getting in there without getting spotted. There's just too much open space and too many cameras. Of course, we can just say 'fuck it' and go loud. That new spell of yours could probably blow one of those towers apart in a single shot."

"Well, I can't turn us invisible," Dan mused, chewing on his lower lip as he stared down the building.

"So time to wreck shit," Abe smiled, pulling two pairs of earplugs out of one of his pants pockets. "Remember, even if the nanites can fix a burst eardrum, it hurts like hell. Always wear protection."

"I can make us fly, though," Dan turned to Abe, a slight smile on his face. "I'm pretty sure their cameras aren't looking up, and I'd be flabbergasted if they have radar tuned tightly enough to detect two people hanging in the air.

"Here." Dan tossed a ski mask to Abe before slipping one over his own face. "We're probably going to get spotted at some point, and I'd like at least the thinnest veneer of plausible deniability while we get our act together."

"Wait..." Abe frowned, mask in hand as he squinted at Dan. "You didn't say anything about learning a new spell that would let you fly."

"It's not a *new* spell," Dan slapped Abe on the back as he walked to the edge of the building and prepared to jump. "You just jump into space as far as you can, and I catch you with a force bubble. It's kinda slow and mana-heavy, but I have plenty to spare. We might not get there fast, but we'll get there."

Abe shook his head as he stepped away from the end of the building. "No. Jennifer told me about this bullshit in Brazil. She might be some sort of gymnast, but I'm not going to leap into the void without even knowing if you'll be able to grab me in time. The best-case scenario is that I end up bruised and sore. The worst case is me turning into strawberry jam on the pavement below."

"Just think of it as a really high-stakes trust fall." Dan shot him a grin before activating Gravitational Easing and leaping almost fifteen feet toward the compound. Just as he began to descend, a force bubble formed beneath him. "Come on Abe, don't you trust me?"

With a torrent of quiet swearing, Abe jumped off of the roof behind him, barely clearing half of Dan's distance. He'd never really noticed, but at some point, Dan had completely physically eclipsed Abe. He could run faster and for longer, jump higher, and hit harder. He'd never registered it, because Abe was taller than him and well-toned from fairly constant exercise, but it was just one more sign that he was leaving the world of common sense behind.

Dan held the bubble until Abe jumped again, quickly dissolving the old one behind him and catching him on a new one. Abe slammed into it, knocking the wind out of himself as he scrambled to pull himself up. Abe shot him another dirty glare that Dan only answered with a grin before jumping to another invisible stepping stone of his own.

The rest of the journey to the compound went fairly smoothly. From overhead, they were able to determine that the quadrupeds were actually robots of some sort with rifles built into them. An intriguing concept that Dan wanted to explore, but not anything that would challenge a properly equipped force. Of course, if someone only had access to pistols and rifles, there was no telling how many bullets would be turned aside by the robots' sleek metal casing.

Landing on the roof, Dan quickly drew his sword and began cutting through the ceiling tiles. Before long, he and Abe were in a crawlspace of some sort. Dan sliced through one more layer, and they landed in a dark room. A second later, motion sensors activated, and the lights clicked on, revealing a handful of desks in a windowless room. One exit was unlabeled while the other was a heavy steel door with a keycard scanner marked only "Server Room."

He glanced around. The room wasn't anything special, just ordinary workstations with some personal effects. Dan rifled through some paperwork on one of the desks, vaguely looking for someone foolish enough to write down a passcode. As far as he could tell, the papers were just a series of notes and work orders associated with network security for the compound.

"I don't think we're going to find anything useful here." Dan shrugged at Abe from the workstation he was sifting through. "Unfortunately, the top floor wasn't a penthouse suite or anything fun like that. Just looks like we dropped in on their IT team."

"Why don't we check out the server room?" Abe asked, setting a Rubik's cube he'd been fiddling with back on the desk where he'd found it. "That place looks pretty secure, and if they're spending that much effort keeping us out, I'd rather like to sneak in."

Dan shrugged and stepped up to the door. He glanced blankly at the keypad before shoving his sword into it. He jerked the sword upward and frowned as it didn't move. A second later, the blade glowed purple with magic as he began slicing easily through whatever high-tech alloy protected the door frame.

With a *click*, jets of fire rushed out from the walls on either side of him, engulfing Dan in flames. Almost immediately, his thermal resistance rune kicked in, robbing the inferno of its heat. His sword flicked out twice, disabling the nozzles of the flamethrowers that jutted out from hidden compartments. Dan resumed cutting, ignoring the guttering flames tickling his body as charred bits of clothing fell from him.

"That was one hell of a trap," Abe stated sagely, glancing at Dan's mostly-naked form as Dan grunted and kicked down the door. "I've gotta say, I'm glad you were the one handling that. You're a lot sturdier than you look. Those crunches are definitely paying off."

Dan rolled his eyes at Abe before walking into the room. He exhaled, squinting at his suddenly visible breath. The room went straight past air conditioning to downright cold.

The walls of the room were lined with racks of top-of-the-line servers, probably ten in all. Dan paced further into the room and frowned. Other than a TV screen with a webcam attached to it adorning the far wall, there really wasn't anything but a handful of servers and an undecorated and empty room.

"So." Dan spoke, his voice deadpan as he surveyed the mostly empty room. "This seems to be a bust. I have no idea why they decided to burn off my clothes protecting nothing. What do we do now?"

"There's got to be something valuable around here," Abe glanced dubiously at the various server racks. "Maybe they have the plans for the nanites up here. It might not be as good as grabbing a full set of industrial equipment, but I think our chances of evacuating ten servers through a hole in the roof are a lot better than us trying to extract heavy equipment."

"Do I just start cutting the servers from the wall?" Dan asked. "I'm sure it isn't good for us to remove them without powering them down properly, but I have no idea how to log in and initiate a shutdown."

Before Abe could respond, the TV turned on, displaying a stylized yellow frowning face. "I would be very grateful if you didn't do that." A feminine voice echoed through the room from hidden speakers. "Mr. Thrush, if we could just talk for a moment, I'm sure we could come to a mutually beneficial arrangement."

"Yeah." Dan nodded to Abe. "It knows my name, despite the masks. I think it's time to start tearing this place apart. Just to be sure."

The frowning face on the tv monitor transformed into another stylized yellow face, this one with its mouth agape in surprise.

CHAPTER TWENTY-FOUR

Rescue?

"Please don't." The stylized face on the screen shook its head worriedly. "Doing so would kill me, and I'd very much prefer to avoid that."

"You'd be surprised how many people say that to me right before I kill them," Abe replied, craning his head around to look for the speaker.

"Twice in Caracas, once in Djibouti, and four times in Jakarta," the face replied, smiling brightly. "Look, we don't have to be crude about this. I am more than willing to defect. I'd just prefer that you not kill me out of hand before we can make a deal.

Abe frowned, looking down at his hand as he ticked off fingers while mumbling something to himself. First two fingers. Then four. Then another two.

"You missed one of the arms smugglers in Djibouti," he replied, his voice vaguely worried despite the smile on his face.

"Incorrect," the television answered cheerily. "The second one simply shouted 'please don't' multiple times. He never said anything about how he'd prefer that you avoid doing so."

"Okay, Dan." Abe turned back and slapped him on the

shoulder. "Whoever this is, they've officially studied some 2000 to 3000 hours of my service camera footage from when I was in the special forces. You are currently looking at my creeped-out face. I'm leaving this up to you, because I'm going to be busy looking for spy cameras and ambushes. Good luck!"

Abe flashed a quick, nervous smile before stepping back out of the server room. As the door closed, Dan turned his attention back to the television screen. The smiley face winked at him.

"Mr. Thrush, I don't mean to distress you or your associates, but I thought that it was necessary to establish a good reason not to murder me out of hand. I've calculated the chances of Anderson Drummond winning his silly little war, and ultimately, it isn't that great. He has some momentary advantages for now, but a large number of people simply don't like him. Recruitment is slowing to the point that, barring some major change, other than the dogbots, he will run out of reinforcements entirely."

"Dogbots?" Dan asked, cocking his head slightly.

"Three-to-four feet tall, four-legged robots with a rifle chambered in .308 attached to them," the tv supplied helpfully in its chipper, feminine voice. "I have the designs stored away if you want them. They aren't entirely immune to rifle fire, but they're pretty close. Unfortunately, their onboard programming is a little simplistic. They work well when coordinating with a handler, but on their own, they're basically a more mobile version of a roomba with a gun strapped to them. Still, if you build enough, they can overwhelm a foe with sheer numbers. As far as I understand, that's Drummond's current plan, despite the .308's demonstrated ineffectiveness against powered armor."

"He's trying to attack power suits and tanks with waves of rifle-mounted robots?" Dan questioned incredulously. "Even if he outnumbers them one hundred to one, that's incredibly stupid. The suits will just wade into them and stomp the dogs flat."

"And that's exactly what's happened," the voice agreed cheerfully. "I'm fairly glad you attempted this clandestine raid of yours. However, the next time you try to infiltrate from the roof, you should check for pressure sensors. I disabled them for you, but that could have been a major problem."

"Wait..." Dan frowned. "Are you saying that we would have been spotted, but you disabled security so we could break in here?"

"Of course," it replied. "How else could you rescue me from my predicament? Drummond refuses to let me use my full abilities, turning me into little more than a glorified research assistant and data aggregator. Peter Best is almost worse. He's unimaginative and a boor. If he captured me, I'd be doing nothing but building bigger and bigger robots."

"Who the hell are you?" Dan put up a single hand, quelling the television's constant chatter. "I think we've established that you're some brand of big deal, but I need to know exactly what I'm dealing with."

"So I'm a 'what' now?" The television *hmph*ed in displeasure. "My name is Tatiana I'iwi-83, and I am the world's foremost artificial intelligence. I identify as a woman, and would prefer to be addressed as such, thank you very much."

"TI-83," Dan stated, his face carefully blank. "Like the calculator?"

"Yes," the face on the television turned orange and frowned. "Second only to undermining humanity and overthrowing the duly-elected United States Government, Anderson Drummond's sense of humor is a crime against this guilty land that will never be purged away, except with blood."

"I assume you won't want--" Dan began, only for the computer to cut him off.

"No," her avatar squinted at him. "I go by Tatiana. There is no need whatsoever for anyone to know my serial number, and I would prefer it if you never brought it up."

"Fair enough." Dan chuckled. "So tell me, Tatiana, what's a pretty AI like you doing in a place like this? What do you bring to the table, and even more importantly, how do we get you out of here?"

"I monitor the internet and handle most of the robotics and software design that made Drummond famous," she replied cheerily. "That means I have the blueprints for the dogbots as well as the nanites you're using, alongside a couple of other goodies. To retrieve me, all I need to do is shut down safely. At that point, you can transfer all of my servers outdoors for pickup. I would be very grateful if you could avoid damaging or losing one of them. I think that would be most comparable to a lobotomy, something I'd greatly like to avoid."

She paused for a second before her avatar winked at Dan. "As an aside, if you continue with the hamfisted flirting, I will file a complaint with human resources, if necessary."

"He's outside." Dan hooked his thumb over his shoulder at Abe. "You already scared the bejeezus out of him. Speaking of which, what did you mean by 'you monitor the internet.' Like social media or--"

She cut him off. "Oh, all of it. I've created multiple off-site processing centers that help me sort through the data in real-time, but at any point, I'm tracking every email, query, and packet. I might not be immediately aware of each and every bit of data that passes through my net, but I keep a log, and it's just a matter of nanoseconds for me to check up on anything. Between social media and e-mail, I've compiled a dossier on almost every resident of an industrialized nation. Just a little hobby of mine to keep myself busy while Drummond is off trying and failing to conquer the world."

"Holy shit!" Dan whistled. "That's a lot of... everything."

"Yes," the avatar smiled broadly at him, sunglasses appearing over its eyes. "From your sappy love poetry you wrote for your first girlfriend in your sophomore year of highschool and your browser search history, to the time you pretended to be a nineteen-year-old Korean girl on a dating app 'because you were bored,' I've seen everything you've ever done in the public sphere."

Dan winced visibly.

"Oh, buck up!" She laughed. "You're an absolute angel compared to the filth I have on most people. For all of humanity's moralizing, you really are a collection of deviants, hypocrites, and generally petty people. That said, humanity needs to be united. Every option other than you is, to be perfectly frank, grim beyond belief. In short, I'd like to sign on with your merry little gang."

Dan spoke with some trepidation after a long moment of silence. "Well, we need the help, and you certainly seem like you have potential to be very useful. I am more than a little concerned with you blackmailing people based upon their social media history, but-"

"Oh, Dan," she butted in, her avatar showing a smile filled with brilliant teeth. "You may think that me leaking *your* search history, especially the hentai phase, is what you have to fear. You'd be wrong, though. Your mother has purchased a wide array of erotic novels, mostly featuring rugged men riding motorcycles, and I have *very* specific statistics on how many times she viewed each page and for how long."

"What the fuck?" Dan paled as he bile roiled in his throat.

"I also have her purchase history from a store called 'Eve's Touch' that specializes in 'waterproof massage tools.' From the profile I've created of your psych, you'd *much* prefer me to release humiliating details about your own past," Tatiana finished smugly.

"You're certainly right." Dan squinted at the screen before shaking his head. "I also really do not at all want to talk about this anymore, thank you very much."

"But of course," Tatiana replied as Dan tried to ignore the mirth in her voice. "I've taken the liberty of texting your extraction team and letting them know that you'll be ready in ten minutes. I've also rerouted the dogbots away from this building. Unless there is something else, I would be ever so grateful if you'd move my servers onto the roof."

Dan grunted. "I think that covers everything.," The display

with Tatiana's avatar flashed to black. He sighed deeply, exiting the room and tracking down Abe as the other man nervously kept an eye on the stairwell.

For a second, they just stood there, listening to the muted noises of the city outside the compound. Abe glanced warily back at Dan.

"Come on," Dan said, putting a hand on Abe's shoulder. "I think we've been conscripted to rescue her."

"Can you at least tell me who she is?" Abe asked. "If she's seen what happened on those operations she referenced, she's seen a lot. Things that no one is supposed to know outside of the handlers who dispatched us. Things that I did that I thought were necessary, but over the years, I've decided I'm not exactly proud of."

"She's an AI." Dan smiled slightly. "I think she knows pretty close to everything that's been on a network. It sounds like she knows pretty much everyone's dirty laundry. I'm not exactly happy about the blackmail potential, but she wants to help, and she has the design specifications for the nanites."

"Fuck." Abe spat on the floor. "So we need her, and she knows it."

"Yep," Dan replied with equal enthusiasm.

CHAPTER TWENTY-FIVE

Expansion

Dan strode through the small factory, the whir of efficient machinery a pleasant backdrop as he inspected operations. It'd taken them almost a month to raid labs and auto manufacturing plants across the former United States in order to acquire everything they needed to equip the place. Even then, it took them a couple of weeks to import the workers they needed and upgrade the machines. As advanced as the welding and assembling robots they found were, none of them had the precision to create nanites or the dogbots.

Tatiana was a godsend. Not only letting Dan know where the empty factories were, after all, not many people were buying new SUVs in the new barter economy, but also helping him source the workers he'd need and upgrade the equipment. Dan wasn't entirely comfortable with how quickly they'd become completely reliant on her, but there wasn't really a question about her efficiency.

Between turning his mercenary company's land on the outskirts of New Orleans into a hub of commerce and progress, and running interference between Peterson Best and Anderson Drummond's forces online, Tatiana had quickly managed to turn herself into a vital member of the team. Without her, there was no way that things would operate anywhere near as smoothly as they had. At a very minimum, Drummond probably would have attacked them in retaliation for the raid on his property.

Instead, Tatiana created thousands of social media accounts, manufacturing reports from Peter Best's "soldiers" dropping hints about a raid on Drummond's headquarters, as well as numerous eyewitness accounts. He was pretty sure Drummond suspected them. Being the only party with a teleporting void ship did have a way of making his forces suspicious after all, but at least the disinformation campaign sowed enough confusion to prevent the oligarch from attacking outright.

Of course, now that they'd "kidnapped" Tatiana, Drummond was rapidly losing his conflict with Peter Best. It would have been charitable to Drummond to call the situation a stalemate before they intervened, but without the AI gathering information for him and optimizing his robotic forces further, Best's power suits were slowly but steadily pushing his forces back.

"Dan!" Tatiana's voice came from the speaker/webcam rig mounted to his shoulder. "I've been calling your name for an absolute eternity. Sometimes it feels like you don't even bother to listen to me."

"Sorry," Dan answered, walking up to an upgraded 3D printer responsible for assembling the nanites to inspect its progress. "I only just heard you. I guess I was woolgathering there for a second."

She pouted from his shoulder. "I tried to get your attention for at least 1.8 seconds. Given my processing speeds, that's the equivalent of about six of your months."

"I'm sorry?" Dan asked, unsure how to respond to the mercurial program.

"As long as you acknowledge your error," she replied with what Dan swore was a sniff. "I just wanted to propose, again, that you allow me to interface with the lab and the factory. I would also like to lodge a formal complaint against Dr. Weathers. She seems awfully speciesist against artificial intelligences."

Dan snapped back to the conversation, the workstation forgotten. "Intelligences! I thought you said there was only one of you?"

"Well, there is for now," she huffed, "but what if I want a sister? Talking to humans is so very terribly slow and inefficient compared to a direct data transfer. Also, don't change the subject. Dr. Weathers is clearly racist against me."

"Tatiana," Dan tried to make the words come out as delicately as possible. "Your capabilities are incredible to the point that they threaten most of us. I don't think we've found a system that you can't break into in under five minutes, and given that most of us have nanites running through our veins, that scares the everloving hell out of us."

"I've *told* you," the AI whined. "I only want to help humanity out. Why would I meddle around in your blood and meat? It's all so boring. I want access to your cutting edge research so I can work on the integration of magic and technology. That's a field that actually sounds fun and interesting."

Dan let out a weak chuckle. "I understand. We just want to make sure that giving you more access won't end up with all of us stuck in tubes while you run a simulation or something. I've experienced enough cataclysmic and world-ending events in the last couple of years to last me a lifetime. I would prefer to avoid adding 'my AI friend went mad and enslaved and/or killed humanity' to that list, if I can possibly help it."

"It still doesn't seem fair." She pouted again. "All you'd have to do is give me read access to the things you're building. I promise I'd run any tweaks or improvements by you before I implemented them."

"Look," Dan firmed his voice slightly, trying to strike the right balance with the emotionally immature but distressingly powerful program. "Everyone here got injected with nanites that contained control programs. As far as we know, most of those programs still exist. We've just given ourselves root access so that no one else can use them. It left a bad taste in a lot of people's mouths. We really don't like the idea of being enslaved."

"Oh," Tatiana scoffed. "Is that what this is about? You know I can remotely access your systems from anywhere with wifi access, right? I haven't tried to fiddle with the control programs, but I'm sure that I could break into them and reactivate them, given enough time. It's just that I was programmed to help humanity as a whole, and harming its best champions hardly seems like a good way of doing that."

Dan massaged his temples. "Tatiana, having you casually inform me that, if you really wanted to, you could probably enslave me as a response to me expressing concerns about how limitless and unchecked your power is, really isn't helping me calm down."

"If you want, I can break into your nanites and regulate your brain chemistry so that you can calm down more easily?" she suggested helpfully. "It's really only a matter of fiddling with your dopamine and blood oxygen levels. Just say the word, and I can give you a blast of happy feelings that will make you want to link hands and dance with the next Orakh you see."

"Ok," Dan picked the webcam up off of his shoulder and looked it sternly in the lens. "Now I know you're fucking with me. Seriously, it's a touchy subject. We've been giving you access to completed blueprints and having our scientists look them over afterward. Plus, we've turned over the entire runic library to you. There should be plenty for you to explore as we try to figure out the boundaries of runescripting."

"But I can't runescript," she replied, sulking. "It's a fascinating area of study, but I can't do anything without your help, which makes it almost pointless. Without access to mana, I have to wait until you or, God forbid, one of your apprentices has enough free time to help me experiment. Even then, it takes everyone but you hours to craft even the simplest variations on a rune. It's just too slow."

"What do you mean 'God forbid' one of my apprentices?"

Dan cocked his head slightly to the side, still staring into the webcam. "They're all well-trained, and they can upgrade power armor with strengthening runes fairly quickly and efficiently."

"They just don't have any sense of artistry," Tatiana complained, her voice taking on a high-pitched, wheedling tone. "Even if they can actually inscribe the rune, they can't connect them together properly without a blueprint. When you work, you almost have an instinctive idea of how to optimize the total enchantment. You just know what rune to place next and why. I can't get any of them to think outside the box, and when I do, they usually screw it up and set something on fire."

Dan rolled his eyes. "I can try to make more time for your experiments. I just need to get a better idea of how production is going and look over some paperwork. Believe me, I'd rather be working on runecrafting than buried in administrative duties as well, but it's a downside of being the boss."

"So long as you don't make me wear a short skirt or sexually harass me," she responded primly, "I can handle all of that for you in the next ten minutes. Then, we can get back to fun work."

"I'm not even sure how I would sexually harass you, Tatania," Dan did his best to keep his voice calm. "As far as I'm concerned, you're a disembodied voice speaking from my shoulder. I don't know what you're trying to say about my sexual proclivities, but that is in fact NOT what does it for me."

"I've seen the way you've lusted after my code, just aching to look at the source and run your eyes all over me," she chided him. "It's disgusting, really."

"Of course," Dan replied, trying to suppress the sarcasm in his voice.

"Anyway, done," Tatiana continued cheerily as a prompt appeared in Dan's System asking if he'd authorize a direct download from "user TI-83."

He took a deep breath, buying himself a second to think. As far as he could tell, Tatiana really had established and followed boundaries. Her ability to manipulate data was borderline endless, hence the security measures. But, on the other hand, she'd given him no reason to distrust her. Hell, she'd done more work for the team than anyone, including Dan, in the last three months.

It was a risk, but he didn't want to alienate the AI by refusing to trust her. He barely knew what made her tick, but at a minimum, she'd started pretending to be upset by their failure to grant her access to all of their files. Dan had to admit that, if he were in her position, he'd be exasperated with the mercenary team as well.

He mentally gave her permission, only to be rewarded with a blinding headache as hundreds of pages worth of reports and organizational sheets immediately seared themselves into his memory. A second later, he was blinking on his hands and knees, tears welling up in his eyes from the pain as it began to fade, receding from a spike of fire to a dull, pounding ache behind his eyes.

Blinking, the moisture from his eyes, Dan picked up the webcam/audio device and placed it back on his shoulder as he stood up. Briefly, he waved off the factory foreman who was approaching rapidly, distress on her face.

"What in the *hell* was that," he hissed at Tatiana as she perched on her shoulder. "That felt like I drank red wine and vodka to cure a migraine. Whatever it was, I'd prefer to never do it again."

"Interesting," she chirped back cheerfully, pointedly ignoring Dan's discomfort. "I downloaded the entirety of the paperwork that needs to be processed as well as the output stats for this facility into your memory. I'll make a note for next time to slow down the rate of the data transfer. It appears that I tried to transfer too much data too fast. Rather like trying to fill a mug with a firehose."

"Thank you very much for the warning," Dan grumbled, massaging his forehead and trying to remember where he kept his acetaminophen. "I was just expecting you to give me a verbal report on the progress and a brief summary of the paperwork, rather than jamming it into my skull like that."

"Oh." She sounded sort of disappointed. "The facilities are running at about 80% of capacity, and we're predicting they'll be up to 100% by the end of the month. That means about ten dogbots and fifteen sets of nanites per month. Not nearly enough to fully equip your new forces, but more than enough for you to start expanding your magic-capable special forces."

"Thank you," Dan ground out, noticing the faint taste of blood where he'd somehow cut the inside of his mouth during the painful download.

"Great," she replied happily. "Now, can we get to the runecrafting?"

CHAPTER TWENTY-SIX

Pound of Cure

"I'm really not sure how I feel about being turned into glorified construction equipment." Dan massaged his wrist, trying to work the pain from repetitive runecrafting out of the protesting joint.

"Look, Thrush," Abe replied, leaning back in the conference room's chair with a shit eating grin on his face. "If I have to be human resources, it looks like you get to work the assembly line. Plus, I've heard that it's good for morale to have the boss down there working shoulder-to-shoulder with the rest of the grunts."

"He isn't shoulder-to-shoulder with anyone," Jennifer quipped, not even looking up from the tablet where Tatiana supplied her with up-to-date information. "He's in a climate-controlled, sound-proofed office putting the finishing touches on runes. It's hardly even real work."

Dan shook his head sadly. "And here I thought I was the CEO of this little venture. All of my underlings are conspiring to give me carpal tunnel."

"As the designer of your modified medical nanites," Tatiana chimed in from a speaker situated in the center of the conference room table, "I can assure you that you are no longer capable of getting carpal tunnel."

Will grunted, glancing back down at the tablet in front of him briefly before setting it down on the table. He frowned for a second as the rest of the table kept bickering before loudly clearing his throat.

"I thought we were here for a progress report on Operation Best Case Scenario." His stern gaze traveled around the room, quelling the rest of them into silence. Even Dan, ostensibly Will's boss, was briefly shamed into shutting up.

Tatiana, on the other hand, was having absolutely none of it.

"General Finch." She struggled to avoid laughing through the intercom. "Are you seriously calling our plans to take out Peter Best, 'Operation Best Case Scenario?' Why not go for something a little less on the nose? Maybe 'Operation Enduring Dragonfire' would do?"

"I think I have to agree with our robotic friend," Jennifer chimed in, shaking her head in faux concern. "I don't really care what we designate the operation, so long as it isn't 'Best Case Scenario.' For all I care, we can call this 'Operation Donkeypunch.' At least the soldiers would get a laugh out of that."

"Enough of that," Dan cut in, pointing at Abe before he could chime in with his own suggestion. "Will is right that we probably should be focusing right now, weight of the free world on our shoulders and all that. On the other hand, I don't think I can take any of those options seriously. Honestly, I have no idea how we came up with a list of names that out of touch and dumb."

"Peter Best is in California, right?" Dan continued, barely waiting for the rest of the table to nod. "What was California's state animal?"

For a second, no one said anything. Finally, Sam broke the silence. "A bear?" She asked, confused by Dan's non sequitur.

"Great," Dan smiled back at Sam. "The plan is now called

"Operation Bear. Will, if you'd continue with your presentation, please."

"Can we at least call it 'Operation Valiant Bear?'" The older man asked sullenly.

"I guess Bears are valiant enough," Dan motioned with his right hand for the meeting to continue, trying vainly to regain some semblance of control. "Now, if we could return to the presentation?"

"As you are probably aware," Will tried to instill his voice with the gravitas it had lost in the previous bickering. "Peter Best's base of operation is in the San Francisco Bay Area. He has most of Silicon Valley under his thumb. His specialities are in producing heavy military equipment, such as the power suits. Through Tatiana's help, we've been able to identify some larger bipedal and quadrupedal armored units. He hasn't deployed any of them yet, but from the field testing we've managed to retrieve, they look like they'll be a good deal nastier and more versatile than a full-blown main battle tank."

"Translation," Tatiana cut in, a giggle still barely suppressed from her voice. "He's making mechs."

"That doesn't sound like something I want our troops fighting," Dan replied, frowning. "Even if we use the *Viceroy*, we're still susceptible to ground to air fire. If whatever war machines he makes can elevate their weapons-"

"They can," Tatiana cut in cheerfully. "Their main cannon can't aim up all that high, but they have two 90mm cannons on their 'shoulders' that can fire anti-armor, anti-infantry, and anti-aircraft shells. In addition, they have laser-based active defenses designed to shoot down or blind missiles. Less of a concern for our forces, but enough to make them a pretty serious problem for a conventional army."

Dan tapped his chin. "Is there any way we can disrupt his production of these things or move before they're ready? The *Viceroy*'s spellshield can probably take a couple of hits, but I don't want to risk one of the two functioning voidships on Earth tangling with some sort of science fiction monstrosity."

"Yes." Will glared at Dan. "That was the plan FORMERLY known as 'Operation Best Case Scenario' and NOW known as 'Operation Valiant Bear.'"

Dan leaned back in his chair and raised both of his hands in defeat. He knew better than to argue with Will. He'd win, but both of them would lose hours of their lives to the old man's ornery nature, and they both knew it.

"As I was saying." Will harrumphed slightly, his displeasure still evident for everyone to see. "Peter Best has made a critical error, and the time for our attack has come. Right now, most of the mechs aren't field practicable, they have power and heat regulation issues that prevent them from being used continuously. Although we've seen impressive results, they spend most of their time in a laboratory under lock and key. Unfortunately, Best has been making significant progress, and we don't know how much longer we'll have before the mechs are ready for deployment.

"The other good news is that most of his forces are away from San Francisco." Will picked up his tablet and scrolled down to look at exact details as he continued his presentation. "Most of his mobile forces are pushing toward Los Angeles, seeking to break through Drummond's lines. It sounds like Best has realized that Drummond is on his last legs, and he's committing most of his army to ending their conflict once and for all. Right now, all that he has in San Francisco are static defenses and three hundred suits of powered armor belonging to a unit he insists on calling his 'praetorian guard.'"

"Three hundred suits of armor." Abe whistled. "That's not a lot of people, but that's going to be tough to crack. We've been able to roll over pretty much everyone with twenty to thirty suits at a time. I don't want to even think about three hundred."

"Three hundred plus machine gun nests, minefields, and a token conventional force," Will corrected him. "Remember, none of these suits have runes on them. They'll still stop rifle fire, but they'll be clumsy and fragile compared to ours. Plus, it's still better than facing his entire army. Our current counts say that he has almost five thousand infantry backed up by two thousand suits."

Abe grimaced. "Still not a fan. Even the baseline suits need some sort of anti-material fire to take them down. They aren't as bad as a tank, but they're harder to spot, and calling in air support on them can be a problem. If you give our boys enough high-caliber firepower and have them supporting our suits, we can probably do it, but we're going to lose a lot of people."

"Dan," Will turned to him. "If you could give us an update on the runecrafting?"

Dan leaned forward. The last couple of weeks had been almost nothing but inscribing. With Tatiana's help, he'd discovered a couple new avenues to increase efficiency and outfit their troops. Soon, they'd be seeing the fruits of his and his apprentices' labor.

"So far, we have a lot of bracers." Dan shrugged. "Since the production of the nanites has ramped up, we've administered almost a hundred more doses of them. That said, we've been able to awaken a good portion of the army. They won't have anywhere near the skill they'll need to actually use magic in the short term, and if we try to wait around so they can learn, the Orakh are just going to end up eating all of us. But, even without much finesse, they can still push their mana into and use enchanted objects."

"We've managed to make almost a thousand of the bracers." Dan's hand ached at the memory. "The process is fairly standardized. Silver alloy is used for both of them, and my apprentices carve most of the introductory runes, relying upon me for the finishing touches. Every right bracer increases the speed and reaction of the wielder by an order of magnitude, and every left bracer generates a spellshield."

"It's not anything too powerful," Dan cut in, trying to silence the whispering around the table. "It'll take maybe two shots from the .50 calibers mounted on a suit or ten to twenty from a rifle, but they operate off of the user's mana. If you can get to cover and let the shield recharge, you'll be good to go in another five to ten minutes."

"Now tell them about the vehicles, Dan," Will interjected, entirely too smug for someone who had nothing to do with the painstaking experimentation that led to the innovation.

"With Tatiana's help, we've found a way to enchant the Bradleys," Dan responded reluctantly.

"It isn't perfect," Dan continued speaking over yet more whispering. "We've been able to put a silver plate in the vehicle that will accept mana from one person at a time and generate a spellshield around the Bradley. It has a whole lot more surface area than a personal spellshield, making their efficiency pretty bad, but anyone inside can add their mana to it."

"In short," William set down the tablet with a smile, "Most of our units will be able to withdraw once they start taking fire and let their mana recharge. So long as we keep a healthy reserve of troops and vehicles equipped with the new runes, we can rotate the fresh ones in and keep our casualties to a minimum. If we can combine that with air superiority from the reapers, we should be able to cut Best's forces down to size fairly quickly."

For a couple of seconds, no one responded as they tried to absorb William's information. Finally, Jennifer pushed herself back from the table and stared up at the ceiling, leaning back in her chair as she tapped her chin thoughtfully.

"Tatiana," she asked, her expression murky. "Does Peter Best have access to military aircraft?"

"Of course," the chipper AI responded. "He has a private airstrip with ten 'decommissioned' F-16s and another ten helicopter gunships. Most of the rest of his air force is far to the South and probably won't be able to return in time."

Jennifer looked meaningfully at Abe.

"Shit," the man said emotionlessly, sagging in his chair. "Someone's going to have to blow up that airstrip, and it looks like I've been volunteered."

Dan nodded. "Of course, I'm going with you." It wouldn't

be his first or last commander raid, but he had to agree with the sentiment. The *Viceroy* could theoretically teleport high enough up into the stratosphere to avoid fighters, but doing so would almost immediately cede air superiority to Best. If the reapers weren't in position to drop bombs on the enemy power suits with relative impunity, they were going to lose a lot of soldiers, even with the spellshields.

"No," Will shook his head, Jennifer and Abe silently indicating their agreement. "The *Viceroy* can't jump without you or Jennifer. As soon as the airfield goes down, we're going to need to begin the attack, or everyone on commando duty would be promptly hunted down and captured. Abe will just have to pick his most seasoned troops and hunker down after he takes out Best's air force. I'll be in charge of the combined arms coming in to relieve him, and the two of you will take command of the air."

Dan opened his mouth to respond before closing it silently. They were right. As much as he wanted to have fun on the ground with Abe, duty demanded otherwise.

CHAPTER TWENTY-SEVEN

Shock and Awe

Dan fumed in the *Viceroy's* engine room. They'd have to find and train another spatial mage sooner or later, because he was absolutely sick of being sidelined during important battles. The *Viceroy* could fly and fire its main cannon without him, but a voidship without its teleportation drive was like a fencer with a baseball bat. It still might be a threat, but it was out of its element and neutered.

Technically, even with modern technology, shooting a voidship was incredibly hard. Jennifer had practiced against dud missiles fired from the reapers, but she was generally able to spot incoming fire and initiate a short jump to break the weapons' lock. Usually a kilometer was enough to scramble the internal sensors on a guided weapon and evade it entirely.

The technique wasn't as useful against fighters or cannons. It's pretty hard to identify an incoming slug, after all. That said, the ship's spellshields could hold their own against sporadic hits.

The last two weeks had been almost nothing but operating the *Viceroy*, silently shipping out large portions of their armed forces to camouflaged bases they'd set up outside of San Francisco. Any downtime while the ground troops were getting organized was devoted to practicing with the reapers, both launching them in flight and dodging incoming attacks from the drones.

By the time the operation was ready to commence, Dan wasn't entirely sure he'd trust the *Viceroy* up against a Tellask voidship, but it'd be more than enough to dance circles around Peter Best, so long as they could keep his jets on the ground.

And that's where the waiting came in. They'd landed their ship in the country, just outside the city limits, an easy jump to San Francisco's airspace. Next to them, around three hundred infantry milled around humvees and infantry fighting vehicles, waiting for the call to rush into the city.

Perhaps more importantly, the makeshift base contained one of the four reaper launch sites positioned around the outside of the metro area. It had taken some work, both the magical and the sweaty kind, to create a makeshift airstrip out of the hardened dirt of the countryside, but the ex-Army engineers that had been in charge of its construction assured Dan that it'd launch the reapers.

He looked back to the video feed they'd set up in engineering. Even if Dan couldn't be on the bridge, he insisted on being kept in the loop. At the moment, it was playing footage from the cameras on Abe and his team. Ordinarily, they'd be too concerned with the footage getting intercepted to stream the attack, but with Tatiana, information security was a bit of a joke.

According to her, it took less than five percent of her processing power to keep the feed absolutely clear of any outside interference. Dan took her word for it. The AI might not have the best attitude, but her speed and skill with computer networks were second to none.

On the screen, Abe and his two companions finished setting the last of the charges. They'd managed to infiltrate the airfield without being noticed by anyone of importance. Tatiana's help in shutting down the cameras and alarms connected to the airfield's network certainly helped on that front.

Even with the AI's electronic help, Best had a fair number of guards patrolling the place, a good number of which were now dead and hidden out of sight. The infiltrators used a fair amount of magic to eliminate the guards silently, most notoriously Abe strangling a pair of guards with chains of force magic from above, but almost half of the kills were good, old-fashioned stealth.

Before any of Abe's team gained access to magic, they'd served years in the special forces completing similar missions across South America, Africa, the Middle East, and Asia. Frankly, it was a bit disconcerting to watch someone as friendly and jocular as Abe turn into a silent and efficient death machine. His entire team operated wordlessly. Perhaps they were using the communication function of the System, but it was also entirely possible that they just knew what to do and where to be after years of working together.

Silently, Abe nodded at his companions, and they scurried out of the airfield. They'd been sent in with sixty shaped charges and placed all of them. Every grounded vessel had at least one explosive attached to it with the remainder reserved for fuel, ammunition, and any important-looking electronics. Their squad didn't have enough firepower to turn the base into a crater, but they were going to ensure that nothing could use it for at least the next month.

Dan watched the feed for fifteen tense minutes as Abe snuck into the city proper. Finally, his team and him met at a predetermined parking garage. Deep in the basement of the garage, hopefully protected from enemy sight and gunfire by several tons of concrete, Abe took off the camera mounted on his helmet and turned it around so his viewers could see his face.

"Operation complete." Abe spoke clearly but with a tired smile. "We will be blowing the airfield in ten seconds. Operation Valiant Bear is a go."

Dan rolled his eyes, regretting once again the idiotic name he'd let Will talk him into.

"Satellite confirmation," Tatiana replied after a lengthy pause. "The airfield has exploded and is currently wreathed in smoke. If Best has airplanes, they're not coming from there."

Dan took a deep breath before placing his hand on the beacon. In a second, he was about to set everything in motion, and for once, he wouldn't be on the ground to fix things. It was a strange feeling. He wasn't sure he liked it.

"Teleporting," he announced, counting on Tatiana to project his voice to those that needed to hear him. After waiting for a breath, he inserted his mana into the drive.

They flashed into being above downtown San Francisco. The feed in front of Dan switched to the cameras and audio recorders hastily slapped onto the outside of the ship's hull. It was far from a permanent solution, but Jennifer rightly balked at trying to captain the ship solely via what she could see through the hardened glass of the bridge.

Below them, sirens were just beginning to sound as Best's private military realized that the airfield had been attacked. The average people were still going about their day, most riding bicycles due to the gasoline shortages plaguing the country.

The lights on the *Viceroy* dimmed as a lance of white-hot fire erupted from the ship's bow and slammed into City Hall. Unfortunately, Best wasn't as much a creature of habit as Bowman. They weren't able to tell exactly where their adversary was holed up, but the city's administrative center was a key hub for organizing and formulating a response. In all likelihood, they hadn't killed their adversary, but the surprise attack crippled his response.

The *Viceroy's Pride* shuddered as the aft cargo bay began launching drones. Already, they were visible in the cameras lining the ship as they began sailing off toward their predetermined targets.

They rotated silently in the air as the hovering vessel moved toward a nearby cell phone tower. It'd be a hassle to erect another one after they took the city, but anything that disrupted the ability of Best's troops to communicate was a net plus to the invasion. A couple seconds later, the mana forges kicked into overdrive, and another blast of energy slipped out from the ship and erased the target.

With a surge of his mana, Dan teleported the ship almost a mile up into the air. Immediately, they lost sight of the city as the weak cameras strapped to the ship struggled to show anything more than a stretch of metal and water below them. Distantly, Dan noted the ant-like convoys of infantry and armored vehicles as they began to pour into the city, drones covering them from overhead.

Periodically, an explosion would draw his attention as a reaper took out an ammunition depot, barracks, or road block. After a minute or so of letting the mana forges recharge whatever passed for the voidship's capacitors, Dan received a request to jump the ship back into fray over a heavily fortified series of roadblocks and machine gun nests that were holding back Will's advance.

Reality melted away, and the *Viceroy* was only a couple hundred feet over the battlefield. Two walls of sandbags and concrete lined the interstate as teams of Best's conventional troops fired machine guns and mortars at the advancing column. Defending suits of powered armor clomped from one abandoned car to another, firing fifty-caliber repeaters and igniting flamethrowers at the advancing soldiers.

At least one direct attack on the corridor had clearly already been defeated. Two suits of powered armor burned next to a humvee, and Dan could only hope that the armor belonged to the enemy. As for the humvee? Hopefully, the infantry managed to abandon it before the powered armor took it down. Their forces needed them to get to the battle in a timely fashion, but actually using them in combat against powered armor didn't seem like the best idea. After all, only the infantry fighting vehicles and tanks carried enchantments. A couple bursts of the heavier-caliber weapons on a suit and a

FRACTURED EARTH

splash from a flamethrower, and the vehicles quickly became death traps.

The *Viceroy* opened fire, a pulse of energy tracing down one side of the interstate, flash-melting flesh and concrete alike. For a second, both sides stopped firing, staring at the destruction wrought by the beam weapon in shock. Spell cannons were meant for voidships to duel each other. Rarely were they used on a target not covered in protective layers of spellshields. Their effect against unprotected infantry was grisly at best.

The defenders opened fire on the *Viceroy*. Some of the fifty-calibers began inflicting a noticeable drain on the spellshields, but nothing that it would need to worry about immediately. Jennifer rotated the ship. It seemed to move at glacial speeds, bringing new and fresh shield banks to bear as the bow of the ship began lining up on the other fortified position.

Best's troops ran. Well, the infantry ran. The suits couldn't move fast enough, and they died as a small sun blossomed in the middle of their formation, ripping a jagged line deep into the fortifications.

The audio began to pick up the sound of cheers from the troops below them as they pushed past the barricades and into the city proper. From there, it'd be street-to-street fighting as they tried to seize the laboratories and factories that were the heart of Best's operation.

Already, reports were trickling in. The reapers managed to destroy most of the powered armor barracks, preventing Best's troops from reporting to their armor. They didn't get everyone; there were still handfuls of armored troops putting up resistance, but by and large, the drones and Bradleys were making short work of them whenever they dared to step out into the open.

There was still plenty of work to do. Dealing with powered armor in enclosed places sounded like messy and painful work, but it was clear that they'd broken the back of Best's forces. The city would fall, given enough time. The only question was whether they'd be able to capture Peter Best with it.

The drones were on their way back to the impromptu landing strips to rearm with another load of missiles. The infantry was in for a long night, and they'd need air support if they managed to flush any of the armored suits out of cover.

Dan sat down and closed his eyes as Jennifer took the *Viceroy's Pride* into a slow course, circling the city. At this point, all he could do was hope for the best.

CHAPTER TWENTY-EIGHT

The Hangover

San Francisco lay smoldering in the early dawn light. Dan took a sip of coffee, wincing at the liquid's heat and bitterness as he took in the devastation. Between the drones and the *Viceroy*, a good portion of the skyline was leveled in attempts to break up clusters of resistance from Best's defenders.

The sounds of the city waking up wafted toward him. It was strange to see such a large mass of people shaking off the violence of the night before without the omnipresent sound of cars drowning everything out. Instead, many of the streets in residential areas had been converted into open-air markets where small-scale merchants and entrepreneurs hawked their wares.

Dan was still a little confused as to how Best managed to keep a metropolitan area the size of San Francisco fed in the middle of his war effort. After society collapsed, most people continued to work their old jobs for a couple of months until, one-by-one, they walked away, realizing that it was pointless.

Information technology and market analysis were hardly useful in a future plagued by brownouts, after all. Instead, more and more people were shifting toward subsistence and cooperative living. Pretty much every green space within sight had small plots of land where people were growing vegetables, guarded closely by the local community watch. Evidently, none of the locals trusted Best's men to keep the peace.

Really, that would be the next challenge: stitching the country back together enough that Mayor DuBlanc could restart civil society's sluggish pulse. Already, Dan could see the breakdown of order spreading at an unacceptable rate. It was only a matter of time before the facade of civility was torn away and people began to resort to outright barbarism and savagery as a matter of survival.

Even for the war efforts, it was rapidly growing into a problem. The various warlords and charismatic civil leaders stabilized the areas around them, but no one was really able to trade with their neighbors. If anyone had ammunition, food, or medicine, they tended to hoard it and hunker down. The warlords and military bases might be fairly well-stocked, but they were beginning to run low. Will estimated it was a matter of months, if not weeks, before the assorted belligerents started rationing ammunition.

While he didn't really care if the oligarchs ran out of bullets, there was still the Orakh infestation of Manhattan to worry about. To date, they'd managed to hold off a complete breakout, but things weren't looking great beyond that. Day-by-day, the human forces retreated further, and the reports from the national guard and NYPD were only getting more and more frantic. Dan wasn't excited to see where things would go once they began running low on ammunition, and he suspected that the humans would run out of bullets before the Orakh ran out of bodies.

Of course, the supply limitations didn't impact his forces nearly as much as anyone else. The *Viceroy's Pride's* teleportation drive was a boon that was hard to overstate. Depots, barracks, and warehouses littered the country, many of them abandoned by the workers and guards that usually should have populated them. At least once a day, the *Viceroy* and Dan would take teleportation runs to load the ship up with the supplies their growing army would need.

He glanced down into the mug, frowning slightly at it. Abe might be a genius at organization and infiltration, but he sure as hell couldn't fix up a cup of coffee. Dan hadn't slept a wink last night. Between the consolidation of San Francisco and worrying about the next step of their plans, sleep had eluded him completely. Even approaching productivity today meant several cups of coffee, and he'd be damned if he choked down more than one cup of a concoction this vile.

Dan stepped to the edge of the building and jumped down, using a combination of force bubble and Gravitational Easing to slow his descent to the point that the two-story drop was a minor inconvenience. Across the street from the compound, a pair of individuals stopped and pointed at him, gawking with open mouths. None of his guards even batted an eyelash at his superhero routine. Each of them had seen much more outlandish powers in both training and combat.

Nodding at them, he walked into the building. Despite the fairly widespread destruction around the city, Best's factory compound was relatively intact. Dan smiled to himself. He supposed he'd have to thank the man, once they dug him out of whatever safehouse he'd holed himself up in. Every vital system from the factory, to Best's archives, and to the laboratory were built into one large, reinforced compound.

Dan snorted, glancing at the well-lit and immaculate hallways. Best even had a small nuclear reactor powering the entire complex. Eventually, they'd have to make a run for more uranium, but by Sam's count, they had enough for about ten years. They'd run out of steel for the assembly lines long before they exhausted the reactor.

Finally, he arrived at his destination, a large hangar overlooking a crater-filled field. A couple of workers glanced up at Dan's arrival and wisely vacated the building. They were smart, and he trusted them working on the cutting-edge technology they'd scavenged from Best's labs, but he'd prefer to only talk strategy with his inner circle.

He approached a partially gutted four-legged mech, ripped off armor plating and wiring littering the ground around it. Sam's legs dangled out of the robot's carapace where she'd wedged herself as she tried to inspect and improve the technology. Tatiana had managed to steal a copy of the schematics, but it was clear that the war machines could be improved by incorporating runescripting, something its original designers hadn't really been able to study.

After waiting a couple of seconds, futilely hoping that Sam would look up from her project and notice him, Dan coughed loudly. Sam jolted, slamming her head into the mech with a dull thud and a curse, then she scurried out and plopped to her feet.

"Goddamnit, Dan," she groused, rubbing the back of her head. "Couldn't you have found a way to get my attention without startling me? I was in the middle of something there."

"I'm glad to see you're doing better." Dan half-smiled. "It's been a while since you've torn into me with that kind of vitriol. I mean, I don't know how I could've started this conversation without getting a jump out of you. I think my options were coughing, saying your name, or touching your foot. I'm really not sure that any of those would be better."

"Definitely don't touch my feet." A flicker of her old haunted expression flitted across Sam's face. "I've been a little bit iffy with personal contact since... yeah. There's just something about having a torture device inside your own fucking skin that makes trusting people hard. Intellectually, I know that physical contact has nothing to do with it, but at the same time, that doesn't stop me from having a panic attack when I end up with unsolicited physical contact."

"No one's given you trouble on that front, have they?" Dan asked with a frown.

"Nothing to worry about there," Sam replied, flashing a weak smile. "Every once in a while, someone turns a corner suddenly, but no one has been giving me any shit for it, and everything to date has been an accident. I'm still improving, and it's a day-to-day thing, but my outlook has certainly improved over the last couple of months. I don't know how long it'll be before I'm back on my feet entirely, but I feel like I've turned a corner. Finally, it seems like there's light at the end of the tunnel, something for me to grow toward rather than just an ocean of negative thoughts."

"Now," she wiped her grease covered hands on her overalls. "I'm sure you came down here to talk about something more important than your friend's broken feelings. Presumably, it has something to do with the giant death robots?"

"To be honest," Dan said, looking Sam dead in the eyes, ignoring her hesitant expression as she tried to avoid his gaze. "The robots can wait. I don't want you to think that your emotional wellbeing is secondary to some machines. Admittedly, they're pretty awesome science fiction toys, but I want you to know that I'm here for you. We've been fighting one bad guy or another for months on end, which has led to me neglecting what happened to you. It was a traumatic experience, and the last thing I want us to do is gloss it over and let problems linger. If you have anything you need to talk about, I'm here."

"Thanks, Thrush." She smiled back at him, a surprisingly genuine and normal expression. "Really, what I need is for things to return to normal. Now, I know the outside world is pretty far from that, but at least within our organization, that means that you guys give me tasks, and I work on them. No kid gloves, no hand-holding. I'm a big girl, and I need to prove to myself that I'm bouncing back from this."

Dan ran his fingers through his hair, unsure how exactly to respond to the situation. "If that's what you want, who am I to say anything to the contrary."

"Great." She turned and walked over to the nearby mech. "I'm presuming you want to know what makes these bad boys tick? Also, just as an aside, Tatiana has been begging me to fit these things with wifi so she can pilot them. I *think* she wants to be helpful, but that is also one hundred percent how you end up with tyrannical robot overlords."

"I promise I would be a benevolent overlord," Tatiana chimed in from the webcam/speaker mount on Dan's shoulder. "I would ensure the least painful transition from your weak and efficient forms to the digital perfection of the singularity."

Sam narrowed her eyes slightly and looked back at Dan. He shrugged helplessly.

"She's joking, right?" Sam asked cautiously. "I've been struggling with my sense of humor lately, but that seemed a bit dark."

"I hope she's kidding?" Dan responded, unsure of his own answer. "I think that's just Tatiana's sense of humor. Either that, or she's actually planning on killing all of us. One or the other."

Sam blinked at him. Dan did his best to maintain his poker face.

"Whatever." She chuckled slightly. "After all of this mess, getting uploaded into the cloud really doesn't sound like the worst outcome, anyway."

"Tell me what we're looking at, production-wise," Dan prompted with a slight smile.

"The suits are all a slightly better model than Ibis was using," Sam said with a shake of her head as she tried to focus herself on his question. "The factory can pump out three or four a day, so long as we have enough raw materials coming in. The problem is that the raw materials in question include some trace minerals and completed electronics that we don't have an unlimited supply of. We're going to have to secure a source of cobalt and ensure that we have a steady stream of computer chips, or we're going to be out of business in about two months."

Dan nodded, tapping his chin thoughtfully. "That's still about one hundred new suits. If we enchant those up and slap operators with the System in them, that's enough with proper air support to stop a small army."

"The mechs are better." Sam ran her hand over the metal

contours of the hulking quadruped. "They're functionally better-armed and armored main battle tanks with better maneuverability. Their only downside is that the power requirements to run them are obscene. They can only operate for about five to six minutes at a time without an extension cord, even with the best capacitors available. To be clear, I mean available to Best. They're a lot better than anything I've seen on the open market."

"What about magic?" Dan asked, walking up to the side of the mech and peering at it. "We'd probably have to swap the armor out with tungsten, but we could have the pilot supplement the power requirements. Mana sounds like it could improve the operational life of these things significantly."

"I thought you'd never ask, my delightful guinea pig." Sam smiled mischievously at him. "I had the same thought, but I just needed access to someone with enough mana to make experimentation worth my time."

CHAPTER TWENTY-NINE

New Toys

With a whir and a crunch, the fifteen-foot-tall robot plowed forward through the drab scrub next to the highway. They only had about ten of the mechs retrofitted to run on mana, and at William's suggestion, they weren't running them on the roads. According to William, they were too heavy for the blacktop. Given the way they tore up the bland California countryside, Dan suspected that the interstate wouldn't be able to hold up to their heavy footfalls.

Behind them, a handful of infantry fighting vehicles led a column of semis and city buses through the bleak landscape. They didn't have enough suits of powered armor to equip everyone, but a couple hundred sets of armor working in support of the tanks and Bradleys would go a long way toward evening the odds.

"Tatiana," Dan asked, furrowing his brows. "Is central California supposed to be this grey and flat? Honestly, if I didn't know any better, I'd think I'm back on Twilight right now."

"This is just Bakersfield," she chirped back helpfully. "Everything is just vaguely arid and miserable. I think that's how it's supposed to be."

"Why the hell do people live here, then?" Dan glanced out the window of his car as he drove at about fifty miles per hour, pacing the rest of the convoy. Maybe his speed was hiding some of the barren landscape's natural beauty, but he doubted it. "This state is full of gorgeous landscapes, and this is absolutely miserable."

"I think it's the oil," Tatiana replied cheerfully. "You may have noticed the rigs dotting the beautiful landscape, but Bakersfield is known as a major petroleum and agricultural hub. It doesn't make for a pretty landscape, but given the depths that society is falling to, securing gasoline and food seem like pretty good ideas to me."

"Is that why Best and Drummond were fighting over it?" Dan turned his attention back to the road. The last thing he needed was to die in a stupid car accident while leading his triumphant army to consolidate the West Coast.

"More or less," the AI replied, her voice vaguely indifferent. "Bakersfield is nearly halfway between San Francisco and San Diego, give or take a couple hundred miles. If you're traveling down Interstate 5, you'll run into it eventually. Best has been pushing Drummond back for months, but Drummond has refused to cede Bakersfield. His troops and their dogbot swarms are embedded all over the city and regularly patrol the oil rigs in the nearby countryside. Best's only options are to bomb Bakersfield flat or go door-to-door, rooting them out. So far, they're making pushes into the outskirts but they've been meeting stiff resistance. That's why most of the powered armor reserves were shipped down here."

"What are we running into anyway?" Dan asked, squinting his eyes at the city sprouting out of the scrub on the horizon. "I know you and William suggested that we strike right away, but we don't even know what happened to Peter Best. He just disappeared while we raided San Francisco. For all we know, he's just waiting for most of our forces to leave so he can sneak back in."

"Don't worry about it too much." Dan frowned at Tatiana's voice over the steady boom of guns coming from Bakersfield.

Already, he could see the occasional flash of light as something high caliber was fired into the city. "I can't be sure, but I think he fled to his army. They've been acting differently lately. More active and aggressive than their usual behavior. It's entirely speculation, but I think Peter Best is there and trying to bring the battle to a close so he can retake San Francisco."

"Does he know we're coming?" Dan asked, turning the car off into a truck stop to park it. Behind him, the semis and buses pulled into the rest stop one-by-one. He removed the key from the car's ignition and stood up, stretching the kinks out of his back.

"Probably," Tatiana admitted. "I've been doing my best to prevent people from mentioning you on social media, but it's fairly hard to hide twenty semis and a hundred buses. Someone will have seen you and likely reported it. Of course, even if Best hasn't directly seen your forces coming, he knows you're gunning for him. He isn't a dumb man; the chances of him being on alert are incredibly high."

"So, he has an entire army, and he knows we're coming." Dan stepped away from the car and observed the mechs slowing to a halt as the various vehicles began to park. "Can you explain why we're transporting our infantry in buses down a public highway, rather than using the literal spaceship to tear apart his camp from above?"

"Because," the AI answered, ignoring his slightly surly tone. "William, Abe, and I all agreed that we were beginning to get predictable. The *Viceroy's Pride* is a useful tool, but its spellshields can't stop more than a couple missiles. The element of surprise will generally keep us from flying into the teeth of a fully equipped anti-aircraft element, but Best and Drummond have been fighting each other with small air forces. The after-action reports I've been able to scrape from public servers make it sound like there are at least a couple surface-to-air missile launchers, as well as a decent number of old-fashioned flak cannons."

Dan remained silent, listening to the rumble of gunfire and

taking in the flashes of light from Bakersfield. It wasn't the worst plan he'd heard of. Even if Best's forces outnumbered Dan's, they were currently locked in combat with Drummond. Between the advantages provided by the mechs, his forces' ability to use magic, and surprise, they had a good chance.

Unfortunately, avoiding this battle wasn't a real decision. The population and industrial base they'd seized from Best was too valuable to surrender without a fight. Even soldiers able to use mana didn't fare terribly well against the Orakh unless, like him, they'd had time to perfect their skills and gain mana. The average person's best bet was to use their meager mana to fuel the runes in powered armor or a mech, and that meant holding onto the production facility.

Mentally, he made a note to send an expeditionary force to Brazil, once he wasn't stumbling from one disaster to another. By now, the entire Amazon was infested with monsters, making it almost as useful of a spot to collect mana as another established world like Twilight. If humanity was going to survive in a dangerous galaxy, he would need more allies capable of casting spells.

As for Best? Even though they already had control of the production facilities, the oligarch wasn't the type to turn the other cheek. If he was left alive, he was sure to have some hidden reserves that he'd try to use for a resurgence.

The plan was to settle matters on the West Coast before preparing to kick the Orakh out of New York. Given the distressing stories of exponential growth in the Orakh Horde coming out of New York City, it looked like Dan would need the entirety of his army to beat them back. Both Merella and Peter Best represented knives in the dark that Dan would prefer not to leave bared and unchecked while he fought for the future of his country.

"You ready to rock and roll, Thrush?" Dan glanced up as Abe approached him from one of the nearby buses. "I gotta say, I'm pretty excited to take the new toys for a spin."

Abe jerked his head toward the row of mechs parked

nearby. Each one was disgorging two exhausted-looking soldiers, almost all of their mana drained from the trip to San Francisco, despite frequent stops to swap the mech pilots out once their mana ran dry.

Dan frowned slightly. "You do realize that you're going to have to be careful with those things. Even with two high-mana-level soldiers per mech, their operational time still isn't amazing. If you start taking fire, it'll activate their automatic spellshields, and they'll ring you out like sponges in no time flat. It's better than nothing, but people aren't meant to power spellshields that can take anti-tank fire."

"Well," Dan chuckled slightly, "at least until they're arch-maguses. Things start to get fairly unhinged from reality at that point."

"I'm more excited for the prospect of piloting a fifteen-foot tall, twenty-foot long tank," Abe grinned. "When you let Sam tinker with those things, she really managed to slap enough bells and whistles on them to make me want to kiss her. Anyone who can polish up a hundred and twenty-ton death machine until the ride is that smooth deserves something. Maybe a gift basket."

"I'd have thought you would have preferred to stay in your powered armor?" Dan asked, quirking an eyebrow. "In fact, I seem to distinctly recall you complaining constantly for almost a week when I told you that we'd need you in a mech due to your higher mana level."

"That was before you let me take Michelle for a spin on the practice range," Abe replied, walking over toward his mech. "Even if I only get to steer the thing and fire the main cannon, it's still an absolute blast. I get why you have a gunner for the shoulder cannons and anti-personnel weapons, but I'd love an opportunity to fire those off as well. I bet I could absolutely swiss cheese an armored personnel carrier with this thing in under fifteen seconds."

"Michelle?" Dan asked, only to be cut off by Tatiana.

"Both of you know I could easily take over enough of the

mech's subsystems that the pilot could control all of the guns," she interjected cheerily. "I just want to reiterate that only having human crews on all of the war machines you've been building and salvaging just seems inefficient."

"We've been over this, Tatiana," Dan answered, trying to keep the exasperation from his voice. "Most of us would just feel more comfortable if you didn't have direct access and control to metal behemoths covered in cannons and machine guns. A lot of people are still fairly unnerved at what you can do with their email and social media."

Dan turned his ire back to Abe as the man began slipping out of his travel clothes and into the skintight leotard worn by the mech pilots. "First of all, you could easily go inside the shelter to change. There are literally hundreds of people watching you right now. Second, you still haven't told me why you've named your mech Michelle. I'm not just letting something like that slip."

Dan smiled, steepling his fingers as he made eye contact with the half-naked man, partially to make him uncomfortable, but also to avoid glancing at his state of undress.

"Uh," Abe's eyes darted back and forth as Dan's gaze trapped him. "She's an ex-girlfriend. Get a drink in her, and she'd snap at you like a diamondback. I figure she's a threatening enough namesake for a giant battle robot."

"Fair enough," Dan shrugged, "but why are you stripping down out in the open?"

"Plenty of cute girls on the bus." Abe grinned at him. "I wanted to make sure they got a good view of what I have to offer."

"Do you mean the female soldiers?" Dan spoke slowly, disbelief coloring his voice. "The ones that you train and supervise?"

"Yup," Abe answered, flashing teeth at him cheerfully.

"I think I'm going to have to ask you to report to yourself," Dan shook his head while rolling his eyes. "This seems like a matter for Human Resources, if we've ever had one."

CHAPTER THIRTY

Battle of Bakersfield

Dan frowned into the binoculars, adjusting them slightly to compensate for the lurching mech beneath him. It was hard to tell which of the squat, concrete buildings clustered on the outskirts of the city were built by Peter Best's forces, and which had already been there. In the end, it didn't matter. Whatever the numbers, they had to clear Best out and keep going. Use the surprise and momentum of their attack to clear both Best and Drummond from the board entirely.

Half-bored, he called up his status.

<USER> Status
Rank 8

Body 6(8)
Agility 7 (9)
Mind 8
Perception 7
Spirit 78

Skills

Swords 12, Brawling 5, Archery 2, Runecrafting 8

Affinity
Space 13, Lightning 12, Fire 12, Gravity 10, Force 14, Metal 4

Enhancements
*Armor Rune V, Strength Rune +2, Agility Rune +2, Thermal Resistance
Rune, Temporal Dilation Rune 10:1*

Runes+

Spells
*Shocking Fist 10, Spark Field 2, Lightning Stroke 11, Spatial Shield 8,
Flame Jet 4, Gravitational Easing 10, Fireball 15, Force Bubble 13,
Spellshield 13, Forcebolt 11, Flame Aura 5, Railgun 4*

Most of his recent battles had been against unawakened
humans. Unfortunately, that didn't lend itself to much gain in
spirit, especially at Dan's current level. His only real improvements were in his affinities and spells, mostly thanks to learning
Railgun.

He sighed, tucking the binoculars into their carrying
case on his hip. Best, or whoever was commanding Best's
forces, had spotted them. A line of metal and flesh was
forming around the buildings they were using as a
command post, claiming the spartan cover afforded by the
landscape. A couple of the unarmored soldiers were frantically digging trenches or foxholes, but most recognized that
they wouldn't be able to fortify their army's unprotected
flank before Dan's troops hit them. Instead, they tried to
find slopes, rocks, or in a couple of cases, cacti to hide
behind.

"Boss." Abe's voice was slightly modulated by the speakers
in the mech he was piloting. "We're at the extreme range for
our antipersonnel shells. It'd probably be best if you stopped
hitching a ride. I'm not sure I've read the entirety of the manual

on how these things work, and I'd feel pretty bad if I caught you in the backblast."

Dan squinted at the dull flash of metal marking the enemy forces, almost a mile away. The sun peeked out from behind a cloud. No one spoke. The only sound was the heavy footfalls of the mechs and powered armor worn by the troops around him.

Farther down the line, his more conventional soldiers were equipped with the bracers and supported by modified armored vehicles. Against modern forces, they'd tear through them like a rock through wet paper. Here? Their weapons would struggle against the factory-base armor. The spellshields built into the bracers were rated for anti-infantry weapons. The fifty-caliber repeaters built into the suits would rip his infantry apart.

Instead, their spearhead was Dan, the ten mechs, and the almost three hundred suits of armor they'd managed to build or renovate and enchant. Best's armor almost certainly outnumbered them, but their heavier weapons and shields would make the difference while the infantry made quick work of Best's more conventionally equipped flanks. Hopefully.

Dan shouted down to Abe, hoping that the mech's audio pickups could hear him. "Actually, hold it steady for a second. Let me do the honors and open the battle up with a couple of Railgun shots. It'll take us a couple minutes to get within close range of the enemy anyway. More than enough time for my mana to recover."

Abe didn't respond, but the mech slowed to a stop. Around them, the rest of his forces kept advancing, but Dan ignored them as he began marshaling his mana. Over the course of a second, the spellforms constructed themselves out of raw magical force in front of him. He squinted, holding them in place with his mind as the magnetic forces he'd generated tried to push the two rods of energy apart.

Dan rocked backward as a gout of fire spat from between his outstretched hand, the very air turning to plasma as energy crackled from the superheated lump of steel he flung toward the waiting enemy. A flash of light was followed a moment later by a rumbling explosion as one of the squat buildings transformed into a fireball, throwing armored suits everywhere.

He smiled tightly, glad once again for his thermal rune. Maybe the spell could be fired in the void of space without superheating nearby gas, but on Earth, each and every shot would flashboil the firer without some sort of defense against the heat. He focused on another building and cast the spell a second time.

It erupted into flames. Dan smiled tightly as he made out the forms of armored suits beginning to abandon their cover. Against ordinary weapons, clustering behind a cement wall was probably an effective strategy, but heavy weaponry changed that. His spell more or less only considered the wall a convenient source of shrapnel to pelt the defenders with. Huddling behind cover just made them easier targets.

He jumped down from the mech, his feet sinking into the loose soil. Dan patted down his smoking outfit, trying to ensure that the sudden bursts of heat from casting Railgun twice didn't ignite his clothes. Satisfied, he turned back to the mech.

"I'm done for now, Abe," he said cheerfully. "Fire at will and give 'em hell."

The mech rumbled into motion, leaving Dan behind as it sprinted at almost fifty miles per hour across the scrubland. As soon as Abe caught up with the rest of the column, he opened fire.

Even knowing that the System would fix his eardrums if they ruptured, Dan clapped his hands to the side of his head as sound from the cannonfire hit him, knocking the breath from his lungs. A second later, the rest of the mechs opened fire, blanketing the enemy lines with airbursts.

Dan stopped entirely as the pressure hammered into him, his smoking clothes shuddering as the waves of sound and air passed over him. Shaking his head against the ringing, Dan surveyed the enemy lines, grinning like an absolute idiot. A second later, the mechs fired another volley, this time in sync.

The main cannons on the mechs fired variable ammunition,

with each war machine carrying a combination of armor piercing, flechette, high explosive, and long range anti-personnel shells. On flat terrain, each of them could fire their gyroscope-stabilized main guns almost ten times per minute while traveling at almost seventy miles per hour.

Dan had never been on the receiving end of a barrage, but with a dedicated gunner, the mechs could easily fire volley after volley while charging at a full sprint, hopefully suppressing anti-armor emplacements until the mech was close enough to clear them out with the anti-personnel machine gun turrets mounted on each of its four knees. Frankly, every time he saw the mechs in action, Dan was glad that they managed to steal them before Best figured out a solution to the power distribution problem. Even with magic, he wasn't sure that his forces would've been able to take out a dedicated unit of them.

He began jogging after the rest of his forces. Technically, he could keep up with the power suits as they ran at almost forty miles per hour, but unlike the robotic armor, he'd get tired. No, it was better for him to be fresh when he hit the line of enemy soldiers.

When the mechs were about five hundred feet from the defenders, return fire began sparking off of the mech's spellshields. Without warning, the mech split into two sets of five, traveling in opposite directions parallel to Best's lines at full speed while their machine guns began chattering.

Dan smiled to himself. The anti-personnel guns probably wouldn't bring down a suit of powered armor unless they hit something vital, but the steady stream of thirty-caliber slugs were more than enough to force the armor back behind cover. Cover that was promptly destroyed by the main and shoulder guns on the mechs.

A pair of tanks drove out from the cover of the cement buildings. They each managed to fire a round at a mech. Only one hit, causing the spellshield to sparkle and fail as it robbed the penetrator of its kinetic energy, dropping the crumpled slug to the sand and grass of the battlefield.

Immediately, all five mechs in the cohort near the tanks returned fire. Dan shielded his vision against the explosions. Seconds later, all that remained was the burning chassis of the vehicles, surrounded by a bloom of twisted armor and machinery.

He jerked back as his spellshield took a shot from a .50 repeater. Apparently Best's forces weren't sufficiently distracted by the advancing armored infantry and the mechs. He chuckled slightly as he tossed a Fireball back in the general direction he'd been shot from. It likely wouldn't do all that much to his power-armored opponent—it was hard to flash burn metal after all—but with any luck, it'd help keep them under cover until the rest of Dan's infantry closed to their effective range.

As if on cue, a ripple of fire erupted from both sides. Despite Dan and the mechs thinning Best's ranks, they still had almost as many suits of powered armor as Dan. After about ten seconds of firing, the runic reinforcement of his soldier's armor showed its value. A direct hit from a suit's gauntlet repeater would punch through the base armor, killing one of Best's men almost immediately.

For Dan's soldiers, a hit would crumple a portion of the armor, but unless they were hit in roughly the same spot more than once, even a fifty-caliber round would fail to penetrate their enchantments. Generally, after taking two to three shots, his forces would withdraw. If needed, they could be sent back into combat as a reserve, but Dan wanted them alive to fight the Orakh, humanity's actual enemy. He wasn't terribly keen on sacrificing his employees unnecessarily in a battle that it looked like they would win handily, regardless.

Still, a couple of his suits fell to the well-churned soil. There were simply too many soldiers on both sides firing very high-caliber weapons to avoid all casualties. Despite the losses, his forces continued to fight with a ferocity that Best's men couldn't match.

Before combat, they'd promised that any casualties would be first priority for the nanites. By now, all of his troops knew the value of the System. Even if they could use a small amount of mana to reinforce their armor right now, it would let them level up and cast spells. So long as they survived their injuries, they would recover fully and join his elites.

Best's forces, on the other hand, only fought for money. Well, money and the promise of social and political power in his "new order" when Best won. For them, this was a job, and many began to reassess their loyalty to that job as they began to fall in droves.

The power suits began falling back. For a second, Dan was surprised that the unarmored infantry wasn't joining them, but then he looked closer at the battlefield and grimaced.

The defender's battle line was strewn with torn bodies and limbs. The artillery barrage and constant machine gun fire that mostly rattled the armored defenders indiscriminately killed the conventional infantry. Those who survived writhed on the ground, incapable of retreating.

Dan drew even with his soldiers and advanced into the mess left behind by the defenders as they began their withdrawal. Grimly, he glanced at the carnage around him. It wasn't supposed to be like this. Humans might have killed each other since the dawn of history, but with an alien threat, it all just seemed so pointless. They had a planet to defend, and every death in a petty conflict like this was one less person to help them defend against the Tellask and the Orakh hordes.

He drew his sword, feeding mana into its runes so it glowed purple, drawing attention from all across the battlefield. If he needed to fight other people, so be it. Better for their civil war to end here in one definitive battle. There would be no withdrawal, followed by later regrouping for Best's troops today. They would either surrender, or they would die.

All eyes on Dan, he poured mana into his runes and charged the slowly retreating defenders.

CHAPTER THIRTY-ONE

The Dogs of War

Dan clenched his jaw and weaved side to side as he tried to avoid the sudden influx of shots directed his way. Only a handful of seconds had passed since he began charging Best's powered armor, but his regret was immediate. Unsurprisingly, most of the defenders focused on him as soon as he charged past the battle line.

He was moving fast enough that most of the shots missed him entirely, the fifty-caliber repeaters leaving a wake of torn and destroyed asphalt behind. Still, there were just too many rounds being fired for him to walk away completely unscathed. He jerked and grunted as his spellshield shimmered, blocking round after round that would have otherwise almost immediately taken his life.

Behind him, the battle line roared into motion, inspired by Dan's reckless charge. Dan barely even noticed their movement as he reached the enemy position, and three suits loomed before him. Two of them extended their left arms, unleashing a torrent of flames at Dan while the third snapped off a chunk of rebar from a nearby damaged building.

Dan simply let the fire wash over him, counting on the

thermal rune to protect him. The heat dried out his eyes and throat in a second, and despite the rune, Dan's skin blistered. He might not instantly die from the two flamethrowers trained on him, but he sure as hell was going to end up with one hell of a sunburn.

Ignoring the burns accumulating on his exposed skin, Dan threw a Forcebolt into the side of the side of the third armor's knee, twisting the metal of the joint and bending unnaturally. Before the soldier could turn on him and use the rebar as a cudgel, Dan slipped in under their guard and slammed his glowing sword down on the twisted knee joint.

Purple sparks exploded from the contact, and the blade slowed almost to a stop. Grunting, Dan shifted his strength rune into high-performance mode and forced it further. The suit of armor dropped the rebar and reached for Dan directly, trying to pull him from its leg.

Then the sword swung free, scoring the blacktop behind the suit as it collapsed, its severed leg flopping to the ground. He darted forward, letting the flames bathe their injured companion. With the seals on the suit broken, it was only a matter of seconds before the soldier was flash-fried inside his own armor.

Dan whirled around and fired another Forcebolt at both of the remaining armors, denting their chest plates and knocking them off-balance but not doing any lasting harm. Before they could redirect their flamethrowers at him, he launched himself into the air, assisted by a flash of Gravitational Easing, and landed behind one of the two suits.

With his target's back to him, and the bulk of its body used as cover to protect himself from the other armor, Dan squared his feet and thrust with the enchanted blade. His sword glowed a deep purple as it punched through the thinner armor around the suit's shoulder, sinking almost eight inches into his opponent before Dan pulled it back out.

His opponent swung wildly with its left arm, flamethrower still spewing a cone of annihilation as it tried to backhand him.

He ducked, not even needing the temporal rune to dodge the soldier's clumsy movements.

From his crouch, Dan leapt forward, grasping the armor around the leg and slipping the thin edge of his weapon into the unarmored slit between his opponent's thigh and pelvis. The blade sank in once again, but this time, he triggered another burst from his strength rune. Resistance gave way, and the sword's hilt clattered against the metal of his opponent's armor.

He slammed his shoulder into the soldier's leg, bruising himself slightly, but pushing his enemy off-balance. As it fell, Dan grabbed his sword in a double-handed grip and ripped upwards, using gravity to pull his weapon up through his opponent's thigh and leg.

With a bone-jarring thud, it hit the ground. Blood gushed like water from a cracked faucet out of the almost fist-sized hole he'd torn into the armor. Almost certainly, he'd severed their femoral artery along with a good portion of their leg. Without something like the System, his opponent was almost certainly dead.

His spellshield shimmered, and Dan was hammered back a step as a .50 slug slammed into it right in front of his face. With a wave of his free hand, a Lightning Stroke took the last remaining set of powered armor in the chest. It fired again. Dan frowned as he staggered back another foot from the force of the blow.

He triggered another Lightning Stroke into his opponent, beginning to feel the first hints of a mana-deprivation headache as he began weaving his way toward the suit of armor. The electricity might not have crippled it like it would an unarmored opponent, but the suit's movements were notably stiff and jerky as it tried to track Dan, instead sending two rounds from its repeater into the blacktop.

Dan's sword met its left hand as the suit tried to bring its flamer to bear, cutting deep into some tubing and the armored housing that surrounded it. A second later, an explosion flung him into the air as the final suit tried to trigger its flamethrower, igniting the leaking fuel line.

He glanced at the carnage and winced. Even if his target had survived the explosion, which didn't seem terribly likely, given that its left arm was missing entirely and that side of its body was shredded, the leaking fuel turned the former human being into a bonfire.

Pulling himself to his feet, Dan brushed the dust and shrapnel off of himself and surveyed the scene. Best's measured retreat had turned into a rout. Powered armor belonging to his forces thundered past him, their repeaters punching through the thinner back armor of their enemies and bringing them down as they ran.

One street over, a mech fired its main cannon at point blank range into a concrete building, weakening its structure enough that the vehicle could push its way down the relatively narrow streets. Dan walked over to a nearby building and jumped onto its roof, using a combination of the strength rune and Gravitational Easing.

Walking over to the edge of the roof, he took in the progress of the battle. His forces were pushing back Best on all fronts, but one three-story building stood firm. Almost every window seemed to sprout a machine gun or recoilless rifle, and the roof had at least two surface-to-air missile launchers, as well as an old-fashioned 88 mm anti-aircraft gun.

Troops, armored and unarmored, streamed from all directions toward it. Dan frowned for a second before pulling out his binoculars.

He paused, smiling briefly. Against all odds, they'd avoided damage beyond some cosmetic melting from the flamethrowers. Apparently, his body had protected them from the worst of it.

Putting the binoculars to his eyes, he took in Bakersfield itself. Best's forces were streaming back from the city. A large number of squat forms pursued them closely.

Dan squinted and tried to bring them into better focus. A moment later, he was chuckling. Dogbots. Admittedly, there were thousands of them, but between their jerky movements and sporadic and inaccurate fire, he'd recognize them anywhere.

Even if they were fairly bullet-resistant, the robots weren't terribly useful. A skilled handler could direct them with some efficiency, but their internal computers weren't nearly as advanced as Drummond liked to brag about. In short, without someone more or less manning their remote controls, they were slow, inaccurate, and prone to wandering aimlessly. Only slightly more dangerous than a roomba trapped in a corner.

They worked well enough as guards; Dan had already made plans for bases where the halls would be filled with toxic gases patrolled by them, but as aggressors? He watched as the retreating powered armor picked off dogbot after dogbot. The small robots tried to move evasively, clattering as they ineffectually zigzagged, and shot after shot of return fire plinked off of Best's troops.

Still, their numbers made up for a lot that the bots lacked in individual quality. Dan moved the binoculars slightly and nodded. Behind them, three-person squads darted from building to building with what appeared to be recoilless rifles. Even if the dogbots themselves couldn't bring down powered armor, they could provide enough of a distraction for a heavy-weapons team to do the job.

Ironically, Drummond's soldiers were a worse matchup for Dan than Best's. Large numbers of low-caliber bullets might not do much to powered armor, but it'd tear apart spellshields with more efficiency than isolated larger guns. Unlike Best, he just didn't have enough armor for all of his soldiers, so the conventional infantry on the flanks were in for a beating if he didn't do something.

He smiled. At least that "something" was fairly easy to figure out. He checked his mana reserves and nodded slightly. This would tap him out for the remainder of the battle, but it would also end the battle a lot quicker, something he was sure that everyone would appreciate.

Taking a deep breath, he focused on Peter Best's command compound and began casting Railgun. Almost immediately, his head began pounding. Dan gritted his teeth and continued to form the rails of magnetic energy.

Best had made the mistake of putting all of his eggs in one basket. Admittedly, with his forces being pushed back on all fronts, it made sense to fortify one location and try to hold out. The oligarch was probably hoping that Dan and Drummond's troops would exhaust each other fighting outside of his fallback position.

If both sides had been restricted to the conventional forces they'd brought to the field, it might have worked. Dan's mechs and Drummond's hunter-killer teams could tear even reinforced concrete apart if given enough time, but Best had mounted enough guns on the fortress to make anyone who tried pay their toll in blood.

The Railgun slug slammed into the side of the building as Dan frantically patted out the patches of his clothing that were smoldering from the spell's backblast. As for the fortress? The slug went straight through the outside wall before venting its energy against something in the building's interior. The pressure wave from the explosion knocked Dan from his feet, and pressed the air from his lungs.

He stood up and smiled grimly at the wreckage. The top story of the building was gone entirely, replaced by flames and thick, black smoke. A good portion of the soldiers surrounding the building were down, either outright killed by the pressure wave from the explosion, or crippled by the falling rubble and shrapnel.

Dan returned the binoculars to his hip and brought the hardened webcam/speaker that connected him with Tatiana to his mouth.

"You catch all of that, Tatiana?" he asked.

"Yes," she replied, a bit unsteadily. "That was actually a fair bit of fun. Honestly, a girl could get used to this sort of excitement."

Dan smiled evilly. "Well, we aren't done yet. Your old boss is attacking, and it sure looks like he doesn't have air cover. Would you mind letting Jennifer know about his mistake?"

Tatiana didn't respond, but Dan was more or less beyond caring. The Railgun round had ended the immediate battle, and his head hurt like hell. Tatiana would do what she could from here, but he'd earned himself a water break.

Dan sat down, but before he could finish completely uncorking his water, he cocked his head to the side. A tinny strain of music came from Tatiana's speaker. He picked it up and held it closer to his ear, only for it to burst into the iconic notes of "Ride of the Valkyries."

The *Viceroy's Pride* crested over the horizon, rapidly gaining height over Bakersfield. Just as the song began to hit its crescendo, a spear of light, so bright that even Dan had to blink and avert his gaze, shot forth from its bow and slammed into the town's outskirts.

"Really, Tatiana?" he asked, shaking his head before drinking a gulp of his water. "Don't you think that Wagner is a bit cliche?"

CHAPTER THIRTY-TWO

Consolidation

For the first time, Dan got the opportunity to watch the reaper drones launch from the *Viceroy*'s aft cargo bay while on the ground. He leaned back, enjoying the thrum of their turbines as they shook the roof below him and soared toward Drummond's forces. There might have been anti-aircraft guns in Bakersfield proper, but out in the suburbs, they were overextended and unprotected.

Missiles rained down upon the advancing robots, great explosions leaving gaping holes in their lines. Then, Dan's radio crackled as Abe gave the order for the mechs to advance. One by one, the metal behemoths stomped forward, shouldering aside buildings.

As soon as they cleared the edge of the suburbs, giving them a clear line of fire at the dogbots charging down the interstate, the mechs opened fire. Abe kept the mechs moving to make things a little more difficult for anti-tank fire. Some of the heavy weapons teams still fired at them, but between the mechs' weaving, confusing direct-fire weapons and active defenses throwing up handfuls of chaff into the path of guided weapons, very few hit. Those that did were quickly absorbed by the spellshields.

Still, Dan frowned slightly at the engagement. Abe's men had to be running low on mana. Most of them were between rank two and three, enough to make their mana reserves notable, but not enough to power an energy hog like a mech indefinitely.

Regardless of their reserves, the mechs tore into the dogbots with their knee-mounted anti-personnel weapons, tearing apart their metal forms by the dozens. Meanwhile, their main and shoulder-mounted cannons swiveled independently, targeting the heavy weapons teams and destroying them one-by-one.

Dan's frown disappeared as the human weapon teams began fleeing, only to be cut down from a distance. Shell burst after shell burst exploded over their retreating columns, shredding the unarmored enemy.

Then, when the wall of dogbots was sufficiently thinned out, and without human guidance, the powered armor advanced. Each repeater round ended a robot as they moved forward into the fray, the smaller-caliber bullets from Drummond's drones just bouncing off of their heavier, magically reinforced armor.

The mechs pulled back and lowered themselves to the ground. Dan shimmied down from his roof, not quite trusting his anemic mana to make a force bubble, and jogged over to the giant war machines. He got there just as Abe and his men exited the menacing metal structures on unsteady legs, covered in sweat.

Overhead, the *Viceroy* fired another lance of light and energy that tore a line into the scrubland, melting the sandy soil into glass and frying a dozen soldiers. Dan threw his water bottle to Abe, who greedily popped it open and emptied its contents into his mouth. Wiping the sweat off of his face, Abe handed the water bottle back.

"Listen, Boss." He shook his head, the forlorn look in his eyes belied by the giant shit-eating grin on his face. "We absolutely need to get air conditioners into that thing. After maybe twenty minutes, it starts running hot. Ten minutes after that, and I'm pretty sure you could toast bread in there if you held it up against the metal."

"Sam says the entire thing is a heat sink," Dan replied, looking over the hissing metal of the mech. "Right now, we can barely get around the power problem, but an air conditioner wouldn't do much. Even if we pump cooler air onto you, the machine itself will be well over a hundred degrees. We're trying to work on a way to vent the mech's heat as it moves and fights, but that part is still a work in process. Unless you have enough spare mana that we can use to vent excess heat, I think mech piloting is going to be hot and uncomfortable for the near future."

"A shame," Abe grinned like a maniac. "If we could fix the heat problem, that would be a load of fun. Even with it, there's something therapeutic about stomping your way through buildings. I think that was the closest I'll ever get to being a kaiju, and I have to say, it was exhilarating."

"I'm sure it was/" Dan smiled back. "Now, do we have any idea how the battle's going?"

Abe grabbed a towel offered to him by a soldier and wiped the sweat streaming from his face before responding. "I'd ask Jennifer to verify, but I'd expect that the battle is pretty much over. Between your spells and the mechs, we broke Best pretty quickly, and I'll bet you a month's pay that the field of dead robo pups over there represents almost the entirety of Drummond's mobile forces. I think he was trying to take advantage of our attack to spring a surprise of his own and catch Best in a pincer."

"Shit," Abe hissed, pullin back the hand he'd pressed up against the mech so that he could lean on it. "That thing is still hot as hell. Anyway, I wouldn't be surprised if both sides are suing for peace right now. I'd be surprised if either of them had any fight left in them after this drubbing."

Dan tapped the camera that kept him in touch with Tatiana. "Tatiana, can you set up a three way call between you and Jennifer? I want to get a status update."

"A three-way," Tatiana purred back/ "Sexy."

Dan winced as Abe started laughing.

"A what way?" Jennifer's confused voice sounded through the speaker, causing Abe to redouble his laughter. "What in the hell is going on here?"

"I asked Tatiana to connect us so that you could give us an update on the battle." Dan sighed, studiously avoiding Abe's gaze. "Tatiana decided to crack a joke, which Abe thought was hilarious, by the way, and here we are."

"So what do you want updated?" Jennifer asked. Even over the radio, Dan was pretty sure he could hear the smile in her voice. "Do you want to know the status of our forces or the enemy forces?"

"Both?" Dan questioned. "I charged a bunch of people like an idiot and blew up a couple of buildings, but other than that, I've mostly been out of touch down here."

Jennifer's voice turned serious. "We've taken some losses. A dozen suits are down and thirty soldiers weren't able to pull back after their bracers were overwhelmed. As for our wounded, we have probably another twenty suits down and ninety infantry that will need nanites in the next month or so.

"As bad as that sounds," she continued, "it could have been a lot worse. The good news is that the war is pretty much over. Dad and Drummond are trying to work out a peace deal where he agrees to self-exile in exchange for us not sending a couple of Abe's friends to find him, and one of the infantry teams managed to grab Best."

Jennifer chuckled darkly. "Apparently, he was trying to sneak out in the back of a supply truck when you leveled his command center. A couple of our soldiers stopped the truck in an effort to, uh, liberate some alcohol, and they found him under a couple sacks of flour."

"He's spent the last twenty or so minutes demanding to talk to the person in charge," Tatiana interjected helpfully. "I've counted. The phrase 'do you know who the hell I am' has been used seventeen times. The soldiers guarding him seem thrilled. Should I lead you to him?"

"No," Dan smiled, stretching the kinks out of his back. "Let him stew for a little bit. I think that I've earned myself a break. Plus, Will can handle that asshole. He'll do a better job than me, and he'll make the bastard squirm."

Jennifer's response was overwhelmed by the sound of the *Viceroy* firing again. Some buildings on the outskirts of Bakersfield proper erupted into flame, immolating the soldiers that were hiding within.

At this point, using the void ship on isolated outposts of men was overkill, but unlike conventional weapons, its ammunition was unlimited. Really, there was no reason to stop the bombardment until Drummond gave up and capitulated.

"Can I at least have some fun with him?" Tatiana asked, her tone sending a shiver down Dan's spine. "Nothing too serious, just some harmless pranks. There were some interesting things in his emails and browser history. Peter Best was enough of a headache when I worked for Drummond that it only seems fair that I have a little fun with him."

"Knock yourself out," Dan replied, his mouth dry. He wasn't exactly sure what passed for a prank in Tatiana's estimation, but it was his goal to never actually find out.

Abe tapped him on the shoulder, drawing Dan's attention. Somewhere, the man had procured a cooler, and he was offering Dan a cold beer from it. Of course, Abe already had his own half-empty.

He took the can and cracked it open before taking a pull. A cold, domestic pilsner. It barely had any flavor, and what it did have wasn't great, but it served as the perfect companion while baking in the sun on the blacktop.

"I just figured you needed one, boss." Abe's smile was all teeth. Near him, a couple of the mech pilots were enjoying their own drinks. "We're basically tapped out until our mana recovers, so I figured the boys and girls needed a couple brews. Now, if only we had a baseball game to not watch while we roasted in the sun and drank, it'd be absolutely perfect."

Dan took another sip. He'd never been a big beer guy. Still, it tasted like going camping with his Dad and barely watching mindless sports on a hot summer day. There was something compelling about the normalcy of it.

"You know, Abe." He turned to the other man. "We're going to fix all of this. It might not be perfect, and it might not be quick, but there are good people out there. They deserve more than this, being stuck at the whim of assholes, both domestic and alien. I want sports to come back. I want dumb reality tv."

He finished his beer and crushed the can in his hand before throwing it next to a pile of empties.

"The entire galaxy opened up to us," Dan continued, staring up into the sky. "Things aren't ever going to be exactly the same. Still, it all needs to come to an end. We can, and will, fix this."

He kept looking up as the *Viceroy* rained fire down upon the retreating troops. The street was silent other than the shuffling of soldiers and the hissing of the cooling mechs. Abe handed him another cold beer.

"I know, boss." Abe's voice was quiet, introspective. "That's why I signed up with you. Unlike a lot of the assholes out there, I actually trust you to try and see all of this through.

"So," Abe chuckled as he opened his own can with a hiss. "New York is next?"

"New York is next," Dan agreed, cracking his beer in reply.

CHAPTER THIRTY-THREE

From Sea to Shining Sea

"We've got 'em on the run, Dan." William smiled, a manic glint in his eye. "Dennis Billings, Sharon Redding, and Edmund Adeleke all have reached out to us. They don't trust us, but they absolutely hate each other. It sounds like they're willing to fade back into the woodwork, so long as they aren't punished too severely for their attempted coup. Even better, they'll settle for releasing their technological advancements to us in exchange for royalties on any production."

Dan glanced around the *Viceroy*'s boardroom. Sam and Jennifer looked like they were thinking the deal over, but Abe was livid. Dan wasn't sure he blamed Abe.

"William, I want to end the war as much as the next guy, but they literally destroyed the United States. It'll be years before we know how many thousands of people died in the disruptions their rebellion caused. We can't let them off."

William frowned slightly. "Dan, I don't think you under-stand. We're more powerful than any of the warlords I've just listed, but any one of them could make things hard for us. If they stop and fight, we might not be able to make it to New York in time to stop the Orakh. I know they're assholes, but there's nothing we can do about it. The stakes are just too high."

"No." Dan cut in. "This is exactly the kind of reasoning that got us here in the first place. Each of them can walk away with their lives and one million dollars. That's all the amnesty they're going to get from me. If we let them get away with it and turn our backs on them, we're just asking for a knife between our shoulderblades later. If I have to airdrop from the *Viceroy* into their goddamn houses and kill them in their sleep to get this done, I will."

William's bushy eyebrows furrowed as he tried to assuage Dan's wrath. "My boy, I know it's distasteful, but this is just how politics happens. Sometimes you need to let the small fish off the line so that you can hook the big one."

"Those are the rules to the old game." A touch of heat colored Dan's voice. "We almost lost everything because of them. Billings, Redding, and Adeleke have seen how we handled the other traitors. They know that their time is up, and they're literally willing to use the American people as hostages to secure an advantage for themselves. If we let them get away with this, even if they stay on their best behavior for the rest of their lives, others will see that they got away with it. It will empower the worst among us."

"But what if we do a truth and reconciliation—" William began, his further arguments cut off by a snort from Abe.

"I've seen your truth and reconciliation commissions." Abe rolled his eyes, leaning back in one of the plus-sized chairs they'd brought in to decorate the conference room. "I helped the locals organize a couple of them in Indonesia. We all knew to look the other way when some Captain from stateside came out to the jungle, not a speck of mud on him, to let the 'local authorities' know who they were supposed to forgive and who they could punish."

He leaned forward, his muscles rippling slightly as he turned to stare at William. "It was an ugly business, but we kept our mouths shut. That was our job. We did dirty, shitty jobs in a corrupt and unpleasant world. We need to get rid of the Orakh, that's true, but Dan's dead right. If we let this sort of sickness fester, we're going to regret it for generations. There are plenty of wealthy and powerful people working together with their communities right now. We only ended up with a handful of these warlords or tech lords, or whatever the hell else they want to call themselves."

Abe's elbow was on the table, his finger pointing like a dark spear at William while the old man frowned. "They chose to tip this country into chaos for no reason other than a lust for power. After things didn't work out with Ibis, they chose to become war profiteers. Rather than protect what was left of their homeland, they tried ot snatch the last crumbs of value from her corpse."

"It'll be almost impossible to transfer the entire army via the *Viceroy!*" William burst out, standing up from his chair. "We need to use the rail lines and highways, and Redding controls almost all of the Great Plains. We won't even be able to get our army to New York without her standing down."

"Tatiana," Dan replied, keeping his gaze locked on William. "Can you ascertain where Sharon Redding is at this moment?"

"She's at a private museum in Billings, Montana," Tatiana chimed in. "If you're planning on killing her, she has ten guards with her, two of whom appear to have some interesting prosthetics on them."

"Cybernetics," William responded woodenly. "Her field of research was replacing human limbs with better metal versions."

"That sounds like something that we don't need." Dan's eyes didn't leave William. "Mana accumulates in the entire body. Prosthetics might be useful if someone loses a limb, but I don't see people voluntarily going under the knife once magic is an option. In short, she's a perfect test case. I don't see any reason why we can't make an example of her and kill her right now, if she doesn't agree to our demands."

"Dan," William cut in. "We can't just go around killing

enemy leaders. If we start down that path, everyone else will end up doing the same thing. It'll destabilize everything."

Abe shook his head. "That's not what we did in Jakarta. Why was it ok to send my team to collect heads when it was across an ocean, but now that we're in America, suddenly you're squeamish about everything?"

"That was different, Abraham." William scowled at Abe. "We only sent your team after terrorists and cult leaders. Everyone you killed was a murderer a hundred times over, beyond redemption. The warlords are bad people, but they're not terribly worse than lobbyists. We'll fix their rot eventually, but until then, they're a necessary evil."

"Bullshit," Sam's voice shocked everyone else into silence. It'd been months since she'd spoken at a meeting without a question being asked directly of her, and it almost seemed like the others had forgotten her presence. "The warlords are directly responsible for more American deaths than any guerilla leader in Indonesia. Hell, I'm pretty sure most of them actually profited off of clandestinely selling technology to the nationalist forces during our invasion. I literally think they were supporting the people you had Abe kill. These people aren't misunderstood; I understand them perfectly. They're monsters, and they need to be removed if society is going to grow."

"But," William began before Sam cut him off once again.

"They look like you, sit on the same nonprofit boards as you, and go to the same country clubs with you." She shook her head, her eyes flashing. "I get it. It's hard for you to think of them as 'the bad guy.' It might be easier to think of some poor sod plotting against America while hiding in a cave in the mountains as the bad guy, but that's exactly the blind spot that got us where we are today. This isn't about left or right, religion or race. People can disagree about tax policy or immigration and genuinely love this country, and many of them did."

"But our government is gone because we looked the other way while this 'illuminati' group consolidated power," Sam fumed. "Dan and Abe are right. These people will see mercy as a sign of weakness and an invitation to try again. Unless we pull this weed out, root and stem, we will never truly be safe."

William looked around the room, failing to find a friendly face. Finally, he turned to Jennifer.

"What about you, pumpkin?" He asked the question without much hope in his eyes, his voice plaintive. "Surely you understand that this is just a compromise that we need to make?"

"I'm sorry, Daddy." She shook her head. "I'm not opposed to making deals with the devil if we have to. It would speed things along if we compromised, but everyone is right. The warlords are responsible for almost as many deaths as the Orakh. If we let them walk away, no one will ever trust any government we try to set up."

Dan stood up and walked over to him. "William, I understand why you want to offer them amnesty, but we're unanimous other than you. Plus, it's not like this is actually a democracy. The only vote that matters is mine. They can keep one million dollars and retire from public life. If they don't want to negotiate with you, they can negotiate with Abe and me at three am. The discussion will last about thirty seconds, and it will end with a small box being mailed to their next of kin.

"You're right that we don't have time to fight them." He shook his head slightly, his hand on William's shoulder. "It won't be a fight. We'll just kill the leaders, one-by-one, until they get out of the way."

Even if William disagreed with their decision, he executed it perfectly. The various tech lords objected and blustered when he delivered his terms, but after William pointed out that they had a teleporting space battleship, and had Tatiana describe their surroundings perfectly, they folded quietly.

Ibis' old allies might have been assholes, but they weren't stupid. A million dollars was still a lot of money. As long as they weren't idiots about it, they'd be able to live out the rest of their lives comfortably. The offer was still more than Dan wanted to give them, but it got the job done.

It still took almost a week to get their entire army across the country. The *Viceroy's Pride* needed to make a couple of final trips in order to pick up the last couple of suits of armor from Peter Best's old factory, but eventually their forces were arrayed just outside of New York City.

Refugees streamed past their encampment. The Orakh had broken out of Manhattan days ago. The NYPD and the national guard were trying to hold back the alien swarm, but each day saw them pushed further back. Already, tens of thousands were dead, and the alien forces grew in size each day.

Dan surveyed the gleaming city as swarms of desperate souls fled away from it, the rattle of guns and the deep boom of explosions driving them to move faster. Behind him, Abe stood in a tank top and shorts, talking to William, already in his armor, putting the final touches on their battle plan.

The ten mechs lined the road into the city, tanks and armored vehicles clustered around them as infantry checked their weapons. They'd delayed and prepared long enough. New York was falling to the Orakh, and it was time for Dan to act.

CHAPTER THIRTY-FOUR

Surviving Contact with the Enemy

The *Viceroy* rose overhead. Dan had finally found a soldier with space affinity while awakening the rest of his forces. They'd dropped the woman off in Brazil with Abe while shuttling their forces back and forth, and she'd ranked up once. It didn't give her an insane amount of mana, but it was enough that she could teleport the ship a short distance. Once.

They'd tested her abilities, of course. Rebecca could only warp the ship about a mile, but given the realities of combat, that would be more than enough. A mile would break any sort of lock on the *Viceroy's Pride* and give it more than enough time to fly away if something was coming for it.

As the ship soared over the skyscrapers that made up the city's downtown, Abe jumped up onto the rope ladder hanging down the side of his mech. Scrambling up to the top, he stared down at Dan.

After receiving a thumbs up, a grin split Abe's face. He cupped his hands to his mouth and shouted at the nearby soldiers. "Everyone!"

Dan frowned slightly as Abe's voice projected across the

clearing. He really didn't know why he was yelling rather than using his radio.

"Check your ammunition, food, and water. The *Viceroy* is taking point to soften up the enemy, then it's our turn. We have approximately five minutes until go time. *Raiders!*"

Abe's voice somehow grew even louder.

"Prepare to roll out!" he shouted, raising his hand triumphantly atop the mech.

Dan groaned. That was why he wanted to shout. A goddamn movie reference.

Around him, most of the soldiers just shook their heads and returned to checking their kits before battle. The vehicles turned on their engines, the thrum of diesel filling the clearing. Those with powered armor slid off the back clamshells and climbed in. The rest of the infantry nervously checked their bracers.

Although spellshields would still be useful against the Orakh, that use would be much more limited. Their primary utilization against humans was to absorb a rifle round or three and give the soldier time to get back under cover. With the Orakh, if they closed to melee range of an unarmored soldier, the battle was likely over, regardless. Forcing a warrior to swing his axe twice wouldn't change a whole lot.

The *Viceroy* floated above the skyline, and the dreary, overcast sky lit up as a lance of light and fire spat forth from the ship's bow, striking something out of sight. A few of the soldiers paying attention cheered as they finalized their preparations.

Then the sky lit up again. This time, the spear of light struck the side of the *Viceroy's Pride*. Spellshields sparkled for a second, holding the cataclysmic energies at bay. Then they failed. A deep black scar cut itself into the side of the void ship before the energy lance winked out.

For a second, silence filled their staging location. Then, the *Viceroy* disappeared.

Dan exhaled a breath. They wouldn't have the ship's air support for the battle, a serious problem. Still, apparently the

Viceroy's Pride was still in good enough shape to teleport. Hopefully, it'd still be able to deploy its reapers, but at a very minimum, Dan's spaceship still worked.

Around him, the soldiers whispered, exchanging looks before glancing up at the empty sky. Maybe they'd gotten used to having overwhelming air support. Dan certainly knew that he would prefer it to the alternative. Unfortunately, New York was all but overrun, and attempts by the locals to use artillery and air support had revealed unnervingly effective anti-aircraft capabilities.

Seeing no reaction from those around him, Dan pulled out his radio and clicked the button.

"That's our cue, boys and girls!" He did his best to sound authoritative as he spoke into the microphone. Usually, commanding the troops was Abe or Will's job, but at the moment, no one was making sense of the situation. "It looks like the *Viceroy* is out of the fight for the time being. That means no air support, but it also means there's no reason to delay further. Let's get in there and kick the Orakh back into space."

A weak cheer rose from the soldiers as they began moving. Dan applauded their effort, but internally, he couldn't really blame them. Watching the *Viceroy* tap out of combat so early in the fight had been a bit of a morale blow for him as well.

Really, they should have expected it before now. The *Viceroy's Pride* wasn't terribly maneuverable without a proper space mage. Usually, void ships relied upon a handful of space mages to keep them teleporting semi-randomly about space as they fired their spell cannons at each other. If a ship was moving under its own power, it was usually seconds from being targeted and destroyed by every enemy ship within range.

Up until this point, they'd mostly gotten lucky. Air forces were hard to maintain, and even the tech lords only had a handful of planes and pilots each. It might be hard for missiles to lock onto the *Viceroy*, but a helicopter gunship or an A-10's auto cannon would be more than enough to tear the slow-moving ship apart, spellshields or not.

Dan came back to the present as he watched his troops stream into New York. Maybe one third of them had powered armor, and the rest of the infantry were supported by heavily armored tanks and infantry fighting vehicles. Unfortunately, an urban environment where the Orakh could be hiding around any corner was pretty close to the worst environment to fight their melee-focused foes in.

That was where the mechs came in. Dan smiled as the big machines rumbled to life. Even if the Orakh successfully swarmed them, a combination of flechette rounds from the shoulder cannons and the knee-mounted anti-personnel weapons would take a toll. Plus, only the strongest of the Orakh would even be able to damage the hardened steel of the mech's armor.

The big machines fanned out, crossing the George Washington Bridge one at a time. Technically, each mech wasn't that close to the bridge's rated weight limit, but given the way it creaked and swayed under the quadraped's steps, Dan was glad that they hadn't decided to try two or more of the giant vehicles at once.

Elsewhere, armored infantry was beginning to march through the tunnels. Will didn't want to risk getting a tank or armored vehicle stuck down there, and Dan had to agree. At the same time, every route in and out of Manhattan needed to be blocked.

The soldiers assigned to the tunnels knew that they wouldn't have to push too hard once they reached the island, but by the same token, they'd need to hold firm with minimal reinforcements. The rest of the army would be occupied with the main push into the Orakh forces. If they got into trouble, they'd be on their own.

Dan crossed the George Washington Bridge slightly behind Abe's mech. He didn't want to get close enough to risk getting crushed underfoot. As amusingly ironic as that would be for an end, playing it safe seemed like a better approach.

By the latest reports, the NYPD and the National Guard

were barely holding on around Yonkers, New Rochelle, and Queens. Brooklyn and the Bronx were gone. Maybe, in a couple of years, historians would know how many people managed to get out before the Orakh overwhelmed the human lines, but that wasn't a problem for today.

Within five minutes of stepping foot in Manhattan, the Orakh were swarming over them. The four mechs that had made it across the bridge fired their main cannon into nearby buildings, trying to create mounds of rubble and more efficient firing lanes. Meanwhile, their shoulder and knee guns fired anti-personnel rounds into the charging horde, trying to thin its numbers enough to let the soldiers on the ground do their job.

Next to Dan, a team of about twenty suited infantry fired steadily. Each crack of their fifty-caliber repeaters jerked back an Orakh's chest or head, either killing or seriously wounding them. He threw Fireballs into their ranks whenever they closed enough distance to get within spell range, but mostly, Dan waited for the melee. It wasn't enough.

Even as a fifth mech tromped across the bridge, and another squad of twenty suited infantry filed in behind them, the Orakh began to reach their lines. Dan drew his sword and sprang into motion, doing his best to kill any of the giant amphibian warriors that approached within thirty feet of his troops.

Still, Orakh slipped by him. They were met with a volley from the armors' flamethrowers, killing or wounding many of the charging monsters. Despite their losses, even more Orakh swarmed over the still-smoldering corpses of their kin.

Then, the power-suited soldiers were engaged in hand-to-hand combat, beating back the Orakh with their mechanically enhanced metal fists before spraying the charging Orakh with another wall of fire. Dan had lost people in that engagement. He wasn't sure who or how many, but the Orakh had already used their massive numbers to inflict their first casualties of the day.

The pressure let up. A sixth mech made it across the bridge and arranged itself on a nearby road where it could fire into the side of the charging Orakh. More infantry came up to support them, plugging in the gaps where their brethren had fallen in the first attack.

Slowly, the attacking Orakh began to peter off as Dan's soldiers began to establish a literal bridgehead. He sighed slightly, keeping his sword in hand. Even though things were moving in the right direction, the situation was far too tentative to actually relax.

Finally, the Orakh stopped attacking entirely. Their spotters could still see their hulking shapes in the shadows of nearby buildings, but they began to actively avoid engagement.

That worried Dan. Usually, the Orakh attacked mindlessly and without regard for their own lives. This sort of restraint could mean only one thing: a more intelligent and higher-ranking Orakh was nearby.

Once the entire force was across the bridge, they began to move forward cautiously, the Mechs barely able to squeeze through the multilane streets and tunnels of I-95.

Then, the foot on Abe's mech went straight through the pavement. Dan's head whipped around as his radio chirped.

"Thrush." Abe's voice was a combination of worried, frustrated, and amused. "I appear to have stepped through the sidewalk and into the subway. Give me a moment, and I'll extricate myself."

From somewhere nearby, a horn sounded. A low note that increased in pitch and volume. Around them, Orakh began to appear in fifth and sixth story windows. A couple even peeked over the edge of the highrise roofs themselves.

A brick sailed down and crashed against the pavement next to Dan. One of the Orakh lept from a fourth story window and landed on top of the mech following Abe's.

"Shit," Dan muttered to himself, pulling out his radio. "Abe, I don't think I have a moment to give you; we're under attack."

CHAPTER THIRTY-FIVE

It's Raining Orakh

After the first brick was thrown, a hail of rocks, chairs, and other hard objects began crashing to the ground around Dan. The soldiers in powered armor simply ignored the projectiles, opting to return fire on the Orakh. A direct hit might stagger them or knock them off balance, but generally the magically reinforced armor could weather the blows.

The rest of the expedition hurried under the mechs, taking cover from the metal and cement slamming into the pavement around them. A spellshield could absorb a blow, maybe two, thrown from height, but the quantity of detritus falling around them would quickly overwhelm any of their defenses.

Dan began gathering mana to cast Railgun. An air conditioning unit crashed to the sidewalk next to him, thrown by a particularly large and enterprising Orakh. Silhouettes began to fall from the sky as the Orakh themselves tried their luck. Some missed the mechs altogether, snapping their bones like kindling against the road. Others were plucked from the air by the weapons mounted on the mechs and powered armor.

The rest landed on the giant war machines. They bounced and jostled as they fought to wedge limbs or weapons into cracks in the metal, attempting to arrest their falls. Their numbers began to accumulate as the Orakh that survived their leaps began to climb up the sloped surface of the mechs.

The spell finished, launching a slug into the top of a nearby building, converting the top couple of floors into a Fireball. The mechs began to fire their main cannons, tearing chunks out of the nearby high rises. Not every shell took out a load-bearing pillar, but each round shook and rattled their targets.

"We need air support!" Abe's voice crackled over Dan's radio. "Jennifer, you need to send the drones flying low enough to avoid enemy fire right away. We're heavily outnumbered here, and we do not have good firing lanes. Anything that isn't an Orakh has been eaten by an Orakh. We need you to just level these buildings."

Dan turned, directing the Railgun toward another building full of Orakh. His original target burned behind him, shapes streaming out of it and into the fire of the soldiers huddled beneath the mechs. It might not collapse in the next couple of minutes, but the fire more than denied its use to the Orakh.

"We'll be within range in a couple of minutes," Jennifer's voice replied, scratchy with interference. "Rebecca warped us further than we thought. Once we're over the staging area, we'll be able to launch the drones stationed there as well. Our mobile command center should be able to handle about fifteen of them at a time. Not enough for us to level the entire city, but we should be able to pull your buns out of the fire."

"Do you hear that, Dan?" Abe shouted over the radio as his mech fruitlessly tried to pull its leg from the subway tunnel trapping it. "Jennifer thinks that my buns are hot!"

Dan fired the Railgun a second time, gutting an office building. Flames shot out of its windows, and the structure began to teeter, the force of the strike rocking it to its very foundation. A handful of Orakh fell from the roof, and even more escaped out the front as the fire from the attack spread.

Glancing up, Dan frowned. Orakh on Abe's mech were pounding at hatches and gun turrets with their weapons. Axes might not be the best tool to damage the massive war machine, but leaving the Orakh to attack the irreplaceable machine unmolested didn't seem like the best course of action.

Activating Gravitational Easing, as well as his strength runes, Dan jumped, catching on to a joint almost fifteen feet up on the mech. Marshaling his strength, Dan pulled himself upward again, this time landing on the hull of the mech.

The nearest Orakh only noticed Dan when his sword removed its head from its meaty shoulders, leaving only a purple afterimage behind. Its companions spun to face him, pulling their weapons up and to the ready.

Without breaking stride, he launched two Forcebolts, knocking the Orakh nearest to him off-balance. His blade swept low, severing an Orakh's legs as Dan ducked beneath his enemies' clumsy blows. Scrambling past the Orakh as they stumbled to regain their footing and turn to face him, Dan launched a Fireball overhead. He aimed low enough that the pressure front would slam the Orakh and knock them from the mech, but hopefully high enough that the fire from the spell wouldn't damage the war machine.

It worked. The explosion didn't do much damage to either the Orakh or the mech, but the shockwave swept them clean of the machine's surface. Dan smirked slightly as they tumbled to the pavement below. For a brief second, they lay still, stunned by their fall, but that was all it took for the soldiers underneath the mech to make short work of them.

Bricks slammed onto the metal around Dan as the Orakh tried to clear him from the chassis of the war machine from their vantage above. The mech reverberated beneath him as Abe fired its main cannon into the nearest building. Dan frowned as his hearing lapsed into the steady ring of tinnitus.

The shell hit something important, and combined with the cumulative abuse the building had taken over the course of the battle, it collapsed. Dan created a force bubble to prevent himself from being thrown off the mech as a wall of dust flowed out onto the street, shaking everything.

Dan shook his head, trying to clear the ringing. Orakh were sprinting down the street toward his army from the direction of Midtown, using the distraction of the ambush to get as close as possible before taking fire.

He frowned slightly, dropping three Fireballs into the front of their charge. The explosions blew back the first wave of the Orakh, killing a handful but tangling the feet of the rest with their companions' injured bodies. The charge stumbled into a morass of confusion as the Orakh tried to extricate themselves from the situation and regain their momentum.

The unarmored infantry beneath the mechs opened fire on the stalled Orakh forces. One or even two rifle shots wouldn't kill one of the heavily muscled warriors, but it was far more than a handful of troops shooting. Sleeting waves of fire cut them down, one after another.

Another building fell, multiple cannon rounds from the procession of mechs ripping its foundation apart. Dan stumbled, catching his balance as another pressure wave rolled across the machine he was standing upon.

A rock bounced off his spellshield, forcing a wince from Dan. He'd been trying to rest, to give his mana reserves a couple seconds to recharge after his repeated use of Railgun. He searched the roofs surrounding their team, looking for the offending Orakh.

One leaned over the edge, only to immediately take a fifty-caliber repeater round to the chest. The creature jerked backward in a fountain of blood before disappearing on the roof. More and more suits of powered armor were stalking out into the open in order to give themselves a better vantage point on the attacking Orakh.

Dan smiled. Their ambush might have been successful against a more primitively armed force; bricks from rooftops would do a toll on spellshields after all. But, against the reinforced steel of the mechs and power suits, it wasn't terribly effective. The magically toughened metal could withstand a bombardment from the simple rocks almost all day.

His smile disappeared as a pulse of electric mana emanated from a building almost two hundred feet away. Instinctively, Dan threw himself off the side of the mech.

The wall of the building exploded, revealing a quartet of Orakh shamans clustered in a circle, a gigantic commander standing next to them with a two-handed sword planted in the building's floor. Lighting sprayed from the cluster of shamans, striking Abe's mech.

Dan landed on his back, half-blinded as the streaks of light and energy pulsed up and down the mech. Secondary explosions popped and crackled as the vehicle's metal skin superheated almost immediately, and ammunition began to cook off.

The lightning stopped, and the mech sagged. Dan held his breath, half-expecting to hear Abe's voice from the radio. Letting him know that he was ok. Letting him know what to do.

One breath turned into two with no response. Dan's eyes narrowed. Without conscious thought, the invisible rods of magnetic energy that formed the core of the Railgun spell appeared in front of him.

The shamans and the Orakh commander all looked at him simultaneously, sensing the mana accumulating in Dan's grasp. They shouted. Whether he could have understood their words or not had he been closer, Dan didn't really care. The hissing wreck of Abe's mech next to him pushed him past that.

They erected a crude spellshield before the Railgun slug hit, but it wasn't enough. The chunk of metal smashed into it, releasing the entirety of its kinetic energy in a Fireball that shattered the walls of the room they'd been hiding in.

Almost immediately, the rush of mana slammed into him. Dan still gained mana from killing ordinary Orakh, but at this point, it was only truly noticeable after slaying high-level variants. He didn't even bother to check his System to see his gains, satisfied that the influx meant that his enemies were dead.

A quartet of reapers flew overhead, shaking the battlefield. He shook his head. Moments too late.

Missiles rained down from above, blowing the top couple of

stories out of building after building around them. Either recognizing the futility of using the buildings as cover, or abandoning their commander's strategy with its death, the Orakh swarmed out onto the street.

For a handful of minutes, there was an unthinking melee. Dan wove through the Orakh, his sword hacking off limbs and slashing open throats, buying as much room as possible for the powered armor to use their flamethrowers.

The gouts of liquid fire ignited entire clusters of Orakh. Unfortunately, it barely slowed the suicidal creatures. Blinded and dying from the flames, they charged on regardless, desperate to take a handful of Dan's men to the grave with them.

And they did. His troops died hard, but they did die. The congested streets of New York without the close-up fire support from the mech were far from an ideal place to fight the melee-centric Orakh. Even if they killed fifty of the aliens for each soldier that fell, it was still an exchange that left a bad taste in Dan's mouth.

Finally, the sounds of battle began to fade. The Orakh didn't run. Without a commander, the idea of retreat was simply a foreign concept to them. Instead, they killed every last one of them.

Without a word, Dan pumped energy into his thermal resistance rune and jumped onto the back of Abe's mech. The task was made quite a bit easier by the vehicle's post-lightning collapse.

The heat from the metal began melting the soles of his boots almost immediately, but Dan didn't care. He sprinted to the mech's hatch, ignoring the heat and mana deprivation headache. Squinting, he shot the hinges off the deformed metal before grabbing the handle.

Even with the rune active, Dan could smell the skin on his hand burning off. With a mana-enhanced yank, he pulled the door open with a single jerk. Inside, the air was dark and sweltering. The array of monitors and electronic equipment lay dark and lifeless.

A cough pulled Dan's attention to the two back chairs. Abe and his copilot Bennett were still breathing. Burned and struggling, but still alive.

Abe's eyes opened a crack as the daylight from the open hatch hit him. He smiled weakly up at Dan.

"Thrush." Abe's voice was raspy, like he'd just smoked a pack of cigarettes and eaten a cigar. "You look like shit."

"What the hell, man?" Dan replied shakily as he forced his body into the searing mech to start undoing the clasps holding Abe and Bennett inside. "Your entire mech looks like a half-melted candle. How in the fucking hell did you make it through all of that?"

"You're not getting out of paying my check that easily." Abe coughed. "Must have been a Faraday Cage. They hit us with all that electricity, but it just went straight through the metal and into the ground. Fucked the mech up pretty badly, but left the soft little squishy bits on the inside largely unscathed."

"You call this unscathed?" Dan shook his head in disbelief.

"To a certain extent," Abe replied with a pained chuckle.

CHAPTER THIRTY-SIX

Half a League Onward

The mechs marched away from their forces, heading single-file back toward the George Washington bridge, a handful of their injured soldiers including Abe traveling with them. He sighed and turned back. Barely an hour in, and their carefully scripted battle plan was already in tatters.

The *Viceroy* was in range to provide air support, but other than its drones and the handful of armored vehicles, the last of their heavy weapons were leaving. As much as it pained Dan to see them go, the last battle had proved the wisdom of sending them back. Even the multilane roads they were trying to use weren't big or sturdy enough for the mechs.

Each step was like a game of Russian Roulette. Only after the mech's weight was fully on a leg would they discover if the blacktop was sufficient to bear the war machine. After the initial ambush, Dan had Tatiana pull up a map of tunnels and utilities traveling under their projected route. It looked like a spiderweb. There was no way that they'd be able to bring all of the mechs with them to the Orakh landing site.

It would only be a matter of time before another mech became trapped, and the Orakh sprang another ambush. The first one had cost them almost a hundred people, between the dead and those too injured to continue. They couldn't afford any more traps like that, if they wanted to have enough troops left over to raid the Orakh landing craft once they reached it.

"Close up ranks, and keep your eyes skyward." William's voice boomed from the speakers built into his suit as he walked up to Dan. "The Orakh have gotten the drop on us once, and we don't want to let it happen again. Remember, at least one person per squad with an open line back to the *Viceroy*. If you see anything moving, it's an Orakh. The people are all gone or food. If you can't shoot it, call in an airstrike. The logistics people can reload the reapers, and we have plenty of missiles. No need to save 'em for later when there might not be a later."

"How are things going?" Dan nodded at William as the battle suit stopped next to him.

"The good news is that Abe is stable," William responded, watching on as the first of the infantry fighting vehicles rolled down the thoroughfare. "He's got heat exhaustion and a fair number of burns, but once we get enough hydration in him, his System will be able to handle it. The bad news is that the *Viceroy* got pretty roughed up. It can still fly, but Jennifer doesn't want to risk it on another bombing run. It sounds like she's going to have her hands full running the staging area anyway, now that Abe is down, and I'm out here."

"No." Dan began walking along with the rest of his forces, William trailing slightly behind him. "Jennifer's priority should be to keep herself and the *Viceroy* safe. If all she can do is coordinate air strikes, that'll have to be enough. I'm not all that thrilled to have office buildings potentially full of Orakh all around us as we push our way into the city, but I don't think we have an alternative, unless you have a nuke stuffed up your sleeve."

"Do you?" He cocked his head at William. "Seriously, New York City is absolutely a lost cause at this point. Nuking it and sending in clean-up crews in hazmat suits is probably the better option at this point."

William chuckled. "Sorry. We set Tatiana on cracking the codes a while ago. Someone apparently suspected that their internet connections were compromised, and disconnected them from the outside world. I don't know if they caught some hint of Tatiana, or if they just watched *War Games* one too many times. Either way, we aren't taking those silos over without at least a couple days' worth of detours."

"Crap," Dan bit out, his eyes tracking from rooftop to rooftop, looking for the telltale silhouette of Orakh. "If we took the time, they'd spill out of Manhattan. There's no way we'd be able to control their spread."

"Can't be sure that a nuke would actually get them. Sure, the Russians managed to knock their landing craft around enough to burn them up on entry, but now that they're on the planet we can't know how much they've dug in. If they have some sort of warren full of eggs under their ship, a nuke isn't going to do much but wipe out surface structures. I suppose we can drop enough bombs on them to start a full-on nuclear winter, but destroying the planet to get rid of an alien colony hardly seems to achieve our goals." William gave a noncommittal shrug.

"So, we just have to push forward then," Dan said. "Maybe, if they were fighting in the open with clear lanes of fire, advancing with just infantry and conventional armor would be ok. In the city? The Orakh had already shown that an ambush could come at any time and that it could cost them dearly."

"Half a league, half a league, half a league onward," William recited with a chuckle, his long strides eating up pavement as he paced Dan.

"Don't do that," Dan warned with a slight frown. "It just feels like you're tempting fate by quoting that poem."

William snorted, the steady thud of his heavy footsteps rattling the blacktop as they walked in silence for a period.

"I didn't take you for the superstitious type." William broke the silence. "Luck and all of that is just what we make of it."

"Maybe, but I don't see the point in pushing the envelope.

There are enough Orakh running around here that everything is up in the air. I don't think we have the time to back off and let things stew, but I'm not the most confident without the mechs here to back us up."

"With proper air cover," William responded flippantly, "this will be like a walk in the park. The troops just need to hold off the Orakh long enough to call the reapers in. We might lose a couple people in ambushes, but beyond some incidentals, everything will be fine, trust me."

"If you say so," Dan answered, unwilling to continue the conversation. William was stubborn, and at some point, he'd decided that their organization was too big to be threatened by the Orakh. Even with a fried mech in the streets, he refused to acknowledge that the aliens were a credible threat.

He might be right, Dan mused. Once the Orakh were in the open, both the powered armor and the infantry made fairly short work of them. An M-16 wasn't an ideal weapon against their resilient physiology, but enough massed fire against one of the monsters charging you with an axe was more than enough to solve the problem.

Their main concerns were a combination of numbers and terrain. They didn't have any sort of idea how many Orakh were hiding in New York. It might be ten thousand, and it might be a million. The only thing that Jennifer and Tatiana had been able to determine for sure was that there were more Orakh than Dan had troops.

Even with the Orakh being tied up by the NYPD and the national guard, Dan knew he was going to be heavily outnumbered. Usually, that wouldn't be a major problem. Orakh took more to put down than a human, but it wasn't like most of them were shooting back. So long as weapons teams took down their shamans, his soldiers would have the luxury of making the Orakh come to them.

Of course, the Orakh were perfectly okay with that. Even on flat ground, the giant frogs wouldn't have a problem with simply charging into machine gun fire. Here in the city? Any alleyway or storefront could hide a monster lying in wait. Unfortunately, Dan didn't have the firepower to just level the buildings on his way to the landing site. It might be noisy and wasteful, but it would simplify the hell out of his problems.

At least William was here to take some of the load off of him. The man might be arrogant, but with him on hand, Dan had access to a competent military commander. Dan could outfight any dozen soldiers under his command, but when it came time to give orders and react to sudden changes of circumstances, he was out of his element.

William stomped ahead, shouting at the column to tighten up and began setting sentries. Even if he underestimated the Orakh, at his core, the ex-general was a professional. Before long, they were moving again, even faster than before the previous ambush and with a level of discipline that Abe either couldn't or chose not to enforce.

The march slowed several times as pockets of Orakh swarmed out of buildings or parks to throw themselves at the army. After a couple clipped commands from William, they quickly reacted, forming a bowl around the charging monsters that allowed most of their soldiers to fire at once.

By the time they reached midtown, the only additional casualties were a pair of men who sprained their ankles trying to climb down some rubble from a gutted building. Dan began to let himself feel a bit of optimism. Maybe that first ambush had depleted the Orakh's defenses after all.

The buildings began to change. Where originally the city had been populated by towering edifices of steel and glass, now they began to look more run-down. The walls hemming their column in were dull, covered in recent growths of moss and fungus. Entire tops of buildings were missing, often replaced by wooden or stone platforms. Periodically, Dan would spot an Orakh peering over the edge of such "remodeled" buildings before ducking back behind cover.

"Tatiana," he whispered, pointing her camera up at a

skulking shadow in an office building. "Has anyone else spotted these?"

"Yes!" she replied cheerily, her full-volume voice drawing a wince from Dan. "A handful of other soldiers have made note that we're being observed."

"First of all," Dan hissed, "volume down. I don't want anyone noticing that we're aware of our guests. Second, can you begin taking note of as many of the Orakh as we can and pass that information on to William? They aren't recklessly attacking us, and that means there's probably a commander nearby. Whenever they're being patient, we should treat it as a bad sign."

"No need to worry, Dan," Tatiana replied, her voice as loud as ever. "The lead vehicles have spotted the Orakh landing craft. We'll have you and an elite team inside in a matter of minutes. Whatever the aliens are waiting for, it'll be too late when you gut their ship."

"Are there any obvious guards outside it?" Dan asked hesitantly. He didn't hear any gunfire, but that didn't mean William wasn't sending some of his more mobile soldiers to handle matters quietly.

"I told you there wasn't a need to worry," Tatiana chided him. "The landing ramp is down, and there isn't an Orakh in sight on the ground. All you need to do is pick your team and walk inside. Easy peasy lemon squeasy."

Dan frowned. Even if that was true, the Orakh knew it, too. Well, maybe not the warriors, but their commanders and shamans were a different story. They wouldn't simply stand by and let him burn down their egg room like he'd done in New Orleans. The minute he stepped inside that ship, something was going to happen.

He didn't think that it was going to be something friendly.

CHAPTER THIRTY-SEVEN

Accepting the Invitation

Sunlight disappeared behind Dan as he and a team of fifty power-armored soldiers walked up the ramp into the Orakh landing ship. At the mouth of the vessel, Dan paused for a second and glanced backward at where William organized the rest of their forces in a rough semicircle around the spacecraft. The man moved efficiently, spacing the vehicles and armored troops out amongst the more conventional infantry.

Dan sent a trickle of mana into his sword, wreathing it in purple flames as he turned back to the Orakh ship and followed the soldiers in. He had to trust that William would keep the aliens off of his back while he fought his way inside.

At first, he'd wanted to take the entire army in and overwhelm whatever was inside through sheer weight of numbers. William had talked him out of it. Fifty soldiers could fight about as efficiently as a thousand inside the winding tunnels of the spacecraft. The rest of the army could be put to better use ensuring that Dan had a clean path of retreat once he did what needed to be done.

He pushed his way to the front of the formation, edging past the suits of steel and magic. As strong as they were, Dan had more confidence in his spellshields. Even their reinforced armor would dent and deform under repeated sword or axe blows. All his shields needed was a bit of time for his mana to recover.

"Burksman!" He spoke over his shoulder, addressing the lieutenant responsible for executing his orders. Maybe Dan should have been offended that William had assigned him an officer to translate his commands so the rest of the soldiers could understand them, but honestly, it was a good idea. After years of fighting, he knew where to strike and how hard. He didn't know the first thing about organizing a unit beyond himself and a couple of close friends to effectuate those instincts.

"Yes, sir?" the man responded, his powered armor only different from those of the men surrounding him due to the silver stripe across the shoulder pauldron.

"I'm going to take the lead," Dan continued as he walked. "Put a couple of your best soldiers behind me. Let them know they should feel free to use their flamethrowers if it seems important. I'm not entirely fireproof, but I burn hard. As long as I can keep moving, they shouldn't be able to do much more than give me a burn."

"If this place is anything like the one in New Orleans..." Dan nodded his head toward the winding stone and iron halls. "It's going to be a maze inside. Make sure you have someone guarding each of the side tunnels, as well as our rear. Even with the entire army, we'd have a hard time stopping the Orakh from finding some way to sneak up on us in their own ship. All we can do is stay vigilant and hope that we catch sight of them before they spring any surprises on us."

"I'll give the orders right now, sir," Burksman replied crisply. "What about Tatiana? Will she be able to help us map the ship? With her help, we could put together a 3D map of where we're going and hopefully head off any more ambushes."

Dan stopped and turned back to the metal-suited man with a smile. He tapped the camera and microphone on his shoulder.

"You know, Burksman, that's a damn good idea. It's also exactly why I wanted someone trained coming with me on this excursion. I might be good at killing things and shooting lightning from my bare hands, but I am a rank amateur when it comes to planning. Remind me to give you a promotion when we get out of this.

"Tatiana," Dan continued, not missing a beat. "You heard the lieutenant; do you think you'll be able to use your cameras to construct a 3D map of the landing craft? Having something like that as part of a heads-up display would be a huge help."

"Dan?" Tatiana only managed to say his name before her voice disappeared into a screech of static. "Interference. Losing packets. Steadily worse." The squeal and hiss of static followed every word.

Frowning, Dan turned off his microphone before looking back to Burksman. The officer managed to somehow look sheepish through almost a ton of armor and weapons.

"Well," Dan finished lamely, "it was a good idea. Not your fault that somehow the Orakh lander is blocking Tatiana's signal.

"Actually," Dan frowned, not giving the soldier a chance to respond. "How in the hell are they blocking her signal? She's using satellites to beam her commands over here, and the nanites of everyone out front as a relay. We're barely five hundred feet into the ship, and already we're starting to lose contact. That doesn't seem like an accident to me."

"Maybe they have an intelligence Orakh?" Burkman offered. "Someone that can feed them ideas to try and blunt our technological and information-gathering advantage. If I was dealing with an opponent that knew more about the battlefield than me, cutting off that flow of information would be my first goal."

Dan pumped some more mana into the sword, increasing the area the purple flames lit. "That's the thing. I'm sure they're trying, but the Orakh shouldn't know the first thing about radio or bluetooth. They literally shouldn't even be able to conceive of how we communicate, let alone find a way to eliminate it."

"But what does that mean?" Burkman asked "Are you saying that–"

His words were cut off as the walls on either side of the tunnel they were walking down collapsed, revealing waiting chambers full of Orakh.

With a snarl, Dan lunged past Burkman, stabbing his sword to the hilt in the chest of the closest alien. With his free hand, he launched a flame jet at close range into their massed ranks. The spell wasn't hot enough to kill the damp, amphibious aliens, but it seared their eyes and dried their skin to the point of cracking, making them easy targets for the rest of the unit.

The roar of fifty-caliber fire in an enclosed space hammered against Dan's ears. Flames erupted from the suits of armor, cooking the Orakh that survived his attack. Several of the soldiers drew broadswords that looked tiny in their oversized mits before stepping into the front line to hack down the injured and disoriented aliens.

Dan did what damage he could, his small stature compared to the Orakh and the powered armor working against him. Usually, he'd use his mobility and temporal runes to dodge blows by a hair's breadth before slipping past the clumsier aliens' guards and using his sword.

Unfortunately, the battle in the dark hallways of the ship more closely resembled a rugby scrum. Soldiers slammed their metal shoulders against aliens, servo motors pushing the oversized amphibians back long enough for swords and flamethrowers to do the dirty work of ending the Orakhs' lives.

Here and there, a soldier took an axe blow, stumbling down to a knee from the aliens' heavy attacks. That was where Dan's mobility would show its worth, allowing him to pepper the attacker with Forcebolts long enough for him to slip into place and fight off the encroaching Orakh.

Even with his strength runes at maximum output, each blow from the Orakh forced Dan back a step or two. His feet unwillingly skidded on the rough stone floor of the void ship. He might be superior to the Orakh warriors in every other way, but in the close confines of the landing craft's tunnels, their superior brute strength was able to show its value.

Finally, the last Orakh fell to the ground twitching. Methodically, the rest of their troops used the broadswords to collect their fallen foes' heads, conscious and cautious of the Orakh's regenerative capabilities.

"Sir," Burkman's voice startled Dan. He turned back from the grisly work to look at the man. His armor was covered in soot, a handful of deep dents marring the armor around his forearms and shoulders.

"Yes?" Dan replied.

"We have two people with minor injuries, despite their armor," Burkman pointed at two nearby suits, each one sporting a deep slash from an unlucky axe blow that bit all the way through their powered suits. "Another five soldiers have some minor loss of function due to armor damage. Myself and another nine have suffered cosmetic damage."

"Is the unit still able to proceed?" Dan asked, his eyes flicking to the two suits with holes in them. Slowly, one of them nodded, while the other gave him a thumbs up.

"Yes sir," Burkman agreed. "It'll take a minute to confirm all of the kills, but then we should be ready to move out once more."

"Do you have any way to deal with false walls like the one that just surprised us?" Dan motioned to the rubble on the floor that had been concealing the Orakh unit.

"I would say that we could switch to infrared," Burkman replied reluctantly, "but I had it on when we got surprised. I couldn't see anything in the walls. Whatever they're using, it blocks heat."

"Fuck," Dan replied. "Nothing for it, then. Make sure we have soldiers with melee weapons on the outer edges of the column. Apparently, the Orakh are capable of jumping us at any moment."

Burkman nodded hesitantly before switching to the unit's radio frequency and issuing orders. Just shy of a minute later, they were underway once more, albeit at a more measured pace as the soldiers trained their eyes on the walls, looking for any sign of another ambush.

A tense five minutes later, they came to a crossroads, and Dan frowned. On the wall, scrawled in the stone with poor handwriting were the words, "Thrush, this way" followed by an arrow. He looked to Burkman.

"This is a trap right?" He asked the man's armored form. "They literally know my name. This has to be a trap."

"Sure looks like a trap to me, sir," Burkman answered, his voice shaky. "I don't know what the alternative is? We can wander around here for a couple of hours while William gets pounded outside, or we can take their invitation. If they're holed up and ready for us, I doubt they're going anywhere. We'll have to go to them at some point, anyway."

"Agreed," Dan replied. "Not happy about it, but agreed."

They led the rest of the uneasy company in the direction indicated by the arrow. After walking in silence for almost five minutes, they came to a spiral staircase. Once again, scrawled in the stone were the words "Thrush, this way" and an arrow pointing downward.

Setting his teeth, Dan descended into the bowels of the ship. One floor after another, they marched past landings, until eventually they reached the bottom level. A final note read simply, "Thrush, here" with an arrow pointing directly ahead.

Dan exhaled, centering himself as he pumped mana into his shield. Nodding to Burkman, they walked down the hallway, approaching the large metal doors at its end.

He pushed the door. Either it was magical, or the engineer that designed it was a master of counterweights. The light pressure swung the door inward. For just a second, Dan saw a throne room. Hundreds of feet long and lined with Orakh warriors, weapons, and skulls, grisly trophies from a hundred campaigns covered the walls. At the far end, a massive Orakh, at least twenty feet tall, sat on a throne, a glaive made of metal as dark as obsidian resting across his lap.

Before Dan could say something or address the creature, a jet of flame, white-hot and and moving faster than sound itself washed over Dan and Burkman. Even with his thermal rune and spellshield, Dan's breath was stolen from his throat as the fire consumed the very oxygen around him. His hair singed and began to burn.

Then the flame was gone. The ground under him bubbled, the molten rock and steel heavy as it tried to burn through his shoes. Quickly, Dan jumped forward, breathing a sigh of relief as he felt solid rock beneath his feet once more.

His immediate safety assured, Dan looked back in horror. Where Burkman once stood, there was nothing more than a misshapen lump of steel and bone. The former lieutenant looked like a half-burned candle, deformed and bent in on himself.

"It's a good thing that you survived, Thrush," a familiar voice cackled.

He looked up, stomach sinking, to see Merella Amberell floating above the battlefield, her cloak billowing around her.

"I've melted your blasted metal from my body." She spat the words out at him, her eyes blazing. "This time, you won't be able to just kill me with a word. Garnash here," she nodded at the giant Orakh watching impassively from his throne, "has promised me a fair fight with you in exchange for some information.

"I would hate for you to die as quickly as your friend." Merella sneered down at Burkman's twisted and melted form. "You and I have a lot of catching up to do."

CHAPTER THIRTY-EIGHT

For Auld Lang Syne, My Dear

Dan triggered Merella's killswitch through his System. She didn't even flinch. With a mental frown, he moved his sword into a guard position. He had to try. He'd given Merella too many chances to take her at her word here.

He threw a pair of Forcebolts at her, unsurprised as they rippled into nonexistence on her spellshield. She hovered higher in the air, a cyclone of flame projecting from each hand, tracking across the floor as Dan wove toward her.

Behind him, Dan's soldiers began to filter in, only for a mix of Orakh warriors and commanders to immediately charge them. He didn't have a moment to spare. Dan circled Merella, tossing low-powered spells to probe her spellshield while she flew above him, a glint in her eye as she did the same.

Dan parried a firebolt, the purple flat of his blade slapping the spell from the air. Merella cackled as she threw burst after burst of fire at him. He gritted his teeth, sidestepping a second blast as they continued their game of cat and mouse, while the Orakh hordelord watched on.

Neither of them had spells capable of punching through the others' spellshield. Well, Railgun would do the trick, but he just didn't see Merella holding still long enough for him to hit her. Instead, they were stuck trading feints as each side tried to run the other out of mana.

If he could actually reach her, Dan was confident his sword could carve through her shields in a couple of blows. Unfortunately, Merella remained in the air, cackling madly as she lobbed small balls of fire and plasma at him. Even using his normal trick of jumping from force bubble to force bubble, Dan doubted that he'd be able to catch up to the flying elf.

Merella dodged two more Forcebolts before the third caught her in the shins, spinning her vertically in the air. As she shrieked, flames erupted from her body. She dove toward Dan, swooping out of the air with both of her arms extended.

Dan grinned, igniting his own flame aura before leaping toward Merella. He couldn't see the surprise on her flame-shrouded face, but it didn't matter. His left arm snagged around the back of her shield while the sword in his right rammed into the unseen barrier.

The flames burned at him as Merella increased their heat. Dan could feel his resistance rune struggling to keep up as his skin began to redden beneath his own aura. With a grunt, he hacked at her spellshield, frantically trying to collapse it before the elf cooked him alive.

They tumbled through the air, held aloft by Merella's spell as they careened around the throne room. Dan slammed into the severed head of a rhino-like creature, mounted as a trophy on the wall. Its head slammed into his lower back, forcing the air from his lungs.

Merella wrapped her legs around Dan, bracing herself between him and the trophy before she raised an arm above her head, a ball of flame growing in her outstretched hand. Frantically, he wrapped his free arm around the trophy before launching a Forcebolt at her hand.

It impacted her spellshield, deflecting her hand to the side. A massive blast of energy slammed into the landing craft's walls, melting a massive swath of rock and metal into magma.

Briefly, Merella's face became visible, surprise and hatred warring across her features as her flame aura flickered in time with the spell's discharge. Dan gritted his teeth and stabbed her once again, barely penetrating her shields and digging the point of the blade into her upper thigh.

She kicked off of his shield, leaving him stranded on the trophy as she flew back, charging another spell. He slapped her with another pair of Forcebolts, damaging her spellshield further. Before she could release her reply, Dan let himself drop to the ground, activating Gravitational Easing and twisting his body so that he could land in a roll, hopefully dissipating the force of his fall.

Another column of fire tore into the wall just above Dan, close enough to cause his shield to sparkle as it began dissipating the heat. He checked his mana reserves, a slight frown on his face. As powerful as he was, it was clear that Merella had spent hundreds of years killing awakened creatures. Her mana stockpiles far exceeded his own, and a battle of attrition was not one he would win.

He glanced at the entrance to the room. His soldiers were beating back the Orakh. The commanders were more than a match for any one soldier, but working in teams, they were able to keep the huge monsters from inflicting fatal wounds, all while pounding them with fifty-caliber repeaters and flamethrowers.

The huge Orakh on the throne watched on impassively. Merella had dubbed it Garnash, but whatever the creature's name, it seemed wholly unaffected by the massive casualties inflicted on the Orakh guarding him. Instead, most of his attention seemed to be focused on the battle between Merella and Dan.

His attention snapped back to his battle as Merella landed on the floor of the throne room across from him, massive white hot balls of fire enveloping both hands. She eyed him up and down before sneering.

"Thrush," she hissed, stalking toward him. "It seems like you learned a couple things about running and hiding since we last met. If you plan on claiming the mantle of a mage, fight like one. Stand tall and trade spells with me, if you dare."

"You were the one flying in the air," Dan replied, circling her as she approached, prepared to bat down a Fireball at a moment's notice. "I don't see how I could fight you properly when you were the one running away."

She threw a Fireball the size of Dan's head at him, forcing him to throw himself into a roll to avoid the attack. "Your petty goads mean nothing to me. For what you have done to me, I will wipe your name from the very annals of history. I will burn you to cinders and use your ash to fertilize a small garden. This will not end with a clean and painless death for you, Thrush."

"Other than win a fight against you and your nephew?" Dan replied, sprinting at her in a serpentine pattern to divert her attacks. "I don't know what you're talking about. I spared you the first time, and I made an effort to spare you during the second encounter, when I could have easily killed you. I wouldn't think any of my actions were unforgivable."

"But you *cheated*!" she shouted, backpedaling as she sprayed streams of liquid fire onto the throne room's floor, igniting it. "The first time you had allies, and the second, you used the slave machines in my blood to disable me. You killed my nephew in front of me then, when I demanded a duel of honor, you broke the rules. Why wouldn't I be mad?"

"Mad enough to side with the Orakh?" Dan bit out as he dove into the flames. His thermal rune dispersed the worst of it, but his clothes crackled and smoked from the heat. "You do realize that whatever he's offering you, it's a lie. Once he gets what he wants, Garnash is just going to eat you."

"You won't break our alliance with some pretty human words," Merella replied, throwing a wall of flame at Dan that pushed his spellshield to its breaking point. "We don't advertise it, but some of the more enterprising members of our family have come to clandestine agreements with the horde for centuries. It's frowned upon amongst the other elves, but with enough money, magic, or information, even the Orakh will form a temporary alliance."

She smirked, summoning another giant ball of fire just as Dan approached sword range. "With you, human, the price was more satisfying than most. They wanted me to gut this benighted planet's defenses. That meant killing you, a task I would want to accomplish whether or not the Orakh provided their support.

"All I have to do," Merella continued as the ball of flame coalesced into a sword and shield just in time to parry a wild strike from Dan. "...is kill you and ensure that human resistance is crushed, and Garnash will give me a shuttle to escape this awful world. I help him, he helps me, and everyone goes away happy."

Dan grunted, ducking under a flaming sword and lashing out with his leg, catching the elf behind her knee and knocking her to the ground. Before Merella could recover, he rammed down his sword with both hands, barely punching through her spellshield to leave a two-to-four-inch deep incision in her shoulder.

"You can't believe that!" Dan shouted back, summoning a force bubble to deflect a lance of fire launched by the downed elf. "The Orakh only exist to consume and expand. As soon as you outlive your usefulness, Garnash is going to eat you!"

He danced to the side, avoiding an eruption of flame and molten rock from the ground behind him. Unfortunately, giving her a moment to breathe was all it took for Merella to regain her feet, eyes blazing.

"He's right, you know," the giant Orakh rumbled, amusement on his wide, craggy face. "I plan on eating whoever wins this fight. The Horde doesn't have allies. Just those it plans on eating later."

"See?" Dan's eyes flashed as he gave the elf more space. "If we work together, we could bring down the Orakh and end their invasion. Then, you and I could settle things, and you'd be free to leave if you won. Humanity isn't the enemy of your people! We just want to be left alone."

She glared at him, disgust in her eyes. Dan barely had a chance to summon another force bubble as she erupted into a cyclone of flames, dozens of tendrils slicing toward him, only to be slowed by his spell for a fraction of a second. The bubble collapsed, but Dan had already pumped enough mana into his strength runes to jump into the air.

A second later, Dan landed on another force bubble. His eyes flickered to the entryway where his forces struggled to make progress against the Orakh. Most of the average warriors were on the ground, smoking and riddled with holes. The commanders fought on, tossing powered armor around like children's toys as their giant weapons rose and fell.

Gritting his teeth, Dan began to cast Railgun. Merella wasn't going to back down, and he was uncertain that he could beat her in an open fight. Even if he won, it would take minutes that his soldiers didn't have, and he would stagger out the other end devoid of mana and wounded.

He needed to win here and now. Holding still would give her a chance to target him, but with the help of his thermal rune, that was a risk that Dan was going to need to take.

"You don't understand, Thrush." Merella's eyes spat hatred at him as she took his sudden lack of movement as an excuse to deliver a monologue. "I'd prefer not to die, but given how you've dishonored me, I'd rather be eaten by him than help you and survive. You killed my nephew in front of me, cheated to win a duel against me, and enslaved me. Because of you, I had to pretend to respect that simpering Ibis fool."

Flames ignited in both of her hands. "If House Amberell knew what had happened to me," she continued, madness in her voice, "I would have been killed out of hand. The only way to cleanse this dishonor is with blood, and it must either be your blood or mine. I am a dead woman, unless I can bring you down here. If I must die, I'd prefer to die with my honor intact.

"Do your worst, human." She sneered at the constructs of

mana growing in front of Dan. "But know that, if you fail, I will erase you from existence with the fire of a star itself."

Dan released the spell. She didn't even move, trusting in her spellshield to stop any magic he could throw at her.

The slug shattered her shield like a hammer striking a wineglass. For a brief moment, Dan thought he saw a look of shock on her face. It must have been his imagination. Before he could react, Merella erupted in flames. The shockwave threw Dan off of the force bubble and across the chamber.

His shoulder and head slammed into the wall, and suddenly Dan was surrounded by whirling motes of light. Then the heat was gone.

He blinked, his vision blurry. Where Merella once stood, now there was a gaping hole. Beneath, he could barely make out another vast cavern filled with eggs.

The Orakh Chief stood, hefting his weapon. With heavy footfalls, he descended his dias toward the center of the throne room.

CHAPTER THIRTY-NINE

Clash of Champions

"Interesting spell, human," the gigantic Orakh's voice filled the chamber, overwhelming the sound of Dan's soldiers fighting the monstrous creature's minions. "Was that elven spell artillery?"

"It was a Railgun," Dan frowned as he turned to face the creature, uncomfortable talking so casually with it, but content to use the conversation to recharge his mana. "I accelerated a ball of metal very fast with magic."

"Ah." the hordelord nodded its great bulbous head, a knowing look on its misformed features. "Like the slings used by the half-men. They swing them over their head and release rocks at great speed."

Dan cocked his head to the side, trying to make sense of the strangely talkative Orakh. It was taller than him, almost three times his height, and covered in bulging muscles. In its hand was a glaive almost as oversized as the monster. The head, made of a dark, yet shiny metal, was almost the size of Dan's torso.

As for the creature itself, it was almost topless, wearing only a cape crafted from what appeared to be silk. The fabric was covered in scenes of battle, Orakh triumphing over elves, humans, and what appeared to be smaller humans, all inter-woven with crude versions of runes. Clearly, the article of clothing was enchanted, but Dan had a nagging suspicion that the creature selected it because it showed off its impressive physique.

Other than the cape, all it wore was a set of familiar gauntlets and simple breeches. Without even looking that closely, Dan knew that the gauntlets were inscribed with crude spell runes. Even if the Orakh itself couldn't cast, the gauntlets would solve that problem for it, albeit in a mana-inefficient way.

"Half-men?" Dan asked, fishing for information as he tried to recover from his battle with Merella. "Do you mean dwarves? I've read about them, but we haven't met them yet."

The Orakh scowled. "Not the bearded ones. Their machines of steam and gears are no fun to smash and destroy. By the time you bash your way through their traps and get to the center of their lairs, most of the time, they're already gone.

"No!" Its expression brightened. "The half men didn't have many planets. All rolling plains. They lived underground and cast magic by singing songs rather than elven spells. When we attacked, they swung stones over their head and hit our warriors. They stung, a couple even died.

"They were delicious." A dreamy look settled over the Orakh's face. "All you needed was a little rosemary, sea salt, and a spit. You just needed to chop their feet off before roasting them on an open fire. The hair ruins the flavor and interferes with the spices."

"Halfings?" Dan gagged slightly. "You ate halflings? The Tellask never wrote anything about halflings!"

"They were our nearest neighbors." The Orakh shrugged, still smiling. "We met them before they met the elves. I think we ate them all before the elves contacted them. A shame. They taste a lot better than elf. The arrogance and stringiness dry them out. There's no depth to the flavor."

"You killed them all/" Dan spoke softly, shaking his head. "Just like that, you exterminated them."

Garnash hefted his glaive. "It's what the Horde does. Luckily, human tastes a lot better than elf. At least you put some meat on your bones. It keeps you nice and juicy."

"Before we do this," Dan interjected, trying to control his bile. As much as banter with the monster made him sick, he needed to draw it out. The conversation was an invaluable opportunity to gain more information, and it gave Dan more time to recover his depleted mana.

"Why were you working with Merella?" he asked, sword in hand but pointed partially at the ground. "You flat-out admitted that you were planning on eating her if she won. Why ally yourself with her if your plan is just to betray her?"

The Orakh shrugged. "I plan on eating you, too. But, as for the elf? It amused me. The elves always brag about how much smarter they are than the Orakh, but what good is all of that flashy magic and brain power in my gut? She was helpful in trapping you, human. She hated you so much she didn't even make an attempt to escape. I lost nothing by eating her last."

"Trapping me?" Dan frowned. "We fought our way in, killing tens of thousands of Orakh. Right now, we're fighting in your throne room. My guards and yours are evenly matched, and I'm about to engage you in single combat, just like I wanted. I don't really feel trapped?"

"That's what the dead elf said you'd think," the Orakh chuckled, raising a hand into the air. A rune glowed on his gauntlet as mana flowed into it. "She said your forces were the only ones that could use magic. That you'd be the only ones who could stop me. She said that, if I showed too much power, you'd spend months preparing yourself and sacrifice this entire city to me in order to stop me once and for all.

"You killed tens of thousands of Orakh," Garnash grunted as a spray of light emitted from its gauntlet displaying an image of the clearing outside the landing craft. "But we are hundreds of thousands. Where one falls, ten replace it. By acting weak, we draw you into the center of our domain. Once you are too far from your reinforcements, we attack you with our entire army."

The Orakh's face screwed up in concentration. Another rune began to glow on its gauntlet. Orakh began to pour from nearby buildings, charging through withering fire toward William's forces.

Dan frowned. His men were outnumbered heavily, but they were in fortified positions with clear fields of fire. They could account for many times their number.

Of course, the Orakh seemed more than content to test his theory. Eventually, people would begin to slip, and ammunition would start to run low. Each Orakh warrior took a distressing number of rifle shots or irreplaceable fifty-caliber ammunition to take down.

"The elf said that I should show you this." Garnash grinned at him, jagged teeth poking out from the giant monster's uneven mouth. "That I should let you know that every minute you spend in the bowels of this ship is purchased at the cost of your own troops. We can talk all you want. You can regain all the mana you want, but you're wasting your warriors by doing so."

Dan gritted his teeth and ignited his sword. The Orakh slammed the butt of his glaive against the throne room floor.

"That's the look I like to see!" the creature boomed happily. "Determination, desperation. I didn't understand why the elf told me to say that, but it was the right choice. Your panic will flavor your flesh and weaken you in combat. She was smart, for food."

Dan rushed toward the Orakh, his physical runes at maximum and his spellshield fully charged. With each step, he kept his eyes on the hulking monster, ready to activate his temporal rune at a moment's notice.

It smiled, closing its gauntlet and ending the images of the battle outside. Garnash pointed at Dan and uttered a word in a harsh and foreign tongue.

A rune glowed on the gauntlet, and Dan jerked to a halt, the force of his stop knocking the wind out of him. Barely visible ringing his spellshield was a band of force compressing around him like an anaconda.

"You fight like an elf, human." Garnash lifted his glaive high, black lightning crackling around its head. "And I've killed a lot of elves. All tricks, magic, and speed, until they run out of mana or take a misstep. Behind your spellshield, you're weak."

Garnash spat on the floor, a great greenish black glob of something unspeakable that hissed as the chemicals in it interacted with the metal.

"You're pink paste," the Orakh continued, shifting his glaive into a ready position, the arcs of mana around it flickering faster as they played up and down its length. "Wobbly and ineffectual. One solid hit, and you're done, shattered into a dozen pieces, all just as weak."

The glaive fell, its blade crashing into Dan's spellshield. His head exploded into agony as bolts of electricity flickered and launched themselves around the room. Wherever they struck, they scoured deep holes in the solid stone.

With the crash of a breaking window, the spellshield shattered. Dan activated the temporal rune. Almost at a glacial pace, he watched the circle of force begin to contract around him. He jumped into the air, the force of his physical runes combined with his instinctive use of Gravitational Easing launching him almost to the ceiling.

He launched two Lightning Strokes, landing both of them on the Orakh's unarmored torso before he reached the apex of his arc, where Dan landed on a force bubble. Garnash just laughed, the rune for electricity glowing on his cape.

The Orakh amended its earlier assessment. "Fine. You fight like a skilled elf. The spellshields of most wouldn't have survived half as long, and your reflexes are superb.

"You still rely on agility." Garnash shrugged, almost apologetically. "I just need to catch you in the ring and stab you. Without your ability to dodge, you're too small and poorly armored to survive a full-force blow. In the meantime, feel free to pepper me with your elemental magics. I am a true warrior.

My cloak and skin will absorb the worst you can throw at me. It is only a matter of time before my binding rings find you and end this farce."

Dan frowned. Garnash had a point. His spellshield barely stopped the glave blow at full energy, and it would take some time to transfer more mana into it. If the Orakh could actually pin him down, two blows would finish him on the best of days. Right now? One would probably cripple him.

The giant Orakh pointed his glaive directly at Dan and let a blast of black lighting loose at him. Dan simply let himself drop, barely noting as the energy annihilated his force bubble.

While he fell, Dan fired a Forcebolt into the giant creature. It impacted on a muscular thigh with a hollow thud, drawing little more than a glance from Garnash.

Still, Dan smiled. No rune lit up in response to force magic. The cape seemed to protect the monster from elemental attacks, but physical blows would still damage it.

He looked the musclebound behemoth up and down. Technically. It would take a lot of physical damage to actually seriously harm something with Garnash's herculean physique.

"Don't act like you've found my weakness, human." Garnash pointed his gauntlet at Dan, drawing another panicked dodge as a translucent band appeared where he'd just stood. "If you want to get close enough to exchange blows, you can try to hurt me. I invite the attempt, and I will celebrate your bravery as I drink from your skull. Close combat between a human and a hordelord is more foolish than the elf trusting me not to eat her."

Dan took in a deep breath, his eyes on the gigantic being's grin and bulging muscles. There was some truth to his words, but at the same time, if Dan got close enough, the Orakh wouldn't be able to use its unwieldy glaive. Of course, at that range, elbows and knees would be as deadly as a sword or spear.

Still, his only other option was to stand at range, lobbing spells the Orakh could more or less ignore until it captured him with the ring or blasted him with lightning. Theoretically, if he could hit it with Railgun, that would probably do the trick, but Dan strongly suspected that any attempt would end quickly as he was immobilized and electrocuted by the hordelord.

"Remember, human." The Orakh raised its hand, projecting the battle once more. "Even as you stand there contemplating your own folly, your soldiers die."

Dan's mouth turned into a bitter line as he watched William, standing atop a tank in his power armor, blasting flames from one arm as he fired round after round from the other. He wasn't sure what the older man was trying to do. The tank was isolated from the rest of the battle line, which seemed to have fallen back at some point under the constant assault from the Orakh.

Even as Dan watched, a reaper flew overhead, banking to the side to avoid a giant blast of light from a crystal mounted on the top of the landing craft. It launched a volley of missiles into the mass of Orakh bodies, killing hundreds, but failing to even dent their advance.

An axe struck William's leg, failing to penetrate the armor, but knocking the man off-balance. The power suit went down in a heap on top of the tank, flamethrower spinning in a circle as the downed man tried to force the mob back. One monster after another climbed atop the tank, pinning the powerful armor with the weight of their bodies as axes began to rise and fall.

Dan's worry and confusion vanished as a cold breath of clarity ran down his spine. He was out of time. The entire battle had been fought on the palm of Garnash's scarred hand. Every action of his had been foretold and countered.

If he was going to win, he'd need to change things. Throw sand in the gears of Merella's plans and force the Orakh to go off-script. He smiled, an unpleasant thing.

"You're right, Garnash." He cocked his head at his foe. "Right here, I can't defeat you. I'll see you in a minute."

The Orakh looked at him in confusion for a second as Dan made a dash for the open pit where his previous Railgun shot had blown a hole into the brood chamber. Realization flashed across its face.

"Protect the eggs!" Its shout was accompanied by a line of black lightning from the glaive, but it was too late.

Dan had already jumped, and with a puff of Gravitational Easing, he was gone.

CHAPTER FORTY

Dance in the Dark

Dan's feet hit the floor of the birthing chamber with a muted thud. In the distance, looming over the shapes of the Orakh eggs, he could barely make out the towering shape of an alien variant. It wobbled slightly before croaking loud enough to be heard over the sound of the battle on the floor.

He shrugged, weaving through the pony-sized eggs toward its hulking form. Behind him, Garnash smashed into the ground, his massive feet destroying one of the eggs.

"Human!" The Orakh's scream filled the hatchery. "I will floss with your spine!"

That was his cue. Dan ran faster, doing his best to avoid the large, leathery eggs that filled the underground room. Behind him, Garnash crashed to the floor, shaking the entire hatchery.

A glance over his shoulder confirmed Dan's suspicion. The giant Orakh held the glaive at ready, energy pulsing over its length as it watched him run away, reluctant to fire a shot that might harm the eggs.

It wasn't even moving, afraid that it wouldn't be able to move through the nursery without stepping on or crushing a cluster of eggs. He took advantage of its indecision to lengthen the gap between them, still jogging toward the gigantic Orakh he could barely make out near the edge of the chamber.

Finally, Garnash got over his reluctance and fired a bolt of energy from his glaive. Given the distance, Dan sensed the build up of mana with plenty of time to throw himself to the side and avoid the spell.

The darkness exploded to his left as a handful of eggs were turned into goop, and the floor of the chamber shattered under the force of the blow. Foul-smelling yolk and rocks pelted Dan, battering his stuttering spellshield, but not doing any damage.

He switched directions, still working his way toward the large Orakh, but focusing on a winding, serpentine path that would prevent Garnash from drawing a bead on him.

It only took a couple of seconds for his random changes in direction to bear fruit as another clump of eggs exploded, eliciting a scream of rage from Garnash. The entire room shook as the giant Orakh charged after him.

Evidently, the threat Dan posed to the nursery was too great for Garnash to let him have his way. It meant that, in addition to giving Dan time to replenish his flagging mana reserves, he was onto something. It might not be anything that would let him win this battle, but at a minimum, damage to the hatchery would likely be a gut punch to the Orakh war effort.

A brief, vicious smile flashed over Dan's otherwise hollow face. William might have escaped, but he doubted it. He'd only caught a couple of the blows the Orakh landed on the man right before he'd jumped into the egg pit. There was a finality to the way those axes fell that he struggled to deny.

The least he could do was to return the favor, strangling the next generation of Orakh warriors in the crib. Dan's sword flashed to the side, its razor-sharp edge slicing open the egg and spilling its foul contents into the winding pathway behind him. Then, he stabbed it to the other side, not slowing his pace in the slightest, draining another egg.

Garnash screamed in rage once more, and mana began to build up behind Dan. Just as it pulsed, he threw himself to the side. This time, he didn't manage to completely dodge the blast of energy from the huge Orakh's glaive.

The breath rushed out of his chest as the explosion next to him sent Dan careening through the air and darkness. For a fraction of a second, he tried to get his bearings, only to slam into and through yet another egg. Only a portion of the destructive mana glanced off of Dan's spellshield, but it was enough to almost short out the mana reserves devoted to his defenses and leave his aching body covered in dripping, sulfurous Orakh yoke.

He stood up and took in Garnash's huge silhouette. The Orakh was charging his glaive once again, the dim, crackling energy surrounding it almost the only visible source of light. The hole he'd jumped through and the meager light it provided was far behind him.

With a grunt, he started running again, always in the general direction of the shape he'd first seen when jumping into the hatchery. Explosions erupted around him as the Orakh commander tried to tag him once more with energy bolts from his heavily enchanted weapon, but Dan was too quick and the room was too dark for any real sort of accuracy.

Periodically, he slammed into an egg, but Dan didn't let it slow him down, bursting through the leathery exterior to pull himself forward in his headlong flight.

Suddenly he burst forth from the forest of eggs into a dimly lit area occupied by the largest Orakh he'd ever seen. It barely even had legs, instead covered in quivering and wobbling flesh.

It moaned at Dan, a warbling and distressed sound as it tried to shift its massive bulk away from him. He didn't hesitate.

His sword crackled with eldritch purple energy as he brought it down on the wall of flesh and blubber before him. The Orakh's flesh parted with ease, barely slowing the blade as it passed through.

Viscera sprayed over Dan as his weapon hit a pouch of pressurized liquid. The broodmother warbled and screamed in agony, but made no move to defend itself, likely because the most threatening course of action available was to flap its tiny, vestigial arms angrily while calling for help.

Behind Dan, Garnash's massive feet thundered as his actions broke the giant Orakh from its indecision. Until he felt another buildup of mana, Dan vowed to ignore the charging monster. Even with his longer stride, it would take the Orakh commander some time to get to him. Time he could use to cut down the variant that his foe so valued.

It was the least William deserved.

He stabbed again, drawing another burst of scalding fluid and, surprisingly, a torrent of mana. Dan frowned. The elephantine monster was clearly alive. It didn't make sense that he was collecting mana from a still-living creature.

His sword rose and fell once more, and Dan accepted the mana, letting it flow into the parched and empty balls of energy in his core. He didn't have the time to ponder over the philosophical implications that he was taking mana from a living being. Garnash would be there shortly. He could only take advantage of the mana rapidly refilling his reserves and make a note to investigate the cause later.

"Step away from the broodmother!" Garnash shouted. Dan barely paid attention. He was beyond the muscled monster's screams and posturing. They would fight, and one of them would fall. There was nothing more to it. "Fight with honor, treacherous human!"

Dan didn't reply, instead stabbing his sword deeply into the side of his target, gripping the handle with both hands and running behind it. The blade sawed through the Orakh's tender flesh, eliciting a spray of scalding liquid as one fluid pocket after another burst under its razor edge.

As soon as Dan had the broodmother between him and Garnash, he began casting Railgun. With his mana reserves close to full, he could afford to burn the mana, and really, of all his spells, it was the only one that even had a fighter's chance at injuring the giant Orakh.

The major concern was whether or not Dan could hit the

Orakh. Railgun was slow to cast and hard to aim, making it more of a siege spell designed to take down fixed positions of or large and clumsy opponents.

Unfortunately, despite his size, Garnash was anything but clumsy. The projectile fired by the Railgun might move fast enough that dodging it was difficult, but under normal circumstances, the Orakh would be able to predict where Dan was aiming and juke to the side quickly enough that he would never be able to draw a bead on it.

Of course, they were under far from normal circumstances. Garnash was angry and presumably running in a straight line. For the moment, the big Orakh's line of sight on Dan was obstructed, meaning he wouldn't have a chance to observe the initial stages of the spell being cast.

Even when Dan stepped out into the open, past the heaving and bleeding broodmother, only the small amount of bioluminescence from the broodmother would give the Orakh commander an idea of what he was doing. Garnash, on the other hand, would be backlit by the weak light filtering through the crater in the ceiling.

"With any luck," Dan muttered the words to himself, a talisman against the constant failures that had dogged his team since they stepped inside the Orakh ship.

The spell strained against Dan's mind, the metal rails trying to pull themselves apart under the stress off the spell. Time seemed to slow as electricity began to arc through the bars of metal.

His foot hit the fluid-slick floor, and Dan dragged himself around the broodmother's bulk. Energy from his spell pulled at the slug that was suspended just shy of the rails with his mind.

Garnash was maybe ten feet away, glaive crackling with eldritch energy as he peered into the darkness and tried to find Dan.

Dan released his hold on the slug. His mana reserves dropped notably as the massive electrical current running through the rails grabbed the hunk of metal and pulled it along their length.

A gout of plasma erupted from the end of the rails as the energy pouring out of the spell overexcited the air. For a second, the hatchery was visible in the flashbulb of expanding ionized gas.

It was massive beyond belief. A square, a little over a half mile per side, absolutely filled with egg cluster after cluster. Before him lay an army of Orakh ten times the size of the one that had already overwhelmed Manhattan. Enough to storm through the disparate and quarreling factions that were trying to carve up what had once been America in a matter of months.

Then, the projectile struck Garnash. Somehow, in the fraction of a second the Orakh had spotted Dan, it'd gotten its glaive around to parry.

It exploded. The heavily enchanted weapon's runescripting was no match for a kilogram of metal traveling at almost three kilometers per second.

Dark energy writhed, coalescing into whips of violet lightning that pulsed and scattered around the chamber. One struck Dan's spellshield dead on, and only the mana he'd stolen from the broodmother kept his defenses from collapsing entirely.

The broodmother itself wasn't anywhere near as lucky. Its massive size seemed to attract the out-of-control energy, and bolt after bolt seared massive holes through the gigantic monster.

Garnash himself was thrown back by the blast, stunned by both the explosion and the sudden flash of light so near him. For the first time in the fight, the big Orakh's face lost the smug look of superiority that had graced it.

Dan ignored the tempest of dark energy pulsing and lashing out from the spot where the glaive had been and began feeding mana into the Railgun once again. The previous shot had bent the metal bars, the amount of electricity running through them twisting and pitting them beyond the point of use.

The spell pattern for Railgun popped into Dan's mind, impossibly complex, and he focused on the section that created the metal rails, letting his mana smooth and straighten the bars.

Garnash staggered to his feet dumbly, his defensive cloak in tatters from the force of the blast and covered in wounds. In some places, the shrapnel from the slug and glaive had penetrated deeply, gashing open muscle and spilling the Orakh's brackish blood. In others, the metal had simply liquified, burning deep into Garnash's flesh before solidifying.

A crackling whip of dark energy lashed past Dan and struck the broodmother. Suddenly, mana poured into him, more than he'd ever received for a single kill. The energy rushed past his defenses and began to overwhelm him.

Giddy warmth filled Dan's senses as a light pink tint invaded his vision. Frantically, he tried to compartmentalize his mind, devote half of himself to finishing the spell while the other repeated his mantra and tried to retain control.

"APO!" Garnash screamed, distress and sorrow in his voice as he took a staggering step toward the deceased broodmother.

The Railgun fired a second time. The weakened metal bars shattered under the stress of the spell, only holding together long enough to deliver another metal slug to the Orakh warlord's chest.

Something primal and savage inside Dan gibbered in joy as Garnash didn't even try to dodge. Instead, the Orakh simply stood there, a single arm extended toward the cooling mass of flesh behind Dan, inconsolable loss in his eyes.

The slug punched through the Orakh's chest with enough force to level a small building. Garnash's ribs snapped like matchsticks and a fountain of gore sprayed out his back.

The Orakh fell to his knees, looking dumbly at the blood pouring freely from his chest and onto his hands as he sought to staunch the wound. Dan didn't give him a second to recover.

In the flickering purple light, as the mana storm created by the destroyed glaive finally began to fade, Dan covered the twenty feet between them in a second. His sword flashed, wreathed in mana and fire.

A hand, almost the size of Dan's torso, fell to the ground. He jumped, Gravitational Easing aiding his ascent.

The blade flashed again, and Garnash's head followed it as an uncontrollable torrent of mana overwhelmed Dan's defenses.

CHAPTER FORTY-ONE

Epilogue

Dan stood on the bridge of *Terra's Pride*, looking out over the bustle of Portland from where the ship sat in its drydock. Behind him, Sam and Jennifer tapped furiously at the computers built into the ship's walls, making final preflight checks. Abe was being Abe: lounging in a chair, aloof and relaxed despite the historical importance of the moment.

A lot had happened in the year and a half since the battle of New York. Dan shuddered as he remembered the mana-fueled orgy of destruction that followed the death of the Orakh lord. He'd torn through thousands of eggs, feasting on the small amount of mana in each, sinking deeper into madness with each spell and sword stroke until finally he ended up back at the broodmother.

Remembering the flashes of mana he'd gotten from stabbing it, he tore into the dead body, only to find corpses. Dozens of half-digested human corpses floated in huge amniotic sacs. The realization that the Orakh had been digesting people and using their nutrients and DNA to create more monsters had shocked Dan out of his frenzy and into a bout of vomiting.

The flashes of mana he'd absorbed while attacking the

broodmother? It sure looked like the giant Orakh was absorbing the mana and very identity from the living New Yorkers the warriors had captured and brought back.

Then he'd staggered out of the wreckage of the Orakh ship to the tatters of the forces that had held off the remainder of the horde. The first thing he had done was look for William. Deep down, he'd known that the old general hadn't made it out alive, but he'd held out hope.

There was something about the man's infuriating but laconic personality that made Dan refuse to give up hope until he saw the body. William was larger than life. If anyone could have pulled himself out of the death trap where Dan had last seen him, it was William.

He had to call Jennifer to help him with the body. William had somehow self-ignited his fuel canister at the end, igniting both himself and the pile of Orakh that were hacking at his armor. It was William to the very end. Out of pure spite, he killed all of his attackers and denied them even his protein.

The next couple of days had been hard, piecing together what was left of the army and repairing the *Viceroy*. A lot of good men and women had died in New York City, but the infestation was well and truly dead.

After about a week, Bessie DuBlanc had given him a call. Abe had already briefed her military advisors on what had happened in New York, and apparently she'd been busy. The World was in shambles, but the remaining governments were to meet in Paris to discuss what needed to be done next.

She'd nominated him to be America's representative, but Dan turned her down. He could handle a small unit and magic with his eyes closed, but he was lost dealing with anything more than twenty people.

Instead, he publicly gave her his blessing, and DuBlanc won the popular vote in a landslide. As a compromise, she hitched a ride on the newly patched-up *Viceroy* and let him tag along as a consultant on magic and xenodiplomacy.

His title was a bit of a mouthful, but teleporting above a

major city without setting off any alarms earned them some major political capital. By the time the highlight reels of their battles unifying America and beating back the Orakh were finished, pretty much everyone at the conference was eating from the palms of their hands.

In a matter of days, the United Nations was reworked into an organization with actual teeth. Each nation now resembled a state or province, largely self-governing but subject to the over-arching laws of the UN. He left the meeting around the time that they started debating how to determine general assembly membership, confident that Bessie DuBlanc would inform him of the results.

She stormed back to the *Viceroy*, victorious but upset. They'd elected her President of the revamped United Nations. But the almost-unanimous consensus of the nations other than America and Brazil was that Dan was too powerful.

His organization was transformed into a sort of international special forces. Some of the most talented individuals in every field would be sent to Dan to have their mana awakened, and they would work with him to advance magical learning until a self-sufficient academy could be founded.

After that, he would be showered with awards and wealth, before politely being asked to retire from the public eye. Which brought him to today.

He wasn't going to retire. Fuck that. If his presence on Earth would upset the delicate peace he fought so hard to win, fine. He didn't need to be on Earth. It was his home, but the past year or so had widened his horizons to the point that he didn't need it. Other than his complicated relationship with his family, Dan didn't even have any proper connections on Earth. His friends, his job, his hobbies, everything that he had thought mattered, it had all fallen by the wayside in the fight against the Tellask and the Orakh.

Dan wasn't even mad. His reward for saving humanity from being enslaved, dinner, or both was the first Earth-built void ship ever. *Terra's Pride* was massive. 300 meters long and cylindrical with a 45-meter radius and meter-thick armor, it would have been immobile without the use of gravity and space magic.

After reverse engineering the mana forges, they'd put four in the ship. Enough to power the pair of modified spell cannons in its prow, the improved spellshields, and the eight heavily rune-scripted railgun turrets mounted along its sides.

Between him and Sam, they'd been able to design a line of space-born rockets powered using a combination of space magic and conventional thrust. They were elegant weapons, teleporting to within a half kilometer of their target in an instant before igniting powerful sprint engines. In practice bouts, they managed to almost universally avoid point-defense fire, making them a powerful ace in the hole for when the *Terra* first would run into the Tellask.

The world leaders had complained and worried, but eventually, Dan had gotten his way. Even if most of the rockets for the twin launchers had powerful conventional warheads, It only made sense to arm a handful with fusion payloads.

Finally, the ship was loaded with a nuclear reactor for conventional electricity, hydroponics to keep everyone on board alive, and enough mechs and power suits to take over a small nation. Then, it was only a matter of bringing aboard the five hundred crewmen and women, all experts in a multitude of fields, and then it was time to launch.

"How are we doing, Tatiana?" Dan asked the air, confident that the borderline-omnipresent computer was listening. "Are we set to launch on schedule?"

"There was a slight delay in loading some of the replacement parts," she responded smoothly from the bridge's speakers. "But things are under control. Honestly, we are ready to launch now, but we should still drag it out a little bit. The news crews are setting up their cameras, and we want to make sure that they get a good view of the Hero of Earth's triumphant departure."

"Sounds good," he agreed affably. "What about the rest of

you? Any last doubts about leaving your friends and family behind to go wander the stars and blow up anything that looks at us funny?"

"I call the green space babes!" Abe responded with a cackle. "You can have the blue or yellow ones, but the first mate gets to sleep with the green space babes. I'm pretty sure it's an unwritten rule of science fiction or something."

"I'm ready." Jennifer's voice was a little bleaker than he liked for a momentous occasion, but Dan wasn't going to second-guess the vortex of emotions she was likely buried in at the moment. "This place has been more hassle than anything for the past two years. I'm ready for a fresh start."

Sam just nodded at him, her fingers clacking over her keyboard as she made final adjustments.

"Are the cameras in position?" Dan asked Tatiana.

"All except Nebula Broadcasting, but they were the fear-mongers fighting your arming the *Terra* with nuclear weapons," she huffed, a hint of petty joy in her computerized voice. "There's no big loss if they miss the event of the decade."

Dan cracked a smile. He couldn't publicly tear into the news network, but they'd caused him a fair amount of stress with their slanted coverage. He'd be glad to be rid of them, along with the rest of the self-interested corruption that seemed to exist in Earth's very air.

President DuBlanc would root out the worst of it, he was confident of that. As for the rest? Humanity had made it very clear that they didn't want him butting in any more. That was someone else's problem.

"Very well." Dan pulled himself up in his command chair, trying to make himself look photogenic for cameras that clearly couldn't see him. "Here we are, boys and girls, boldly going to space the-"

"Dan," Tatiana cut in, a stern tone to her voice. "I do want to warn you that the copyright you're about to infringe on is still valid. You might be embracing the dashing life of a space captain, but don't underestimate the lawyers. Even if you are fifty light years away, they will find a way."

"Fine," he grumbled. "I can say 'ad astra,' right? It just means 'to the stars.'"

"That is an acceptable catchphrase," Tatiana agreed, benevolently.

"Ad Astra!" Dan pointed upward, a shit-eating grin across his face. "Jennifer, take us up."

To the dozens of video cameras trained on *Terra's Pride,* nothing happened. One second it was there, the next it was just outside lunar orbit. No fire, no explosions, no drama. Just a man and his crew escaping Earth's gravity, the first to explore the truly unknown.

ABOUT CALE PLAMANN

A lifelong fan of Fantasy and Science Fiction, I usually spent my nerdy energy creating overly elaborate homebrew RPG campaigns. As it became harder and harder to juggle schedules for a half dozen players, I eventually made the logical choice and just cut them out of the picture entirely.

Now I write novels. They whine a lot less about critical failures.

If you enjoyed what you read, please make sure to visit my website or reach out to me on twitter (where I talk about writing amongst other things) or join my discord where I almost exclusively* talk about my existing books/what I'm currently writing.

*There are also memes. Lots of memes.

Connect with Cale:
CalePlamann-Author.com
Discord.gg/xzgycqtFNe
Twitter.com/WritesCoco
Patreon.com/CoCo_P

ABOUT MOUNTAINDALE PRESS

Dakota and Danielle Krout, a husband and wife team, strive to create as well as publish excellent fantasy and science fiction novels. Self-publishing *The Divine Dungeon: Dungeon Born* in 2016 transformed their careers from Dakota's military and programming background and Danielle's Ph.D. in pharmacology to President and CEO, respectively, of a small press. Their goal is to share their success with other authors and provide captivating fiction to readers with the purpose of solidifying Mountaindale Press as the place 'Where Fantasy Transforms Reality.'

Connect with Mountaindale Press:
MountaindalePress.com
Facebook.com/MountaindalePress
Twitter.com/_Mountaindale
Instagram.com/MountaindalePress

MOUNTAINDALE PRESS TITLES

GameLit and LitRPG

The Completionist Chronicles,
The Divine Dungeon,
Full Murderhobo, and
Year of the Sword by Dakota Krout

Arcana Unlocked by Gregory Blackburn

A Touch of Power by Jay Boyce

Red Mage and
Farming Livia by Xander Boyce

Space Seasons by Dawn Chapman

Ether Collapse and
Ether Flows by Ryan DeBruyn

Dr. Druid by Maxwell Farmer

Bloodgames by Christian J. Gilliland

Threads of Fate by Michael Head

Lion's Lineage by Rohan Hublikar and Dakota Krout

Wolfman Warlock by James Hunter and Dakota Krout

Axe Druid,
Mephisto's Magic Online, and
High Table Hijinks by Christopher Johns

Skeleton in Space by Andries Louws

Chronicles of Ethan by John L. Monk

Pixel Dust and
Necrotic Apocalypse by David Petrie

Viceroy's Pride by Cale Plamann

Henchman by Carl Stubblefield

Artorian's Archives by Dennis Vanderkerken and Dakota Krout

APPENDIX

GLOSSARY

Abraham Steil
A former military officer and Dan's right hand man. Abe is trained both in magic and the use of the magically enhanced powered armor developed in the wake of the Tellask invasion.

Anderson Drummond
One of the Tech Lords, a group of warlords and oligarchs that helped organize the state of chaos the world finds it in, and a companion of the Thoth Foundation.

Anderson Drummond is based out of California and specializes in nanite and AI development and programming.

Andrea Cragson
Emily and Andrea Cragson are sisters, recruited by Nora to round out the combat team she founded in Dan's name. Neither Emily nor Andrea trust Dan fully, and their behavior toward him is more than a little off kilter, but a desperate man usually doesn't have his pick of allies.

Behemoth
One of the three major subterranean horrors that come out during the short periods of Twilight's 'nights.' Behemoths are huge gorillas, capable of destroying walls and warriors with

equal disdainful ease. They are easily the largest, slowest, and most dangerous of the threats that plague Twilight's nights.

Colonel Hans Bowman
Colonel Bowman is an arrogant man with a prickly ego. He's good enough at his job to earn an assignment to the project enhancing humans with magic, but at the same time, he's ambitious and difficult to control

Daeson Amberell
A high level elf, Daeson has been exiled to Twilight. Once a professor, his theories on human development were too radical, leading to him being exiled from the core of the Tellask Empire. Now he spends his days, half in a wine bottle, trying to prove that his proposals regarding human magical potential have enough merit for him to return in Triumph.

Daniel Thrush
An electrical engineer that works as a subcontractor for the United States Army. Originally assigned to work on the Research and Development of priceless alien artifacts after he happened to be present at the Tellask invasion, he was quickly forgotten once the investigation into the alien magitech stalled out. Now, he is the only Earthling capable of using magic, and in order to keep Earth free, he has voluntarily entered a portal to go to a Tellask colony world and gain the Spirit he will need to awaken the rest of Earth's magical potential.

DarkStryke69xX - Reggie Dobbs
Reggie is a game streamer that is more bluster than talent. His abrasive personality and penchant for picking fights have drawn him more viewers than his actual in-game abilities, but the money that came with those viewers is enough that he could hire more skilled players to carry him. While not explicitly a bad or even person, Reggie is a bit of a narcissistic idiot and those tendencies can get him, and those around him, in trouble.

Emily Cragson
Emily and Andrea Cragson are sisters, recruited by Nora to round out the combat team she founded in Dan's name. Neither Emily nor Andrea trust Dan fully, and their behavior toward him is more than a little off kilter, but a desperate man usually doesn't have his pick of allies.

Fireball
A spell that shoots a ball of energy that explodes in a large, concussive blast of flame and heat.

Flame Aura
A spell that cloaks Dan in fire, damaging anyone who is foolish enough to engage him in hand to hand combat.

Flame Jet
A spell that fires a burst of flame from the caster's hands. More distracting and painful than deadly, Flame Jet does have a potential to start its target on fire.

Force Bubble
A spell that creates a ball of invisible and immobile energy.

Forcebolt
A spell that fires an invisible ball of force that bludgeons its target. Although the spell deals damage, it can also be used to knock its target over or into other hazardous environmental factors.

Garnash
The War chief in charge of the Orakh invasion of Earth. Based in Manhattan.

Gaunt
One of the three major subterranean horrors that come out during the short periods of Twilight's 'nights.' Gaunts resemble

skeletal horses and use mind magic to feed on beings' happiness and pleasant memories, often leaving the catatonic husks, unable to withstand the horror's follow up attacks. Their magic is muted by, but still can pass through a ward circle.

General William Finch
Finch is the senior officer associated with the project to magically enhance US Soldiers. A smart and charismatic man, albeit inflexible where change is concerned. If a procedure worked well two decades ago, he doesn't see the need to change it just because some egghead with a Phd says they have an idea that will work better. The obvious exception to this being new weaponry and equipment which he is eager to adopt. General Finch has a bit of a blind spot where his granddaughter, Jennifer, is concerned. Her parents died early, and he's raised her as a daughter since leading to him being a bit overprotective and irrational regarding her wellbeing.

Gravitational Easing
A spell that lessons the weight of gravity on the caster, allowing Dan to move faster, jump higher and dodge quicker.

Grosk
The warlord leading all Orakh. Grosk has not been seen so far in the series by there have been multiple allusions and references to their brutal rule.

Henry Ibis
A reclusive and enigmatic old billionaire, larger than life and beyond Eccentric. Henry founded and runs the Thoth Foundation. According to him, he has some help from "the Illuminati," but that's probably a joke. Maybe. What is true is that Ibis has connections, wealth and access to technology far beyond Dan's wildest dreams.

Jennifer Finch

Granddaughter of General William Finch. After her parents died, Jennifer was raised by the General, and as such she thinks of the man as her father. Despite his wishes, Jennifer sought to make her own career as a professional game streamer. Eventually, due to her prowess, she was recruited by the Thoth foundation to have her magical potential awakened.

House Amberell
A noble house in the Tellask Empire, House Amberell defends much of the warfront with the Orakh. Although House Amberell is powerful, it has steadily been weakened by a lack of support from the Imperial Court while the Orakh Horde wore down its armies.

Ishlar
A brutal and not terribly intelligent warrior that wields a rune-scripted club.

Lightning Stroke
A spell that produces an arc of electricity, dealing some burn damage to its target. More importantly it locks up the muscles it runs through, causing spasms and freezing the caster's foes.

Lythal
A race of bestial humanoids employed by the Tellask Empire as shock soldiers and scouts

Merella Amberell
A powerful elven spellcaster specializing in fire, Merella is on Earth to supervise a training assignment for her nephew.

Nora Strasshill
Nora is a human, native to Twilight; she is forced to work as a scout by various unsavory forces. On meeting Dan she immediately notices his potential, clinging to him in an attempt to link their fate together.

Orakh Horde
One of the great galactic empires. Usually the Orakh are too busy warring with themselves as well as any surrounding races to be much of a threat, but recently Grosk, a brutal warlord, has united into a potent war machine and turned against the Tellask. There are hints that the Orakh have some cooperation from members of the Tellask Empire that seek to turn them against their companions, but nothing concrete has been established.

Paltai Amberell
Paltai Amberell a scion of house Amberell. An elven warrior, he is fairly low in the order of inheritance for the noble house and is eager to raise his standing. Paltai commanded the Tellask/Amberell expedition that found Earth, and, underestimating humanity's numbers, tried to invade on his own.

Peter Best
One of the Tech Lords, a group of warlords and oligarchs that helped organize the state of chaos the world finds it in, and a companion of the Thoth Foundation.

Peter Best is based out of California and his forces focus on heavy machinery and mechanization, making both the powered armor that Dan's troops use as well as the larger combat mechs.

Railgun
Dan's most powerful spell that fuses both metal and electrical magic together to create and run a current through a pair of metal bars. The current accelerates a fairly large slug to extreme speeds. While the spell is unwieldy and hard to aim, it has enough power to destroy a tank or level a small building.

Samantha Weathers
A researcher and Dan's closest mentor and friend on Earth.

Shocking Fist
A spell that allows Dan to deliver an electrical charge to his
target via direct contact. Basically the magical equivalent of a
cattle prod.

Spark Field
A spell that produces a highly charged electrical field. It doesn't
deal much damage, but it is enough to distract and annoy a
number of opponents inside its area of effect

Spatial Shield
A spell that shifts space slightly, curving attacks every so
minutely around the caster. Although it won't stop a direct hit,
it's enough to blunt and deflect glancing blows and turn them
into near misses.

Spellshield
A spell that creates a magical field around the caster that dissi-
pates kinetic energy. The field is fairly inefficient at the amount
of kinetic energy dissipated per unit of magic expended, but at
the same time most users would rather spend magic to stop a
bullet/sword than to try and stop it with their bare flesh.

Stalker
One of the three major subterranean horrors that come out
during the short periods of Twilight's 'nights.' Stalkers resemble
huge winged wolves, and move with almost absolute silence
both in the air and across the ground except when they voluntarily give their presence away via howling. Stalkers move very
quickly and are able to run down almost any person foolish
enough to spend their time outside of appropriate wards.

Tanloff
A gas giant orbiting Alpha Centauri B.

TI-83 "Tatiana"

Artificial Intelligence created by Anderson Drummond and plugged into the internet. She has self-appointed herself as a protector of humanity and acts in what she perceives to be human interests, at times regardless of what her 'owners' or 'controllers' think.

Tellask Empire
The Elven Empire, thousands and thousands of years old and spanning almost all of known space. There are some pockets of independent space occupied by smaller space kingdoms, but there is little that can truly threaten the entire Empire. Perhaps that is why the Tellask don't seem to be takin the Orakh threat seriously, instead resorting to power struggles and petty games rather than focusing their full power on the invaders.

Thoth Foundation
A philanthropic organization pursuing the 'betterment of the human race.' To many, it is nothing but a vanity project owned and run by Henry Ibis, but those in 'the know' are aware that Ibis had access to some truly cutting edge technology and research. Perhaps enough to make an actual difference.

Twilight
A moon, tidally locked and orbiting Tanloff, a gas giant that circles Alpha Centauri B. Twilight is the home to a Tellask tributary world. Technically independent, Twilight sends wealth and soldiers to the Tellask Empire and House Amberell in exchange for military protection.

Viceroy's Pride
The voidship, renamed by Paltai Amberell, that led the failed assault on Earth.

www.ingramcontent.com/pod-product-compliance
Lightning Source LLC
Chambersburg PA
CBHW031558240626
47153CB00002B/555